PEOPLE CALL ME BIGGIE.
NOT ALL PEOPLE.
MOM AND SOME TEACHERS
CALL ME HENRY,
BUT FOR THE MOST PART, I'M

BIGGIE

BIGGIE

DEREK E. SULLIVAN

ALBERT WHITMAN & COMPANY
CHICAGO, ILLINOIS

To my three future readers:
Charlie, Henry, and Jack

Library of Congress Cataloging-in-Publication data is on file with the publisher.

Text copyright © 2015 by Derek E. Sullivan
Published in 2015 by Albert Whitman & Company
ISBN 978-0-8075-0727-8

Printed in China.
10 9 8 7 6 5 4 3 2 1 NP 20 19 18 17 16 15 14

Cover design by Jordan Kost

For more information about Albert Whitman & Company,
visit our web site at www.albertwhitman.com.

CHAPTER 1
GETTING TAGGED

People call me Biggie. Not all people. Mom and some teachers call me Henry, but for the most part, I'm Biggie.

Do I like the nickname? No. Of course, I don't. Nor do I care much for Brian Burke, who, nine years ago, thought up the moniker when we were playing tag during second-grade recess. I should have just told him to shut up or said something mean in verbal retaliation, but I didn't. I just stood there, head hung, shoulders fallen, hands swaying in the icy wind of early December.

It would have been so easy to fight back. He was tiny, wore the same ratty, torn Notre Dame T-shirt every day, and loved—and I mean loved—investigating the inside of his nose with his long fingernails.

That day, instead of getting caught up in the cherished elementary school game of *I can be meaner than you*, my lips locked. I stood there like some sap with my eyes focused on trampled snow, which was filled with small shoe prints from seven-year-olds avoiding the flailing arms of the kid who last heard, "You're it."

Even today, I can still remember that day nine years ago when everyone was laughing and snickering the first time Brian said my nickname out loud. Over time, the memory is more the background laughter of my classmates than Brian's repetitive teasing of "You're so big and fat, we should call you Biggie." I learned that Friday that you didn't need to be touched to get tagged.

Do I deserve my nickname? Sure, I'm not going to lie or sugarcoat the situation. I stand six-foot-two and weigh north of three hundred pounds.

Last year, my mom had to start ordering T-shirts online. I'll keep my size to myself, but let's just say there're enough Xs in it to make a porn-store owner blush. For at least a little while longer, I can still get my shorts and jeans at John's Big and Tall, which is located an hour from my hometown of Finch, Iowa (population: a handful). Lately, my jeans, new and old, feel like tourniquets wrapped tightly around my thighs.

How did I get this way? Or a better question: Why have I let myself grow to over three hundred pounds? Simply put: now, I'm invisible. Funny, isn't it? The more I weigh, the less people ride me about it. By living up to my nickname, I have accomplished an amazing feat. I'm the only high school student in the world who doesn't get made fun of on a daily basis.

It doesn't stop there. I'm also the only teenager in America whose parents leave him alone. Millions of people in the world give up the foods they love or drop billions of strands of sweat to avoid being called fat. I have managed to avoid the taunts, glares, and verbal abuse without giving up anything or wasting most of my life on a treadmill. I pull this off by shutting my mouth, staying in my bedroom at home, and sitting in the back of the room at school.

Standing in the shadows of my high school, I have noticed one undeniable fact: high school kids are cruel, mean sons-of-bitches, and not just toward fat people. Nobody is immune to the constant ripping. I can't take a step without hearing some kid make fun of another kid. Every second, students are laughing at someone else's dumb outfit, clumsy behavior, or poorly chosen words. It's not a battle, but a never-ending verbal war. In this conflict, I choose to be a pacifist. To avoid being hit by spoken bullets, I have decided to never point that gun at anyone else. I keep my mouth shut at all costs.

At my desk, I disappear from everyone: the jocks that rip on kids who don't have God-given talent; the do-it-alls, who come to class every day, try out for the spring play, run for student council, and so on; and the sleepers, who rest their heads on desks and could care less about school.

Sure I feel the urge to say something now and then, raise my hand to answer some teacher's question, or say hello to one of the few kids I don't despise at this small-town hellhole, but it's not worth the risk. When you're fat, insults hurt and come in droves, like ammunition from a machine gun. I hate being made fun of for my weight and will do anything—I mean anything—to avoid it, even if that means adding weight.

A funny thing happened a year ago when my weight neared three hundred pounds. People stopped looking at me, staring in disgust, or delicately shaking their heads at the sight of me. In the past year, I have learned that being slightly overweight is a lot more annoying than being obese.

For example, the summer before the start of high school when I weighed around 220 pounds, the football coach called our house every week and told me that if I played for his team and, more importantly, if I committed myself to the weight room, I could play college football as an offensive guard or nose tackle. But sports aren't for me, and I definitely don't need athletics to get into college.

Since my school started giving out *As*, *Bs*, *Cs*, *Ds*, and *Fs* in third grade, I've missed out on getting an *A* once. At the end of my seventh-grade year, my physical education teacher wrote that I didn't participate effectively and gave me an *A*-minus. Participate effectively? What does that mean? The way I see it, if a kid stands there and keeps his mouth shut, he deserves an *A*.

Want another example? Having a thirteen-year-old weighing well over two hundred pounds bugged my mom, so she got me up early and forced me to walk on a treadmill. When I came home from school, she, as if she were on *CSI*, searched my backpack and pockets for junk food wrappers. She worked so hard to keep me from eating junk food that hiding the wrappers from candy bars, hamburgers, and Twinkies took up most of my time. Would it have been easier to just not eat my favorite foods? Probably. But they're my favorite foods. I'm a fat kid who has to stay quiet all the time to avoid constant ridicule. Eating Snickers now and then is the only way I don't go completely insane.

So it didn't surprise me at all when no matter how hard Mom worked, my weight kept rising and rising. Soon, the doctor's office staff weighed me out at 270 pounds. Mom said little the next few days. Then one morning she said she was done begging me to work out and pleading with me to eat healthy. The words were music to my ears. Now, other than making healthy meals, she has stopped being my athletic trainer. No more early-morning door poundings, no more rummaging around in my stuff, no more getting on my case about my weight. I am free to be me.

If I had followed my mom's orders and stopped with the junk food and embraced the exercise plans, I would still be working out in the mornings, living off vegetables, and being all-around miserable, twenty-four hours a day, seven days a week, 365 days a year. Plus, if I look even the slightest bit fit, coaches at sports-obsessed Finch High School would never leave me alone.

Some days, I feel like I'm the only person in Finch who doesn't share a passion for sports. What I don't understand is why someone would want to fail so much for just a small taste of success. For example, Matt "Jet" Wayne, the baseball team's best hitter, batted only .418 this summer. So 58.2 percent of the time he failed, and he's an all-state award winner on the diamond. Wouldn't all of the failure make someone hate sports?

Another thing about me: I'm a perfectionist. Not only have I mastered my school's curriculum and perfected a way to avoid insults,

I have also never missed a day of school in ten years. Not one. I have never been sick a single day in my life. If junk food is so horrible for your health, how do I stay so healthy? I'm sure the anti-junk-food crowd has no answer for that.

Anyway, a real perfectionist could never enjoy sports. Sports are for guys like Brian Burke, who unfortunately stopped picking his nose. As I got bigger and bigger, adding more and more credence to his nickname for me, he got stronger and faster. Ever since sixth grade, he has been the school's top athlete. He's the quarterback, power forward, and starting pitcher. By junior high, Brian wasn't the only one calling me Biggie. Everyone did. Everyone worshipped him—so much that he got to pick his own nickname, a rarity at any high school.

The story goes that his father used to wear a homemade T-shirt to baseball games that had a big yellow jacket—the school's mascot—on it, along with the words *Brian Burke, Finch's Killer Bee*. Brian loved it so much that one day he told everyone to call him Killer, and to this day they still do. Thanks to Brian, he's Killer and I'm Biggie.

CHAPTER 2
KIT KATS

School isn't the only place I remain silent. Four nights a week, I work at Bob's Fuel and Food. Outside the small convenience store sit two gas pumps and inside is just one register. The owner hates spending money, so he schedules only one person at a time. Most workers would complain about having to run the register, cook the food, load the empty shelves, and mop the footprint-filled floors by themselves, but I appreciate my boss's frugality.

I can sit up there and read novels, comic books, and textbooks and rarely be bothered. These days, most people pay at the pump, so all I have to do is call the cops when they drive off without paying, which happens more than people think. Outsiders driving through Finch on their way to Dubuque or Chicago think we don't have policemen in this small town, so they pump and dash. They are all idiots because I write down their license plate numbers before turning on the machines. I doubt they get very far out of town before a state trooper pulls them over.

Every now and then, someone will come in for a twenty-ounce pop, twelve-pack of beer, or a candy bar. Last year, when I was a dumb convenience-store rookie, I would mutter the total bill through the same forced smile I use on school picture day. Then one day I retired the crooked grin and waited for customers to toss a buck or a ten- or twenty-dollar bill on the counter. I just calmly glance at the charge on top of the register. Once they see the total, they get out their cash or debit cards. No small talk needed, wanted, or expected, and no one ever says I'm rude. Here's a secret to all future convenience-store workers: no one wants to talk to you, no matter what the bosses or company motto says.

I love making the food. I cook greasy snacks like chicken fingers and egg rolls. It isn't that much work; I just toss the snacks into a heater below the counter and then place them into small paper carriers or into my belly. I'll admit it; I'm addicted to chicken fingers and egg rolls. One night, I bought thirty of them, but most nights I eat between twelve and fifteen. I used to eat them with blue cheese dip, but lately I've been soaking them in the hot cheese we normally sell with soft pretzels.

While cooking is my favorite job, the highlight of my night is watching Annabelle Rivers shoplift.

Three times a week, Annabelle, a classmate since kindergarten, comes into the store before her shift at Molly's Drive-In. She buys a Monster Lo-Carb energy drink and also drops two Kit Kats in her garbage-bag-size purse. Last year, she used to steal M&M's, and before that, Twix bars, but right now she's swiping Kit Kats.

Annabelle thinks she's so sly. She looks at the candy bar with one eye and me with other. She notices me going to add some egg rolls to the heater and drops the dollar treat into her purse. She then grabs a Lo-Carb and pays for it. I would let her steal that too, but I always go mute when she's around. Someday I'll tell her how I feel.

She does her routine every time she walks into the store, even if there are other customers. I just love to watch the precision she takes in swiping the candy bars. As a perfectionist myself, I appreciate her attention to detail. She comes in and always walks down the first aisle, the one closest to the windows, which are covered with red and blue advertisements for pop, cigarettes, oil, and Little Debbie snacks. She's five-foot-six, so her dark hair with red highlights pokes over the top of the shelf.

Her pace can only be explained as quick walking. She doesn't skip, jog, or run, but she's in a hurry, as if she's trying to move just fast enough that I can't focus on her. She then stares through the glass cooler doors at the pop, single-serving milk containers, and energy drinks before turning ninety degrees to slide like a ninja into the candy aisle.

At this point, no matter what I'm doing, I turn away and pretend to be too busy to watch her every move. Then I hear the cooler door open again. She grabs the Monster drink. How do I know she steals Kit Kats? Well, her precision to detail ends when she pulls the Kit Kat out of her purse when she starts her car.

She comes in every Monday, Tuesday, and Thursday around six fifty. Tonight's Friday so I'm surprised to see her show up. She walks in, sees me texting, and smiles. She doesn't normally even make

9

eye contact with me, so a big smile makes me blush and I stand at attention. Then Mike Robinson, a senior whose only real skill is owning a motorcycle, follows her into the store.

"Please don't be together," I whisper.

Mike and Annabelle giggle together as she hands him two Monster drinks: Lo-Carb and Mean Bean coffee. She stands back as Mike walks up to my counter. He tosses down six bucks in extra-crisp dollar bills. The drinks cost $2.79 apiece and six bucks easily covers them, but there are the two Kit Kats and one Snickers in Annabelle's purse that I have to deal with before letting them get back on his motorcycle.

Annabelle and I have an unspoken cat-and-mouse game that lights up my boring nights behind the counter. But tonight, with him, she's paying. They don't get to laugh about stealing from me, not on his motorcycle.

"Biggie, I need my change," Mike says while my eyes are on Annabelle's purse. I can tell he has never shoplifted before, which surprises me. "My change, forty cents or something."

I ring up the drinks and candy bars. "Nine ninety-eight," I answer.

"For two energy drinks?" he snaps back.

I hold on to the counter to keep from fainting. It's tough for me to admit, but I'm kind of a pushover. I normally don't want a confrontation or to get in the middle of a shouting match, but Annabelle gets free food, not Mike "Never Read a Book Without Pictures in My Life" Robinson.

"The candy bars," I say.

"Biggie!" Annabelle shouts.

"There are no candy bars. You hear me?" Mike says.

Like I do with everyone who doesn't have enough money to pay, I grab the energy drinks off the counter and place them on a small table by the gas reader. My hands shake so much that I half expect the drinks to explode out the pop-top. Turning away from them allows me to get some air. The choppy breaths form a small circle of condensation on the window, which looks out to the parking lot. Watching cars fly by on the highway calms my nerves.

"Forget it, Anna. This fat fuck thinks he's a gas-station god," Mike says.

"Mike, get me the drinks," she commands. "Just pay for the Kit Kats and let's go."

"Look at me!" He picks up the money off the counter.

I slowly twist my neck and see him squeezing the now-crinkled dollar bills like a tube of toothpaste.

"New plan," he continues. "I'm not paying for anything, and if you say something or call the Harpers, I'll tell them I caught you jerking off to those magazines back there."

"Cameras," I whisper with my fingernails pressing into the edge of the countertop.

"What?"

"There're cameras always on the front counter. I'm not allowed to look at them."

"The cameras?" Mike asks.

"No," Annabelle jumps in. "You're both idiots. He means his boss knows if he looks at porn and there are cameras recording us right now, so just pay him."

"I only have six bucks after buying you dinner," he whispers.

"Whatever," she says and tosses a ten on the counter.

My blue eyes connect with her green ones, just like when she walked in few minutes ago. Annabelle has been in this store a hundred times, but tonight is the first time I've really looked at her up close. Although we live in the same town, go to the same school, and sit in the same classes, everything about Annabelle seems to take place at a distance. She always seems far away. But right now, we are eye to eye, inches from each other, and I can't look away. I'm looking at her bangs, pink freckles, and naked red lips.

"My change," she blurts out.

"You don't have to pay," Mike says. "Let's get Dilly Bars instead."

"Give me my Monster, Biggie." She ignores Mike's plan. "I liked you a lot better when you kept your mouth shut. C'mon, baby."

As Annabelle walks out, Mike turns with a little unsolicited advice, "Being an asshole will never get you the girl."

As the door closes, I mutter to myself, "Works for you."

CHAPTER 3
SCHOOL-BASED PHYSICAL ACTIVITIES

As a perfectionist, earning straight *A*s is a must for me, and being valedictorian a requirement. Math, English, science, and social studies are easy *A*s. I don't mind studying or memorizing facts and dates. I enjoy doing assignments. I turn everything in on time and the grades follow. Gym is another issue. PE teachers are egomaniacs who look down on people who don't participate in extracurricular activities. Seeing how I have zero interest in embarrassing myself in sports, I figure out a way to avoid gym class and the possible *B* that comes with it. Before last year, I matched my mom's looping handwriting perfectly in a letter to the gym teacher that ended with the sentence, "Due to potential health concerns, Henry Abbott cannot participate in school-based physical activities." Coach Phillips read it and sent me to the bleachers.

Every time the phone rang the next couple of weeks, my heart skipped a beat, but it was never Coach Phillips. I don't know if my plan worked or if he was tired of watching me ruin every activity.

I needed my time on the bleachers, especially since I had first-period PE. A lot of times I stayed up all night talking in chat rooms and needed first-period gym/study hall to quickly finish math assignments.

If I had asked Mom to write a legitimate note, she would have turned me down and asked, "Why don't you want some exercise?" or "Why don't you want to lose a little weight?"

Mom doesn't understand me. Both her former boyfriend and current husband are standout baseball players and were all-state football, basketball, and baseball athletes in high school. That's another reason why the football coach used to call me into his office a lot—my pedigree.

Do I have breathing issues that keep me from participating in school-based physical activities? Hard to say. I'm exercise-challenged—as in, I never exercise so I don't know if playing dodgeball or kickball would cause me harm. But thirty minutes of school-based physical activities isn't going to make me look like Killer or Jet either. Those two love PE because it's the only way they can make girls fall in love with them.

I know my limitations and my domains. While Killer and Jet can run and catch better than I can, they aren't as intelligent, savvy, or quick-witted. Their skills fit perfectly in Coach Phillips's gym class. Am I jealous of jocks? No way in hell.

* * *

When I climb out of bed on the first day of my junior year, I calmly and quietly pull the zipper open on my backpack and see the envelope containing my forged letter to skip PE for this year safe and secure. After getting dressed, I head downstairs for breakfast.

Mom makes me two English muffins with low-fat marmalade and pours me a glass of puke-colored grapefruit juice. For the past few years, Mom has made sure I eat only healthy foods. The problem is that the muffins and juice don't give me the energy I need to tackle school. Only a Starbucks Doubleshot and Molly's breakfast sandwiches do the trick. Mom's healthy food plays the role of morning appetizer. I'll eat my real breakfast in fifteen minutes.

After swallowing the two muffins, I stand up and search for my backpack. I always set it by the door, but I notice only my shoes sitting there.

"I ripped up the note," Mom's voice says behind me. I turn to see her holding my backpack. "Saw Coach Phillips at the store and he told me in not so many words that I'm a horrible mother for not letting you participate in gym." A small did-you-think-you-could-get-away-with-this? grin slowly switches to a look of pure disappointment: glazed-over eyes, head hanging down, lips circled for sighs of breath.

My heart stops and a little bit of grapefruit juice reemerges on my tongue.

"I told the three girls in your class that babysit your younger brother to email me when you skip gym. The first one that contacts me gets a hundred dollars." She tosses the backpack at me. "Henry, I don't know what else to do. I don't. Everything I've tried, you have battled and battled me on, and I don't know why. Tell me, please tell me why, because I'm at a loss."

A lump in my throat keeps me silent. I can't even force an apology past my dry lips.

"Well, maybe you can write it down—as your handwriting or mine, I don't care."

She doesn't understand. I'm trying to be valedictorian. I'm trying to get college scholarships. There is a method to my madness. If I could just open my mouth and speak, tell her why I do what I do, she would understand.

"I hate gym" are the only words I can sneak through my dry lips.

"You…" She goes silent. I can see her tongue lick her teeth as she searches for words. "Just please go to school and be normal."

＊ ＊ ＊

Everyone stands in a semicircle around Coach Phillips on the makeshift Wiffle ball court in the corner of the school's parking lot. Phillips, who coaches football and baseball, considers Finch's football and baseball fields sacred ground. No one who hasn't earned the right to step on them is allowed to step on them. So gym-class Wiffle ball is in the parking lot. Man, I hate him.

For three years I've avoided this moment. Three years! While I should be thinking about how I'm horrible at sports, how I didn't bring gym clothes, and how Annabelle is in my PE class this year, all I can really think about is how pissed I am at Mom. This disaster is all her fault.

Phillips tosses up a Wiffle ball and catches it.

"Biggie, welcome," he says. "Glad to see you're going to join us this year. Technically, I'm not supposed to let you play in school

16

clothes, but I'll make an exception seeing as how you already owe me a bunch of classes."

His smirk is so pretentious that I want to slap him. What's he all proud about? He didn't find the note. He's the idiot I fooled.

My breathing and sweating pick up. My T-shirt tightens and my jeans, already two sizes too short, bite my ankles and suffocate my knees. My hair starts to itch, making me scratch the center of my head, which only accelerates the sweat dripping down my forehead, cheeks, and chin.

"Can I be excused?" I finally spit out, knowing it's a waste of words.

Coach Phillips grabs my wet hand and places a Wiffle ball in it. "You can pitch, all-time pitcher. All you have to do is stand there and throw the ball. No running at all. You should barely sweat. All right?"

I grab the ball and notice Killer and Annabelle talking to each other on the pitcher's mound. Killer tosses another Wiffle ball up and down, and Annabelle tries to steal it from him. Every time she misses, his laugh gets louder, and she shoves his shoulder.

"Killer, put the ball in the bucket. Biggie's pitching today," Coach says.

"No, Coach, I got it." Killer turns his head and Annabelle swipes the ball and jumps up and down like a two-year-old after cake and ice cream.

"Killer, play short; Biggie's got it," Coach Phillips orders. "Go get the ball from Annabelle."

I'm a statue. Every ounce of my body freezes, even under the ninety-degree heat. Nothing moves, not my hands, feet, or knees. My eyes won't blink and my lungs don't pump air. I suddenly feel light-headed. Any moment now, I am going to pass out and land face-first on black asphalt. My head will crack open and blood will surround me like an ocean around a peninsula. In five, maybe ten minutes I will be dead from blunt force trauma and blood loss. The newspaper will run the headline: *Boy Dies Playing Wiffle Ball.*

People that are too lazy to read the article will be confused. How does a Wiffle ball kill someone?

"Biggie!" Annabelle screams. "Are you pitching or not?"

I nod and she heads to right field. I can't help smiling as I watch her run away. Her butt looks amazing in those shorts. The grin disappears when I remember that I'm the center of attention. I hate the center; I prefer the back of the room.

The Wiffle ball has eight oblong holes, each one the width of a dime. To be honest, I have no idea how to throw a Wiffle ball. My hand is sweating so much that I can't hold the plastic ball tightly in my palm.

Jet steps up to the plate and pounds the tip of the plastic bat on the asphalt. He sticks his tongue out like a thirsty Labrador and jiggles his elbows.

What do I do? Should I put the tips of my fingers in the holes? If so, how many fingers? Do I fire the ball like a baseball or flip it up there like a Frisbee? Should I lob it overhand or underhand? Am I supposed to let everyone hit it or should I try to strike everyone out?

"Biggie, PE is only an hour. Let's go," Coach Phillips shouts.

"Let me pitch, Coach!" Killer yells from shortstop. "He has no idea how to pitch."

Jet smiles as he stands near the plate. He knows what's going to happen. I'm going pitch the ball and he's going to launch it over the fence. I can already hear all the girls chanting, "We love you, Jet! You're so amazing!"

"Today, Biggie!" Coach Phillips yells so loud that the command quiets the chants in my head.

I decide to fire the ball with two of my fingertips on top of holes. I step forward and throw the ball as hard as possible. The ball flies halfway to the plate and bounces off the black asphalt.

"Don't throw it so hard, Biggie," Jet says. "It's just PE. Put it right here." He sticks the bat out to a point where it looks like it's jutting out from his hip.

"It's *only* PE to the stud athletes. To the rest of us, it's hell," I whisper.

I decide to toss the ball hard again, but with three fingertips on the holes and my thumb on solid plastic. I lift my leg an inch or two off the ground before I throw. The ball flies toward Jet like a drunk bird and then, as if the bird has suddenly died, drops straight toward the ground. Jet leans forward, his shoulders dropping with the plastic bat. Almost falling forward, he hits a ground ball to Killer, who scoops it up and throws him out at first.

Nice. Three fingers is the way to go. Michelle, junior class president and an awesome softball player, comes up to the plate. She stares out and waves the bat at me. Wow, someone is taking Wiffle ball seriously. She squints as rays from the September morning sun burn her brown eyes.

I stare at the ball and try to remember where I put my fingers last time. Which holes were they? How much pressure did I place with each finger last time?

I look at Michelle, lift my leg, and fire the ball. Once again, it looks like a strike, but it dips near the plate. Michelle swings and misses. Chuckles fill the air, along with heckles of "Way to hit air" and "Was the sun in your eyes?" Which is actually a dumb one because it is. In gym there is no catcher, so she has to retrieve the ball and throw it back to me. She fires it with a grunt and the ball flutters like a bee stalking a flower.

I spin the ball again and put on the fingertip pressure points. The ball seems smaller now, softer. At first, it felt hard, tight, with no bend or give. Now, it fits perfectly in my fat fingers. I toss another pitch and, once again, the ball drops. Michelle doesn't swing, but Coach Phillips calls the pitch a strike. I smile.

"Michelle, quit being nice to Biggie and hit it," says her boyfriend, Kyle, from first base.

She isn't being nice as much as she's being schooled by the Wiffle ball master. I throw another pitch and Michelle hits a high fly ball to right field where three girls stand and text. Becky, whose dad is my boss, sees the ball coming and drops her iPhone. She flinches, closes her eyes, and uses her forearms to trap the ball up against her flat chest. Her elbows snare the ball like two cob holders securing a hot ear. Becky stands there frozen as Annabelle pulls the ball out from between her arms and throws it back to me.

Batters come and go, and every one either swings and misses

or hits a harmless groundout or fly ball. No one reaches first base. Standing on the sidelines in between innings, I'm feeling my confidence grow and I start to fiddle with an extra ball, changing pressure and release points. During the third inning, I even start throwing the ball sidearm. The more I fiddle with my windup, the more freaking stuff the ball does in the air. After a while, I notice that just moving my bottom finger to the left or to the right will make the ball sink or slice or dart to the left or to the right.

After he grounds out a second time, Jet says, "Is Biggie throwing a perfect game?"

I am.

When the first couple of innings ended and my team came to bat, I sat down. I was hot and tired and still mad at Mom. Now, after the third inning, I'm pacing, impatiently waiting to get back out there. My teammates cheer as Killer and Annabelle smack base hits, but I feel frustrated. Inside, I cheer for outs. I want to get back out there and continue my perfect game. Somehow I am excelling in gym just like I would in history or English or science. Now, I'm on a quest. I have to get everyone out or this whole exercise has been a major waste of time.

After we score five runs, I'm back on the mound. The pacing was a bad idea. I struggle for breath under the blazing sun. My wrists perspire, and the sweat travels down my palm. The ball is wet. I consider acting like a big leaguer and asking for a dry ball. But I keep quiet, dry the ball on my jeans, control my breaths, and ignore the sweat stinging my eyes and concentrate on the task at hand—throwing a perfect game.

Michelle steps back in. I remember her swinging and missing at a pitch near her aqua-green tennis shoes. She doesn't like the ball low. I place the pressure points, pressing down on the plastic at the top, bending the globe-shaped ball ever so slightly, and placing my thumb on the very bottom. I only want the ball to drop, no other movement.

Damn, I wish I had rested during the last half-inning. My legs ache. "Man up," I whisper. I ignore my body and concentrate on perfection. I lift my leg as high as I can—maybe three inches—and snap my wrist when I release the ball, causing the pitch to spin instead of drop. I let it go wrong. The ball just hangs there and I stop breathing. Michelle swings and hits a line drive to left field. My neck snaps as I follow the line drive.

Killer reaches out and catches the ball with his right hand. He slides on the asphalt and rolls over with skid marks busting open down his leg. I can almost hear the sizzle like bacon bouncing on a skillet as he slides on the hot surface. He jumps up, shakes off the pain, and screams to Jet, "No one on your team's going to reach base today." He flips the ball back at me and gives me a nod. I see blood mixed with small pebbles of gravel on his forearm. He takes a deep breath, rolls his neck, and ignores the little pieces of parking lot trapped in the sticky red substance escaping from a series of tiny cuts.

"Last batter!" Coach Phillips yells.

Justin Martinson steps up to the plate. If not for me and my lard ass, he would be the biggest kid in school. But while I say nothing and stay invisible, he's the class clown. He shakes his big ass to make the girls laugh and invents new sound effects for fake farts to get the guys to applaud and shout. I don't know what to expect. He might strike out by taking an overexuberant swing or hit a home run.

Knowing Justin's the last batter calms me, and I get a second wind. I'm able to take a deep, relaxing breath. I stand upright, feeling confident. I squeeze the Wiffle ball with precision like a nurse taking a pulse. I toss the pitch, releasing the ball just above my head. The ball drops, slices, and hovers in space. Justin swings as hard as he can and yells as loud as he can, but the ball barely bounces off the bat.

Like a raindrop, the ball drops straight onto the asphalt, bounces twice, and stops just a few inches in front of home plate. With no catcher, I run toward the spinning ball. As I get within stretching distance of the ball, a sharp pain shoots through my chest. My knees buckle, my neck stiffens, and my eyes slam shut. I don't fall as much as tip over, landing on my right elbow and rolling onto my belly.

Killer grabs the ball and throws out Justin as the hot asphalt leaves grill marks on my forehead. My breaths become choppy as I try to roll over onto my back. Everyone must be looking on in horror as I vibrate like a fish out of water.

"Biggie, you okay?" Coach Phillips says and helps me sit up.

My forearms have stingy pains, and I can't take a long breath or close my mouth without a lump forming in my throat. As the pain in my chest lessens, the sting from my tears mixed with warm sweat intensifies in my eyes.

Why did Mom rip up the note? I struggle to get air. I am dying. Right here in the parking lot, right after throwing a perfect game. Why did Coach make me play? He knows I shouldn't be doing school-based physical activities.

"You'll be all right," Coach says. "Just too much heat." He rubs my shoulder and Michelle brings me some water. She bends down like a World War II nurse and pours the cold liquid into my mouth.

As she leans over me, Michelle places her hand on my chin, and I start to feel better. How do I know? Because I start getting turned on. I know it's sad, but this is the most action I've ever gotten from a Finch girl. She pours some water down the back of my neck. The water feels like razor-blade slivers of ice cutting my neck. "That'll cool you down," she says.

My breathing slowly returns to normal and I feel comfortable enough to close my mouth. Coach and Killer help me up. "Everyone hit the showers," Coach says.

I sit there with my hands on my knees and try to take deep, long, consistent breaths.

Kyle, Michelle, and Annabelle surround me, and Kyle offers a hand to help me up. His Popeye forearms pull me up with little effort.

"Hell of a game," Michelle says. "Hey, Coach Phillips, is there room for Biggie on the baseball team this year?"

"Yeah, I wanna see him pitch!" Annabelle yells.

"Really?" I whisper so quietly I'm not sure anyone heard it but me.

"C'mon, guys, you're going to be late for class," Coach Phillips says. "Biggie, you can have a few more minutes of fresh air, but don't take too long."

"Coach," I say. I want to add, *Annabelle said I should pitch?* But the words settle in my throat. Instead I say, "Thank you. I won't be long."

CHAPTER 4
THE BASEBALL-PLAYING SON

I lie on my bed and wait for my younger half-brother Maddux to get home from spending the summer traveling with my step-dad. Maddux and I get along pretty well. He's a cocky little thing who thinks he's gonna hit seventy home runs in the Major Leagues by the time he's twenty, but for the most part, he's all right. My step-dad is a different story.

In 1990, Jim Kaczor changed the pronunciation of his last name from *Kass-sore* to *Kazer*, so that he could go by the nickname Jim "the Laser" Kaczor. He stole thirty-three bases as a senior at Finch High School and helped the Yellow Jackets win a state title, one of ten Finch has won. He has now played professionally for three organizations, including the San Diego Padres, who called him up for four days in 2004. His lifetime batting average is .100: 1-for-10, a single against the Los Angeles Dodgers on September 29. After singling to right field, he was thrown out trying to steal. So the self-proclaimed Laser has the worst possible stolen-base percentage in major league history: .000

Laser never talks to me. I'm not complaining, just stating a fact. Is it possible for a step-dad to be embarrassed by a child he didn't procreate? All of the Kaczors are baseball players. They're royalty in this town. When I was younger, I always thought Laser would adopt me, but he never has. I guess only baseball players in this town can have the last name Kaczor. If he doesn't want to be my dad, so be it. I don't care.

Eleven years ago, they had Maddux Kaczor, named after former Atlanta Braves pitcher Greg Maddux. In a lot of ways, Maddux is my best friend. We stay up all night playing video games and talking about his road trips.

I like Maddux, not only because he's my brother, but because he doesn't expect anything from me. He doesn't ask questions about school, work, or girls. Outside of calling me Biggie, which I said he could when I went through a Henry's-a-stupid-old-man-name phase, he doesn't make fun of my weight or ask me when I'm going to lose one hundred pounds. When we sneak off to Molly's for chicken fingers, he keeps it to himself. I just wish he was around more. What really sucks is that he's gone in the summer when I have little to do.

Maddux is road-schooled. I can't say he's home-schooled because he's never home. Laser takes him everywhere: out east for minor league baseball, down south for winter ball. Maddux sleeps in his bed in October, November, Christmas, New Year's, and the first few weeks of February. The rest of the year, he sleeps in hotel rooms with his dad.

The Kaczors are also filthy rich. Besides being baseball players, they have a knack for buying farmland cheap and selling it high. Laser doesn't farm, so he sold his 2,400 acres of inheritance to his brothers and used the money to build my mom her 6,000-square-foot dream house and Maddux his own indoor baseball field. The indoor baseball diamond has green-and-white field turf, a dirt pitching mound, a batter's box, bases, and a pitching machine.

Maddux can hit pitches that fly in at 75 miles per hour. He stands straight with his feet parallel to his shoulders, stiff as a miniature green plastic army man. The bat barely moves as he points it straight up at the thirty-foot ceiling. The machine fires the ball, and in one quick motion Maddux drops his back shoulder and smacks the ball off the padded wall just past third base. It's poetry—the perfect swing.

"What's up, Biggie?" Maddux shoves my door open.

"Welcome back," I reply. "How was Victoria?"

"It sucked ass." He jumps onto my bed. "Dad couldn't get on the field, so he's calling it a career."

"What?"

"He retired."

"No shit." I'm shocked by the news. "He just quit, no more majors?"

Maddux shakes his head. "His brothers said he can help out on their farms, plus Coach Phillips offered him a coaching job."

"Wow," I say. "That's big news. Is he okay?"

"Yeah, he's cool. He's thirty-four now and coaches don't play old guys. It's all politics, he claims. What really sucked is that the coach played crappy young guys, so not only did Dad ride the bench, but the team lost all the time. It was the worst summer ever."

"Yeah, I saw he wasn't playing much. I kept asking Mom if he was hurt," I say.

"Nah, he just had a crappy coach." Maddux settles down in front of my PlayStation and turns on the TV.

"Dad's pissed that you were skipping gym." He sifts through video games, searching for right one. "I would hide out here too."

"It's cool," I say. "I went to PE today and actually threw a perfect game."

"What? You played baseball in gym?"

"Well, no, we played Wiffle ball, but no one reached base. I taught myself to throw this badass curveball that no one could hit."

"I could hit it," he claims.

Still feeling the rush of my perfect game, I talk with an ounce of cockiness in my voice, "Maybe. Maybe not."

"Game on," he says, stretching his neck out to get his eyes within an inch of mine.

We walk to the indoor baseball diamond. Despite my smart-ass comments, I'm nervous to pitch to Maddux, afraid he'll smack my perfect pitch all over the building. Facing Killer, Michelle, and Jet is one thing, but getting Maddux, who plays baseball six hours a day every day, to swing and miss is something completely different.

And then I remember we don't have any Wiffle balls. I need to throw a baseball, which is firmer, heavier, and slimier than the Wiffle ball. And there are no holes for my fingertips.

I look at the ball and try to remember where my favorite holes were and put finger pressure in those same spots. The ball's cold from sitting in a white bucket in a dark closet for months. Maddux stands there, motionless. Not even his eyes blink. He shares mannerisms with his dad, including confident shoulders, a straight posture, and a quick, I'm-running-late walk.

He, like Laser, has blue eyes, a perfectly sloped nose, and a small chin that's much thinner than his lips. Their faces start wide at the forehead and then, like a V, thin down to the chin. Unlike his father, Maddux is stocky with big shoulders, forearms, and calves, which he gets from his mother's side of the family.

I wind up and fire the ball at the target behind the plate. Just like in gym class, the ball drops at the last minute. Maddux swings and hits a ground ball.

"Are you throwing knuckleballs?" he asks.

I just shrug my shoulders.

"Throw it again, but harder," he says.

I go through my routine and, this time, throw it harder. Maddux swings and hits the ball off the back wall. Damn it, I think.

"Now throw it slower, but with the same windup," he says.

How can I throw it slower but keep the same windup? What is he talking about? I step back, lift my leg, and push the ball to the plate instead of pitching it. The ball barely reaches the plate and Maddux slaps it back at me. The ball bounces off my shin. I hop twice but quickly lose my balance and drop to my back. How come every time I play sports, I fall down?

Maddux hovers over me as a pink balloon of gum swells from his mouth. After a loud pop he says something really dumb. "I know you were probably joking upstairs, but you're going out for baseball this year."

"No way," I say, climbing to my feet. The pain is gone, but when I press on the welt below my sock, a sharp pain shoots up my leg.

"Why not? You could be a great pitcher with some help," he says.

"Nah, I hate sports."

"Why?"

"It's all about failure," I say. "I can't handle that type of disappointment." I head for the door, limping.

"What if you don't suck?" Maddux shouts at my back.

"No," I shout at the door.

"Just listen. What if you mastered this knuckleball and threw a perfect game?"

"I already threw a perfect game," I say as I reach for the door handle.

"Wiffle ball doesn't count. Biggie, no one in high school throws a knuckleball, at least not a good one. No one would know what to do when they see it. Plus, there would be no scouting reports on you because you're just starting. The other players would be completely off balance."

I resist turning the knob, choosing instead to turn and say, "I don't care."

Twenty feet away, Maddux continues his sales pitch. "If I can fix your windup, you could be a hell of a junkballer. We have nine months to tinker with a few things. Biggie, you could throw a perfect game. I know it. The first in school history. Just think how cool it would be to throw one for real, not just in gym."

"My dad threw a perfect game, I'm sure," I say. "He's in the Iowa High School Baseball Hall of Fame."

Maddux shakes his head. "Aaron never did. No one has. I've memorized the entire Finch record book."

"My dad didn't throw one?"

Maddux smiles. "No one. Stick with me and you'll be the first."

I ponder the thought. Throwing a perfect game, especially after finding out that my dad never did, is appealing. Plus, Annabelle did say she wanted to see me pitch. I am 99 percent sure she was kidding or making fun of me, but what if she wasn't? What if she watches me throw a perfect game and falls in love with me?

"So what do you think, Biggie? Wanna throw a perfect game?" Maddux asks, jumping up and down, giddy with excitement. The way he's shaking, who would believe he hasn't had a teaspoon of sugary pop in six months.

Although I know it's a horrible idea, I don't shake my head and nod instead. Why? Who knows? Maybe I just want to make Maddux happy. Maybe I just want to live in the glow of the perfect game a little longer and believe my ability to manipulate a ball isn't a fluke, but a start of something bigger, something that can't be predicted or prophesized. Maybe I think it's a path toward kissing Annabelle.

No matter the reason, baseball season isn't until the end of the school year, eight months from now, so I know I have nothing to lose by saying okay. I have plenty of time to quit. For now, I'll make the kid jumping up and down in front of me happy.

CHAPTER 5
ANNAROCKS

Annabelle drops two Kit Kats and a Lo-Carb Monster Energy drink on the counter with a small smile and hands me a ten-dollar bill. We don't talk about last Friday or yesterday's perfect game. As I scan the junk food, I want to tell her that I'm going to do everything I can to make her dream of seeing me pitch come true. When I take a quick look at her, I go blank. Instead I say, "I don't care."

"What?"

"The Kit Kats," I mutter. "You can just have them."

"Just give me my change, Biggie."

She walks out and I'm back to doing one of my favorite things: staring out the window at Highway 3. I watch guys drive by with a girl in the passenger seat. One night, I saw twenty-seven straight cars with a guy and girl in the front. Like most workdays, I begin to dream about the day when I take Annabelle on the perfect date, and she sits next to me in my black 2006 Chevy Silverado, which I bought from my uncle when he got a new work truck. I know she loves Chevy trucks. We will drive down to Cedar Falls and eat at McKellen's Steak House. I know she loves their chicken salad and popovers. Finally, we'll drive down the hidden highways and gravel roads of northeastern Iowa, drinking Honey Weiss beer and listening to Def Leppard, a band she saw with her cousin three years ago at the state fair. It was her first concert.

How do I know what Annabelle wants to do on a date? Well, it isn't from social media or overheard conversations after school. What the rest of the school knows about Annabelle is superficial garbage: tweets about getting coffee or being exhausted after a big test. She tweets about current bands and current movies as her favorites, but it's all lies, small concessions she makes in order to fit in the clique of kids who care about Finch High School. She wants to make sure that when friends see her feed, they notice she loves the same stupid things they enjoy. It's all lies.

If people found out what I know about Annabelle they would know that she loves everything old: bands like Def Leppard and Poison, TV shows like *Friends*, *Married with Children*, and *Golden Girls*—which was actually really funny when I gave it a chance.

When teachers ask her what she wants to be when she grows up, she always says real estate agent like her mother and two aunts. Rivers Realty sells most of the homes in Finch. While her mom counts down the days until her only daughter becomes another member of the Rivers Realty family, Annabelle dreams of being a writer. She loves poetry and shares her work with her cousin, who returns friendly compliments, even on the pieces that I feel aren't very good.

Annabelle lives two lives. She tells her Finch friends lies but she tells her cousin, her best friend since age three, her true thoughts, passions, and fears in rants sent with an email account that she started back in seventh grade.

For the past five years, I have known her screen name and password. Her screen name is abrivers, easy to read if you walk by her desk at the perfect time. Figuring out the password took listening skills, patience, a keen eye, and an obsession that wouldn't go away.

I was twelve years old and I had no idea that I loved Annabelle. I knew that her developing chest made me stare uncontrollably. Every day I would watch her whirl strands of her curly hair with a cheap plastic blue pen. If I looked close enough, I could see smudges of lip gloss smeared on the top half of the pen. When she walked by me in the hallway, I tried hard to look her in the eyes, but my gaze always fell to her boobs. I had to blink and turn away before I got busted as the pervert I feared I was becoming. I looked at other girls, but gawked and dreamed of only one: Annabelle Rivers.

At the start of the seventh-grade second semester, everyone got a new schedule. Annabelle and I had life science together. I could see on the top of her desk a grocery-bag-wrapped science book. On the cover, surrounded by pink hearts, green stars, and blue dots, were nine letters: annarocks.

In my room that night, I started scribbling *annarocks* on a notebook page, and I couldn't stop. I just wrote it over and over again: *annarocks, annarocks, annarocks, annarocks*—in different fonts and sizes. I would write one with a big *A* and then one with all small letters. The page must have had a hundred different versions. Finally, with the tiny bit of remaining white space, I scribbled, *Anna rocks me hard all night long*.

I didn't know what it meant, but it caused my heart to skip a beat and made me drop the pad of paper on the floor. As I rolled over on my bed to pick it up, I saw my reflection in my computer monitor. I just stared at it for one minute, then two, then five, until finally a big smile reflected on the black, dusty fourteen-inch screen.

I got up, ignored the pad of paper at my feet, and sat down at my desk. I pushed the on button and the computer started to breathe, welcoming me with its familiar chime. I went to the Gmail homepage, typing in the letters: abrivers in the ID box. With my pinkie, I tabbed my cursor to the password box. Slowly, with rising excitement creating goose bumps on my arms and pulsing static energy on my cheeks, I pressed the keys methodically with the precision of a brain surgeon: a-n-n-a-r-o-c-k-s.

After one long, deep, lung-filling, relaxing breath, I hit Enter.

CHAPTER 6
COMFORTABLE CONVERSATIONS

I have friends. Tons, actually. Over the past four years, I have accumulated a massive number of online friends. I'm not lonely, far from it. Tonight, I'm looking at pictures from my online friend Lucy's seventeenth birthday party.

Lucy lives to have fun. She loves guys and girls who party. She smokes Marlboro Lights and weed, drinks, and stays out late, even on school nights. The only reason she gets online at all is because she's so frenzied after a night of partying that she can't calm down.

In real life, a girl like her and me would never coexist. I would be way too boring with my hatred of face-to-face conversations. She parties. I hate parties. Or at least I assume I'll hate them. Yet we're good friends and I think she likes me. In fact, she likes me so much that she sent me birthday party pictures, one with her eyes closed and lips puckered to offer me a birthday kiss. Technically, she should do that when it's *my* birthday, but I still think it's cute. I love—let me repeat—I love the online world.

It's perfect. I write something out, and before I send the message, I look at every word, syllable, and letter. If I find something I don't like, I can move the cursor, erase, and replace. Online, I can have comfortable conversations without all the sweat, worry, or jitters of face-to-face confrontations.

Too bad the real world doesn't work that way. If it did, I could walk down the hallways at school, see Annabelle, and say, "You look nice in that shirt," which I often think because of her love for cool, colorful, and tight attire. If the world were a chat room, the compliment would hover in the air and allow me time to tinker, correct, and improve my sentence. I could replace *nice* with a powerful word like *great*. I could erase *in that shirt*, which brings to her attention what my eyes are focused on and replace it with something simple, friendly, and to the point, like *today*. If I could turn Finch High School into a chat room, I would talk to Annabelle every day and say things like, "You look great today."

Even with the possibility of pondering words, I still need the necessary information to make a girl fall for me. I don't lie about being overweight. If a girl asks for a picture, I send one, so I can't get by on my looks like Killer or Kyle. I have to be the nice guy, the thoughtful one, and the good listener.

I realize that my mind can't hold statistics on more than a hundred girls, so I have a black three-ring binder that I fill with notes to keep track. It's my personal black book, like all the suave men have in old black-and-white movies. When someone tells me that her dad is being an asshole, I look up notes in her section and find a page titled *Previous father rants*. All girls have daddy issues. I'll reply, "Reminds me of when he took your car without asking a couple weeks ago." She loves that. The more information I know about a person, the better. If I wanted to, I bet I could write autobiographies for fifty people that I've met online.

While I have notes on more than one hundred girls, I can probably toss out most of the notes as girls come and go. They get bored with online dating or get a boyfriend. In some cases, I have to ignore them because of what I like to call "a desire to get too close to me." Online dating is about distance and not making real eye contact. If I wanted to talk and see a girl close up, I would just talk to the girls at my school. When a girl starts talking about meeting or moving here, I ignore them. Their notes stay in the binder though. Why? I guess I just like knowing some girls would stalk me if I gave them the opportunity.

Of the one hundred girls, only a handful really interest me. There's Jamie, a girl from Indiana. She loves movies and wants to be a critic. She probably sees two hundred films a year. I live in a small town with no movie theater, so I don't get to see many new releases, but I don't tell her that. For all she knows, I see two or three movies a week. To keep up this ruse, I have three movie review sites up when we chat. She mentions a movie and I quickly pull up information on the film so we can discuss it. I'm prepared.

Then there's Maddy from Colorado. She loves to take pictures. She sends me tons of photos of mountains, animals, friends, or herself in a new outfit (or sometimes in nothing at all) and waits for my opinion. Sometimes she sends them to my email and sometimes to my phone. No matter where she sends the pictures, I have at least ten minutes to construct the perfect answer. I can't just say, "That's a cool picture." She can see right through that. I need to give interesting, deep answers—I'm the thoughtful one.

Last week, she sent me a picture of her dog standing in front of a red hatchback car. After an hour, I realized that the dog's black eyes matched the color of the worn-out tires on the hatchback. I wrote back that I loved how the smoky color of the dog's eyes matched the rips and tears of the beat-up tires. She texted back a smiley face and later sent me a picture of her boobs as a reward for understanding the importance of backgrounds in photos.

I wish all the girls I talk to loved their bodies as much as Maddy loves hers.

Other than *Don't show up at my doorstep someday*, the only real rule I have for my online girls is—don't call me, ever! This may seem like a dumb rule and maybe it is, but if I let a girl call me, I'm no longer having a comfortable conversation. I need the moments between what she types and texts to prepare my perfect answer. Talking to them on the phone is no different than me talking to Annabelle at school: a situation destined for laughter, weird looks, and ridicule. Plus no one calls anyone. Everyone texts. Slowly but surely, my dream is coming true. The world is turning into a chat room.

Only one online girl calls me: the already discussed, newly seventeen-year-old Lucy from Kansas City, Missouri. She's the only girl to break the rule, to defy me, to do what I told her not to do. See, I give out my number to girls with the stipulation that they only text and send me hot and sexy pictures. No phone calls. And with the exception of Lucy from Kansas City, they obey.

One night about four months ago, my phone rang at three in the morning. Caller ID said *Restricted*. Mostly out of it, I answered and mumbled, "Hello."

"Henry," a female's voice said.

"Who is this?"

"Lucy."

"Oh, okay."

"My car died and I'm stuck on the side of the road waiting for AAA," she said. "Will you talk to me while I wait?"

"Okay" seems to be the only word I can mutter with my eyes closed and my face shoved into a pillow.

We really didn't talk. She went on and on about how horrible her 1982 Ford Escort was acting. Then, she ranted about how this guy who invited her to this college party tried to get her drunk and when she lied to him and said she doesn't drink, he ignored her and talked to another girl. Partway through the story, I fell asleep.

The next morning she called me and said, "Hey, what's up with you passing out on me?"

I wanted to rant and rave about the no-calling rule, but I felt bad about dozing off with her stranded on the side of the road, so I let it slide and opened Pandora's box.

Now she calls a couple times a week, mostly in the middle of the night. It's not that big of a deal because she only expects consciousness from me. She talks and talks and talks and talks. When she calls now, I just balance the phone between cheek and shoulder bones and let her roll. I guess someone could say she's the closest thing I have to a real girlfriend.

"Biggie, let me in!" Maddux pounds on the door.

I quickly send an email telling Lucy how much I love the birthday pictures before unlocking the door.

"What are you doing in here, whacking off to porn?"

"Shut up. You don't even know what *whacking off* or *porn* is," I say.

"Yeah, I do," he says. "The hotels have porn on Channel 1."

"Fine," I say. "So why are you here? Do you wanna play some Minecraft or something?"

"We need to practice the knuckleball some more," Maddux says.

"We've been practicing for two weeks. I need a break," I say. "Not tonight. It's Friday, and I'm talking with my friends."

"Who?" He sticks his head between me and the computer monitor. His hair smells like day-old milk from constant batting practice and zero showers. "Invite them over to be pretend hitters."

"You need to shower," I tell him.

"I will tomorrow." He pulls his head back. "Can your friends come over?"

"My friends don't live here," I say. "They live in other states."

He reaches for the mouse. "Just click off then. They aren't real friends if you can't hang out."

I pull his arm away. "Maddux, get out of here. I'm not in the mood to pitch."

"You know, maybe if you join the team you'll get real friends," he says.

"Screw you. What do you know? I've never seen you with anyone," I say and regret it immediately. This is another reason I hate face-to-face talking—I always end up with my foot in my mouth.

"I don't care. I'll make friends this summer when I play ball," he says. "Then I'll have lots of friends, real friends in Finch, and you'll still be all alone here. If you don't want me to help you, fine. Have fun talking to the screen."

I grab the back of his T-shirt to keep him in the room. "Calm down. I'll get my glove," I say.

"Awesome," he replies and I start to think he just got one over on me. "We need to practice because there's a baseball meeting and open gym tomorrow night at school."

"What meeting?" I ask. "The season doesn't start for nine months."

"Do you not know where you live?" Maddux knows very well I do, but that question isn't expecting an answer. "It's Finch. Baseball's a year-round sport."

CHAPTER 7
NO ROOM FOR ME

My relationship with my step-dad remains complicated. I don't hate him. He loves my mom and my brother, and they are the two most important people in my life. I cannot be mad at someone who makes the rest of my family happy.

I know he doesn't hate me but I also know he hates everything about me. I know he's embarrassed by my weight and doesn't understand why I don't love sports.

When he married my mom, he knew the offspring of Aaron Abbott came with it. He must have thought I was the prize at the bottom of the Cracker Jack box. I was only four then and didn't hate sports like I do today. I'm sure it didn't take long before he found out that sports weren't the be-all and end-all for me like they were for most kids in this town, his hometown. He must have been pissed when I didn't dominate T-ball. He probably still is.

I guess it comes down to this: I put up with him and he puts up with me. I'm his tenant, and he's my landlord.

When I see him talking with Coach Phillips at the baseball meeting Maddux told me to attend, I cringe. With his blue eyes frosted and frozen, he watches me slowly climb to the fifth and final row of the bleachers in the gym. He says nothing. There are no waves or nods. I'm assuming he thought Maddux was kidding when he mentioned my upcoming pitching debut.

The more he stares, the more determined I become to prove him wrong. Yes, I'm at a Finch baseball meeting, I want to yell. My little bastard of a brother says he'll teach me to throw this magical knuckleball that will help me pitch the first perfect game in school history.

Even though I'm determined, I still feel stupid and out of place. Stupid for believing Annabelle was serious when she told Coach Phillips she wanted to see me pitch.

Three rows ahead of me, the rest of the natural baseball players are talking and laughing with each other. Kyle keeps adjusting his blue-and-gold baseball cap. Killer tells a joke with the arm movements of a mime. Everyone belongs here but me. As usual, I'm in the back of the room, quietly sitting by myself and praying that no one will notice me.

Coach Phillips talks, tells bad jokes, and hands out paper-work. As Jet hands back a pile of papers, I shake my head and wonder why I would ever pick a baseball meeting over hanging out in my bedroom. I miss my room so much right now. I love my king-size bed, my twenty-six-inch flat screen mounted on the wall. I love my MacBook. I love my online friends, 215 novels, and 127 comic books.

While I hate baseball, I do understand how it works. As I look down the bleachers, I see so many good hitters. And if—or when—I do take the mound against some other high school, they will have amazing hitters just like Finch does. What am I thinking? There's no way I can throw a perfect game. The idea sounded so interesting, fun, and, most of all, possible when I was talking about it with my brother in the comfort of my house. Now it sounds like a delusion created from hitting my head on the asphalt in gym class. If it wasn't for the forty guys sitting shoulder to shoulder and creating three rows of man-made barricades, I would sneak out. My love of the back row has done me in.

After sitting for an hour, the boys jump up and huddle around Coach Phillips. They chant, "Yellow Jackets," and walk out. A few of them look over at me on the bleachers. They probably think I'm early for a meeting of the nerds or geeks or loners. Wait. Do loners have meetings? I think I'm losing my mind or having my first panic attack.

Coach Phillips breaks my trance. "Biggie, get down here."

I keep sitting there, afraid that if I stand, I'll faint and fall to my death.

"Henry, come here."

Suddenly death doesn't sound so bad, although I would prefer to die in a much cooler way than falling down the bleachers in the school gym. I lift my ass off the seat and wobble down the steps, clinging to the railing for balance. By the time I reach the gym floor, my heart is beating out of my chest.

"Are you here for a reason?" Phillips asks with Laser looking over his shoulder. Both terrify me.

"Pitching" is all I can say.

"I heard," Laser says.

"You must have had fun in gym class, huh?" Coach Phillips asks.

I nod my head slightly. Sweat rolls down my cheek, cold sweat that normally teams with tears. But as of now, I don't feel like crying. Let me repeat. For now, I don't feel like crying. I'm out of my element, my comfort zone. I should want to go home. I should want to sit in my room, but for some reason I can't explain, I say something loud enough for Phillips and the Laser to hear. "I like pitching. I'm good at it."

"Have you ever played baseball before?" Coach asks.

"Maddux, my younger brother has taught me how to pitch." I look right at Laser. "We invented an unhittable pitch."

I squeeze my lips as tightly as possible, look away, and nod.

Coach Phillips walks over to a big, black bag and pulls out a catcher's mitt that he tosses to Kyle and a clean, white baseball. He rubs the ball with his hands as he walks up to me. As he places the ball in my hand, he says, "Show me this unhittable pitch."

Every night for the past two weeks, Maddux and I have sneaked down to the indoor diamond to work on pitching. At first I didn't own a glove, so Maddux had to softly toss the ball back to me. Eventually, I bought one off Craigslist for three dollars. Slowly but surely over the past few nights, I've been able to throw the secret pitch, nicknamed "the Wiffle ball" by Maddux, over and over again for strikes. Maddux says the pitch is part knuckleball, slider, curve, and change up.

I will need that smorgasbord of a pitch if I'm going to get through tonight. As I slip my three-dollar glove on without sneaking a peek at Laser, I try to imagine Maddux catching instead of Kyle. Maddux is a hell of a coach and I know I can throw strikes. I hold the ball in my left hand and put my forefinger firmly on one seam and my ring finger firmly on the other. My bird finger gently rubs the center of the ball and my thumb and pinkie hold the ball tight at the bottom. After a deep breath, I throw the pitch. The ball floats in the air, zigzagging left to right, north to south, and lands in Kyle's glove. His wrist barely moves. Laser gives me a small smile, which helps me breathe easier. At least I know I'm not in trouble.

Kyle throws the ball back. Once again, I put my fingers in the correct spots with the proper pressure and throw the pitch again. Perfect.

"Kyle, roll it!" Coach yells.

Kyle doesn't throw the ball to me this time. Instead, he rolls the ball a few feet out in front of him. It's déjà vu. I'm back in the parking lot playing Wiffle ball.

"Go get it, Biggie," Coach Phillips commands.

I run as fast as I can, pick up the ball, and race back to Coach Phillips. Then, like a professional bowler, he rolls the ball along the basketball floor. Before it stops, Coach tells me to "chase it."

Confused, I turn and look at Coach.

"Biggie, you're pitching, and a throw got past our first baseman. It's your job to back him up and grab the ball before everyone scores. Now go," he says calmly, as if he knows how this story's going to end.

The ball settles against the bleachers on the other side of the gym. I run for it as fast as I can. When I reach the ball, my breaths are choppy, my legs are sore, and my hands shake. I turn and look at Laser. He seems a mile away.

"Throw it in here," Coach yells.

I position myself and fire the ball as hard as I can. It slices and lands nowhere near Coach, Kyle, Maddux, or Laser.

"Bad throw and it took forever," Coach Phillips yells. "Everyone scored."

Shit. My butt lands with a thump on the bleacher.

"Let's try it again, Coach," Kyle says with the ball in his palm.

I can't go again. I can't even walk back to the spot. Saliva rolls out of my mouth and onto my chin like I'm three months old. I spit uncontrollably onto the gym floor. I feel like I'm going to die.

Coach Phillips sits down next to me. "You know, Biggie, more than forty kids will try out for this team and two-thirds of them will hear what you're going to hear, and they have played baseball every summer for a decade. I'm sure you would love to pitch, and for some schools you probably could. But here at Finch, we can't have any rookies. We win championships; we don't hold training camps. Do you understand what I'm telling you?"

"I can do this, sir," I spit out.

"I'm sorry, son," Coach says, "but there's no place for you on my team."

As Coach walks away, Kyle comes over and hands me a plastic water bottle. "You threw some nice strikes, Biggie. It's just too bad you're out of shape. Have you ever thought about getting a personal trainer?"

I hand the cup back to him and lie, "I'm fine."

❊ ❊ ❊

Later that night, I struggle to get to sleep. I keep thinking about the three perfect pitches. For a brief moment, I think a personal trainer may help, but then reality sets in. I can't even run ten feet without almost having a heart attack. I'm way past a personal trainer. I'm a lost cause.

My phone vibrates and Lucy's picture appears with her crooked, cheerful smile, her tiny hazel eyes, and freckles.

"Hey, Lucy," I say.

"I've been waiting all night to ask. How was the meeting? Did you show the coach your pitch?"

Ignoring the question, I mumble, "Lucy, I have to tell you something about me. I'm really, really fat."

"Henry, I've seen your picture." She chuckles.

"No, it's worse than you think. I'm not overweight. I'm not even obese. I'm something worse, off the charts. I can't run, walk right, or throw a ball without falling to the ground to catch my breath. I'm really, really fat and I don't deserve anyone." I hang up on her and drop the phone onto the blanket. With the meat of my palms, I wipe the tears off my cheeks. The phone lights up again and there is Lucy's crooked smile. I press the power button until the phone disappears into the black.

CHAPTER 8
CLOSE YOUR EYES AND THROW

I can't sleep. As slivers of Sunday morning sunshine pierce through open columns between my window blinds, I decide to give up on a good night's rest. For the past five hours, I've gazed at the ceiling. My eyes are bloodshot from tears and lack of sleep. It's no use. My body will not relax, my eyes won't shut, and my brain won't quit replaying what happened last night in the gym.

I need to quit thinking about sports and get back to what makes me great.

Lying on a shelf is my four-hundred-page government textbook with a backdrop of a bald eagle flying next to an American flag. As I stare at the book, calm comes over me. For the first time since I shut my bedroom door five hours ago, I feel like I'm home.

As I read about city government ordinances, my mom turns the doorknob.

"Are you okay?" She peeks inside.

"I'm fine, Mom. Just studying," I answer. Of course I'm fine. I'm sitting in my room. I'm studying for a test that I'll ace. I'm in my zone. I couldn't be happier.

"Jim told me about the meeting." She gives me a look like my grandpa died or something.

I know she's dying to ask me if I will go back again and beg for a spot on the team.

"I just wanted to check it out," I say. "Maddux talked me into it. It was dumb and I'm glad it's over."

Ignoring me, she begins a sales pitch. "Jim said he would teach you how to play if you're serious about being a Yellow Jacket."

"Well, I'm not, so it's fine," I interrupt. "Tell him that's okay."

"I'd just like to see you two do something together," she says. "You never hang out. It would just be nice if you and Jim could get along like he does with Maddux."

"Maddux is his son," I say.

"You're his son too."

"Whatever," I say, knowing I'm right. "Laser hates me. Or at the very least thinks I'm a fat loser. He's just like those jocks at school who think sports make the world spin. Well, sports don't. Governments do, so I'm just going to sit here and learn about the executive branch. If Laser wants to do something with me, why can't he come into my world? Why can't we work on school stuff together? Oh wait. That's right. To him, sports are everything and school is a nuisance, which is probably why Maddux has never been in a school."

"Stop it," Mom commands. "If you want to be homeschooled too, that's fine. Just ask. Nobody said you couldn't get a tutor like Maddux."

"I don't need a tutor. I go to school and I get straights *A*s," I yell loudly even though Mom is a couple of feet away. "I'm sorry for yelling. I'm fine, Mom, really. Just writing an outline."

"Henry Abbott."

My mom never calls me Henry Abbott, so the full name grabs my attention. It's quickly apparent that she hasn't accepted my apology. Henry isn't even my real name, or at least original name. When I was born, Mom, who had just turned seventeen, named me Aaron after my father, who was also seventeen. Both were one month away from starting their senior years of high school. Sixteen months later when my dad's parents presented Mom with papers renouncing his rights to me, Mom changed my name to Henry after my grandfather.

So why is my last name Abbott, even after my biological dad put in writing that he wants nothing to do with me? Well, because Laser has never adopted me. I guess in some ways I don't have a father. I have two contenders, but one left me legally and the other doesn't want me.

When I hear my full name, I quit debating her, throw out the empty bag of chips, and close my government book. I would do anything for Mom.

The indoor diamond sits next to our house but feels so far away from everything I know. It's like our home has two worlds: the baseball world and the Biggie world. Guess where I live? The walk takes me five minutes and Mom follows me the entire way. There's no turning back. I open the door and find Laser at second base placing baseballs into a white bucket.

"Jim!" Mom yells. "Henry wants to play baseball with you."

Laser pulls a baseball out of a bucket and tosses it at me. I rapidly pull on my glove and catch the ball.

"Do you wanna play baseball?" he asks.

"I'm sorry for embarrassing you," I say.

"That's not what I asked," he says.

I'm so nervous, standing in his world, five long minutes from mine, that I forget to throw the ball back and instead let it fall to the ground next to my feet.

"Do you wanna play baseball?" he asks again and fires another ball to me, this time a little harder and sort of sidearm.

I flinch a little but catch the ball. "It's okay," I say.

Laser drops his arms limply. "Jesus Christ, Biggie, could you just answer the question?"

"I'm sorry."

"Don't apologize, just answer the question."

"I did!" I shout. Then I whisper, "But I don't anymore."

"Why did you think you could pitch? You haven't played a single inning of baseball since you were six years old, and you quit T-ball after three games." Laser loves to bring up my short T-ball career.

"I threw a perfect game of Wiffle ball in gym, and Maddux taught me a knuckleball so I could also throw a perfect game in baseball," I quickly mumble, slurring words together. If Laser and I were in a chat room and I had some time to construct an answer and repeat it in a clear voice, I don't know what I would say. I can't honestly answer the question because I don't really know. Would throwing another perfect game be cool? Yes. Would I love to feel the rush of stepping on the mound? Yes. Do I want to give up a home run or turn my head over and over again as the other team racks up hits? Hell no. I don't know what to say.

Laser drops a ball into the bucket. For a second, I think, this is over. He's going to tell me to leave and his interest in me will end before it really starts. But it isn't over. He lifts the bucket, walks over, and drops it next to my left foot.

Although his eyes are peering right into mine, I can still see Mom over his shoulder. I think about her and Maddux and how happy they would be if I played for the Yellow Jackets. I also think about Annabelle and Jet talking about my magic curveball after gym class.

"Look at me." Laser places a baseball in my hand and uses his fingers to bend my arm to a sixty-degree angle. He lifts my left hand behind my ear and brings it forward. "When you throw a baseball properly, you want the ball to almost touch your ear. Okay?"

I must be blankly staring at him because then he says, "Biggie, I need you to say something or at least nod."

I choose to nod, keeping eye contact.

He reaches down and puts his hand behind my right knee and lifts my leg up, pulls it forward half a foot, and places it back down. "Perfectly straight. You need to lift your leg as high as comfortable and step forward out, perfectly straight, and as far as you can. You want your leg to hit the ground at the same time your hand with the ball reaches the side of your head. Plant and release the baseball. The power comes from your legs—which right now feel like a hundred pounds of pudding, but we're going to turn them into tree trunks—and then you'll get your velocity from the muscles in your legs."

I nod a couple more times and begin to sweat. I don't know if it's because I'm nervous or from lifting my leg.

"Stand straight up," he continues. "Feet parallel to your shoulders." He grabs my wrist and spins it, like an evil school nurse taking your pulse. "Place your fingers comfortably tight across the seams. Lift your leg and slowly pull the ball back behind your ear, drop your leg, bring the ball past your ear, and fire. Keep straight and the ball will go straight."

I nod again.

He walks away and I stand there by the bucket of baseballs. He keeps walking and walking. Soon, he's a lot farther away than Maddux or Kyle ever stood when I pitched. He picks up his glove. "Close your eyes tight and go through what I just taught you."

That doesn't make sense. "Close my eyes?" I ask.

"Tight," he shouts. "You'll throw straighter if you think about the steps and not worry about where you're throwing."

That makes no sense, but what have I got to lose? With my eyes closed, I imagine the smile on my mother's face to keep myself calm. After a long, deep breath, I repeat the six steps in my head.

1. Place your fingers comfortably tight across the seams. I remember the step, but I really don't know what "comfortably tight" means, so I just grip it hard.

2. Stand with feet parallel to shoulders. I can't see if they are parallel, but it feels right.

3. Lift my leg and step forward as straight as possible.

4. Bend my elbow and pull it behind my head.

5. Drop my leg and rocket my arm forward at the same time.

6. Release the ball as soon as I plant my foot.

With my eyes closed, I can't see where the ball goes, but I hear the rubber hit off the diamond. I open my eyes and watch the ball bounce past Laser.

"You have to throw a lot harder. C'mon, you weigh three hundred pounds. Show me what you got."

I grab another baseball from the bucket.

"Close your eyes!" he shouts.

I run through the six steps again, and this time I throw it as hard as I can. I open my eyes and the ball bounces to Laser—at least not past him this time.

"Not fast. Don't throw it fast. Throw it *hard*. Pretend like you're throwing it as far as you can, but remember the steps to throw it straight."

With my eyes shut once again, I grab another baseball from the bucket and run through the six steps again, squeezing the ball tightly and grinding my teeth. This time I try to throw it over Laser's head and hit the back wall. Before I can open my eyes, I hear the ball pop into his glove.

"That's great, Henry," Mom says, clapping.

"Again," Laser says.

I pick up a ball and close my eyes. This time, I throw it even harder.

Pop. "Woo-hoo," Mom calls, clapping even louder.

"Again," Laser shouts.

I close my eyes and throw as hard as I can. Now I'm trying to throw the ball through the back wall.

Pop. I love that sound even more than Mom's clapping.

Laser walks up to me. "I thought I saw it last night. Under all of this"—he does an hourglass silhouette with his hands to remind me that I'm obese—"is that concrete block of a boy your father was. The fact that you can pitch like it's no big deal means you got some of his genes. Now we just need to find that concrete block. Not just drop pounds, but replace them with muscle. The good news is that it's only September and high school baseball here in Iowa doesn't start until late May. We will need every one of those days to make you a real ballplayer."

"Coach said—"

Laser interrupts me. "You live in a Kaczor house and you're the only local offspring of Aaron Abbott. Trust me, you'll get another tryout, and when that day comes—and it's month and months and months away—you'll wear gold. If you eat right and work out with me every morning at five a.m., you will wear Finch gold."

I turn my lips up a little to let him know I'll do it.

"Good. See you tomorrow morning at five."

As Laser walks toward Mom, I want to ask him so many questions.

Do you really think I can make it? How much weight loss are we talking about? How long until I can throw fast? Why do you care now? Where were you the past ten years? Why doesn't school matter? Why do you only care about baseball?

All of the questions bounce around in my head, but when I open my mouth, "I don't want to be a failure" comes out.

Laser turns around, and he and Mom stare back at me.

I don't know what I'm saying. The words just come out like there's a man inside of me working my vocal cords. Maybe that's why I'm so fat; someone is living inside me.

Then I realize why I said it and continue, "I want to be the best, not a failure. I want to be great, you know. Can you promise me that?"

"That you'll be great?"

"That I won't be a failure."

"Son, all I can promise you is this: when everything is said and done, you will feel something so wonderful and so addictive that you'll wonder why you waited so long to feel it."

CHAPTER 9
THIS ENDS NOW

I hate my alarm clock. Its beating and pulsing sounds give me a headache as soon as my eyes open. Lifting my arm and pounding the snooze button takes all the energy I can muster at 4:45 a.m. I need the seven minutes between the beeps to wake up. On top of the alarm clock, Mom taps on my door. "Sweetie, Jim's waiting," she says.

This isn't a dream. I'm an athlete now. I climb out of bed and lurch into the bathroom. I fill a Dixie cup full of sink water and take a drink. I repeat this six times. I'm thirsty all the time lately, especially in the morning.

My eyes get only a sliver of space between my eyelids to find Mom and Laser sitting in the living room. He's putting his tennis shoes on and Mom's holding a glass of orange juice, no pulp. She thinks pulp is bad for you. Even after the water, I empty the glass.

"Biggie." Laser hands me a shoe box. "I got you some shoes to work out in. Your mom said your old shoes were worn out."

I open the box and see a pair of Nike shoes: black with one gold swoosh through the middle. They feel so firm and tight, even with the laces untied.

"What do you say?" Mom chirps.

"Thanks, Jim," I say with my eyes now wide open and staring at the shoes. They are kind of cool, but my size fifteen feet can barely squeeze into the size fourteen-and-a-half shoes.

"You want workout shoes to be tight to help keep your feet pointed forward," Laser says. "I thought we would walk a mile. Are you up for it?"

I release a wake-up deep breath and nod optimistically, but I have zero idea how far I can walk.

The walk starts with complete silence. I try to make out how fast I'm walking, so I can then figure out how long the walk will last. My best guess is that a block is approximately one hundred meters. A mile is roughly 1,600 meters. I walk the first block in 127 seconds. I have no idea what Laser's thinking, but I'm counting. I'm doing math. That's a little over two minutes. If I can keep this pace, this walk will last 2,032 seconds or thirty-five minutes. Thirty-five minutes is way too long for him to keep quiet.

Thirty-five minutes is also a pipe dream. The second block seems shorter, yet it takes me 143 seconds to walk it and even that pace is hard for me to keep up with. Soon walking a block is going to take me almost three minutes. Soon I'm going to need to take a break. I'm starting to fear this walk might take all morning.

"Biggie." Laser breaks the silence. "Why did you go out for baseball? And don't tell me it was to throw a perfect game."

60

Well, Laser lasts all of 277 seconds before asking what the hell I'm up to.

"Two weeks ago in gym I threw a perfect game in Wiffle ball," I say. "I told Maddux about it and he said he could teach me to throw a pitch that would be unhittable, allowing me to throw a perfect game. There isn't more to the story than that."

"The knuckleball?"

I nod and struggle to lift my pudding legs, as Laser calls them. I need to take a break, but I'm terrified to say something to him. "The pitch is not really a knuckleball," I say instead. "It's multiple pitches thrown into one. We call it a Wiffle ball."

"Do you have other pitches?"

"A fastball that not really fast," I say.

"You're a big boy with a good pedigree," he says. "I can teach you to throw some heat."

As we cross the three-block mark, I can feel my face turning red and my feet swelling inside the already-too-small shoes. My shoulders must weigh a million pounds.

"You're going to love being on a team," Laser claims. "You'll help them on your good days. They'll help you on your bad days. There's nothing like being on a team."

I move my head up and down to let him know I'm listening. My eyes fill with sweat and my tongue turns to sandpaper. I'm so thirsty. If I don't get something to drink, I'm going to pass out.

"I know that you haven't had good luck with coaches, but you can't let that bother you," Laser says. "I realize that Coach Phillips seems like a jerk after cutting you yesterday, but he's a good coach."

61

I start to breathe slower, louder. The grass in front of Mr. and Mrs. Bowen's house looks so comfortable. I should just fake fainting and take a rest while Laser tries to figure out what to do. No. I can't do that. Cars are driving by, and in a town of a thousand people, word would get out that I passed out. Instead I try to slow the pace down without Laser knowing. How fast am I going now? I've lost count.

I struggle to keep count in my head. Between the choppy breaths, sweat-filled eyes, and Laser's questions, my mind can no longer do math. Is this the fourth block or fifth? How far have I walked? My eyes are more closed than open now and the sweat pools distort my vision and I can't really tell whose house is whose. I don't know where I am.

"I wish I could say the same for your T-ball coach." Laser keeps talking. "Now, he was a straight-up asshole. I never told you this, but I feel really bad for not saying anything."

"*Can we stop?*" I place my hands on my knees. Laser unhooks a water bottle from his belt and hands it to me. How did I not see that earlier? I drink the cold water like I've been stranded on a desert island for fifty years.

"Drink slowly, Biggie," he says. "Getting into playing shape isn't going to be easy, but if you're committed, you'll get there."

My breathing returns to normal after the six ounces of water and the five-minute break. "I'm okay now," I say with little confidence. Laser's not even sweating. He snaps the bottle back to his belt without as much as a sip.

"You know, I was so disappointed when you quit T-ball that I didn't even understand what you were telling me," he says. "Now that

I have Maddux and he's going to play organized baseball, I realize what a jerk your T-ball coach was. To make two overweight six-year-olds race for everyone's amusement—that's horrible. I'm really sorry for not saying anything to him."

I don't accept Laser's apology. Maybe I would've ten years ago when it happened, but he called me a quitter when I, with tears all over my face, said I hated baseball. We had just met and maybe he made a rookie mistake, but I hated him a lot more than my coach that day.

He's sorry now. Well, I don't give a shit.

I need to start counting again. "How far are we?"

"We've walked four blocks. Twelve to go," he says.

I want to die.

After eating Mom's tasteless low-fat yogurt and strawberries for breakfast, I hightail it out of my house with my mind on a sausage-and-bacon-combo breakfast sandwich from Molly's and a twenty-ounce bottle of Mountain Dew to chase down the greasy treat. After walking a mile, I need some protein, caffeine, and carbs to get through the day.

I pull up to the drive-through, order my usual, and wait for *my real breakfast*, not that bird food Mom gave me. Shelly, my favorite drive-through lady, hands me the bag. I open the sack and let the smells and steam wash over my face. I'm in heaven.

I look up and Laser's black Explorer sits right in front of me. "Pull over," he mouths through the windshield.

He followed me. Is he going to play private detective now to make sure I eat only morsels from my mother?

"You forgot your phone," I can hear him say as he walks from his truck to mine.

Although he's holding up the phone, I still give in to the urge to check my pockets for it. The only bump I feel comes from a pen in my left front pocket. The early morning walk took forever and I had to rush to get ready for school.

"Are you even a little bit serious about baseball or was this morning some joke to you?" He tosses my phone onto my lap.

"I was hungry," I muster.

"You just ate five minutes ago," he says.

"That's not enough food. I can't make it through the day."

"That's bullshit," he says. "That's all I had. That's all Maddux had. You don't need to stuff your face all the time."

In the twelve years I've known Laser, I've never been scared of him or worried he'd hit me. Until now. His face has a red glow. I can tell he wants to pound the crap out of me.

He slides the palm of his hand down his face, traveling over his eyes, the brim of his nose, and his lips.

"You have high blood pressure," he says, "It's way too high for a seventeen-year-old. Don't you care at all about your health? Do you want to have a heart attack in your twenties? What's wrong with you?"

I don't answer any of the questions. I just squeeze shut the Molly's bag, holding in the steam.

"You're three hundred pounds, Biggie," he continues. "Three hundred pounds. Listen to that—three hundred pounds. Is there any part of you that is tired of looking—?" Unable to think of a nice word, he stops and shakes his head.

"I'm sorry" is all I can say.

"You better apologize to yourself," he says. "Or to your mom. How can I tell her about this? I mean, you're going to kill her before you kill yourself. She worries so much about you. Do you have any idea how many times she has cried herself to sleep? She goes to the grocery store to buy you healthy food. She gets up early every morning to make you a nice breakfast. And you repay her by sneaking food behind her back."

My eyes look straight ahead, over the steering wheel, on the cars and trucks racing down Main Street. If someone gave me a million dollars, I still wouldn't turn to look at Laser.

"Give me the bag, Biggie," he orders.

I grip it tighter. "No. If I don't eat this, I'll pass out at school."

He squeezes my wrist to loosen my hold, but I keep my fingers locked on the paper bag.

"You will not pass out at school. That's ridiculous. This bag of grease will just make you fat, not healthy."

"You know if people didn't call me fat or Biggie all the time, maybe I would care more about my weight."

"You don't want to be called Biggie?"

"Would you?"

He leans in, rips the bag out of my hands, and says, "This ends now. You are going to play baseball next summer, and you are going to weigh two hundred pounds doing it. You want people to stop calling you Biggie? Well, do you?"

With my eyes focused on the floor at the Mountain Dew that Laser has yet to secure, I offer a small smile.

"God damn it, Biggie, talk!"

"I don't want to be called Biggie anymore."

"You want something in life, you have to earn it. You don't want me, Maddux, your teammates to call you Biggie, then you have to earn it."

He reaches forward, grabs the Mountain Dew, and gets out of the truck.

I drop my head against the steering wheel and grip it tight. As I shake the steering wheel like I might yank it out and grind my teeth, a thought boils inside me and I lean back and scream at top of my lungs.

"*God damn it, Mom. Why did you rip up that note?*"

I dig my fingernails into my forehead and scratch down my face, almost cutting open skin. When I reach my neck, I whisper, "My life's over."

CHAPTER 10
#FRIENDS

I don't sleep much anymore. Most nights, I stay up until two, talking online and then lying in bed until three or three thirty. And since I agreed to get up at five to work out, my nightly shut-eye has dropped to an hour and a half. Thank goodness for the caffeine in Mountain Dew or I would fall asleep in class or behind the wheel.

Tonight all I can think about is Annabelle. Ever since eighth grade, I have known she would be my first date, my first kiss. Now I'm a junior and I've done nothing about it.

Earlier I peeked again at her Gmail account. I know that makes me a creepy stalker, but I have good reasons. One, I'm planning the perfect date, which will be a night she'll never forget. Yes, I'm snooping, but the way I look at it is that when we're eighty years old and reminiscing on how we met, I doubt she'll care how I put together the night we fell in love. Second, I'm addicted to her poetry. She sends all of her poems to her cousin, Margaret, who lives on an air force base in Germany. The first poem of hers I read is called

It Felt Like Being Drunk. The poem itself sucks. It rhymes but the rhymes are not good. The first two lines go like this or something:

Tuesday was a blast. Wednesday sucked ass.
Thursday flat out stunk. Friday, I will get drunk.

I always wonder if she drank when she was a seventh grader or if it is a metaphor for doing something else, something seventh graders do. I don't know how to explain it, but the idea that she might've gotten drunk when she was thirteen made me like her then, and now, five years later, I still like her. I just can't find the perfect time to ask her out.

If I'm going to be Annabelle's boyfriend, I'm going to have to lose weight. I know that. I'm not stupid. She's beautiful—dark hair with red streaks, little nose, green eyes. She's about five-foot-six with massive breasts trapped inside those amazingly tight V-neck shirts, my favorite. She has her ears and nose pierced. The nose piercing, a little silver stud centered on her left nostril, makes me melt every time I see her. She probably weighs around 160 pounds—not anorexic, but not fat either. Since I fell for her five years ago, she's had five boyfriends. Three of them easily weigh more than two hundred pounds, so she doesn't like skinny guys.

I figure if I can get down to 250 pounds, she would go out with me. And if television diet shows have taught me anything, it's that fat people lose weight at a faster rate than skinny people. With Laser training me, I should lose fifty pounds in a few weeks.

Once I reach 250, I need to quit being a pussy and step up and ask her. I have all the research I need; I just need to pull the trigger and ask her out. But how do I do it? How can I ask out someone who I've never had a single conversation with? She comes into the convenience store most nights, so I could just ask her then. But what do I say? *Hey Annabelle, want to go out with me sometime?* No, I need a more open-ended question. It's a girl's reflex to say *no* when asked out by surprise. Maybe I'll ask her what she's doing on Friday night. That's pretty open. She can't say no to that.

But what if she tells me she's going out on a date, which would be worse than her saying no. I guess I could ask her if she's still dating Mike, but then I might come across as her dad, wondering what she's up to. This is so difficult.

My problem is that I'm trying to accomplish this the hard way—in the real world. Nothing good ever happens in the real world—at least not to me.

As I think about her, I feel the urge to see that smile, those eyes, those V-neck shirts. I roll out of bed and flip open my laptop.

I pull up Twitter and log out of my account. As I go to log in with her information, I stop. For years, I've scrolled through her private, protected photos with her password, but now, after the perfect game, I wonder if I could just be her Twitter follower and see the photos that way. I've never sent her a follow request. In fact, I'm not friends with anyone at school on any site. I keep my online and school worlds apart.

Not that I haven't thought about sending her a request. I mean, we do go to school together. I doubt she wouldn't accept it. But then a small part of me worries that she would find it weird that I asked.

Maybe she would take a closer look at me and figure out that I've been logging on to her account for years. Whenever I've considered sending a follow request, I've decided it's better to remain invisible.

But tonight, I send the request. It happens so fast. Half of me wants to take it back, but the other half is curious. What will happen next?

The message comes across the bottom of my screen: *@Annabelle has approved your request.* And then I get another message: *@Annabelle is now following you.* I immediately click on her photos and start scrolling. The pictures are ten times hotter now that I can look at them because she wants me to see them. There's no way I'm sleeping tonight. I'm too excited.

CHAPTER 11
ONE HUNDRED OUNCES OF MOUNTAIN DEW

While Laser never told Mom that I was sneaking junk food, he did convince her to send me to Dr. Pence. There's nothing worse than being fat in a doctor's office. When people walk into a waiting room, they scan the room and wonder what each person has. It's human nature. In most cases, no one knows. But when someone sees a fat ass sitting there squeezed like a sardine into a chair built for someone half his size, it's pretty easy to figure out why he's there—because he's fat.

As I sit there, I watch people look at me and lift some pity smiles. They feel bad for me like it's horrible being fat. I hate those pity smiles. I want to scream, "Don't feel bad for me. I'm a hell of a lot smarter than you."

"Henry Abbott," a nurse shouts out.

"C'mon," Mom says with a rub of my thigh.

The last time I went to this doctor, I weighed 275 pounds. It was February 16, and I told Mom the weight gain was due to Valentine's Day chocolates.

I know the first thing the nurse's going to do is have me step onto a scale, which will likely put me on the wrong side of three hundred. I try to wear baggy clothes, sweatshirts and sweatpants, and stay out of sight, so Mom won't know, that despite her best efforts, I've put on weight. She's not stupid, but I'm sure she believes I've put on five or ten pounds. I doubt she realizes that I've crossed three hundred pounds. The doctor says she should weigh me every couple of weeks, but Mom doesn't. I think it's because when she sees the numbers 270, 280, 290 pop up, she'll start to cry or be embarrassed. Instead she makes me low-calorie meals and hopes the granola, fruit, and baked chicken work wonders.

There's little I can do now. I'm three steps from the scale and all the baggy T-shirts in the world aren't going to help me now.

I step on the scale. It immediately flashes 319 pounds, then drops to 313 before settling at 317, a new record. Wow, I really thought missing out on a week of Molly's and walking a few miles would lower my weight, maybe to even less than 300.

Mom smiles at me as we walk to the exam room to wait for Dr. Pence. Her smile is the same pity smile the old ladies and little girls shared with me in the waiting room.

Dr. Pence is a jackass, know-it-all old man who treats me like a cancer patient. He loves to tell me that if I don't stop eating junk food, I'll die. I would believe him except for the fact that dozens of people come in and buy shit from me every night in the convenience store. All we sell is crap food: potato chips, Twinkies, pop, beer, beef jerky, and greasier food than a fast-food joint. Sure, I eat fried food at Molly's and drink Mountain Dew like water, but so does everyone else in Finch. I wonder if Killer, who loves Dew as much as I do, gets the you're-going-to-die speech.

In the past few years, I have figured out a way to keep from being made fun of at school. All I have to do is keep quiet and to myself. The plan works. Everyone leaves me alone, except for Dr. Pence. He's the only person who talks about my weight, who tells me I'm too big. No matter how hard I try, I can't keep him from mocking me. And he does it in front of my mother. Is he doing his job? Maybe. But that doesn't make me feel any less worthless when I'm in his office. When he knocks on the door, I just want to scream: *Leave me alone!*

Dr. Pence smiles as he sits. I'm not falling for it. I know I'm going to get some typical jackass lecture from him.

"How do you feel, Henry?" he asks.

"Fine. I've been working out, so it's good," I mumble like an idiot.

"You're working out. I'm happy to hear that."

I hate this so much. I want to walk out so bad, but I'm trapped. He's going to ruin my day. I know it. He's going to make my mom cry. I just know it.

"Henry, your high blood pressure has gotten worse, and I assume when we get your blood work back, that your cholesterol will also have gotten worse. You're now six-foot-three and a half inches tall and you weigh three hundred seventeen pounds."

He leans back into his chair and presses down on the edge of the table with the tips of his fingers. I stare at them and try to ignore what he's saying.

"What worries me and your family is that when your mom brought you in here in February, we put you on a diet—remember?"

I say nothing. I just sit there with a blank look on my face. He can look in my eyes, but he's not going to see me sweat.

"Answer him," Mom commands.

With jumbled and practically unrecognizable words, I mumble, "I remember."

"Now your mom says that you've been on this diet for eight months, but I don't see any indication of a person on a diet. What I see here is a person addicted to eating—or a person trying to commit suicide with food."

Out of the corner of my eye, I can see a tear roll down Mom's cheek.

I knew it, I think to myself. *I knew it. I knew it. I knew it. He made her cry.* My mom's crying, which makes me want to cry. I fight it. I can't cry in front of Dr. Pence.

"We're going to run tests next week to see if you have adult-onset diabetes," Pence continues. "I'm scared to death that the results will come back positive. I'm worried that you're doing damage to your heart and especially to your kidneys. Are you thirsty a lot?"

I stay quiet and continue the staring contest. He wouldn't have asked if he didn't already know the answer.

"Henry?" Mom waits for an answer.

I look at my hands. I twist my wrists and stare at my palms as if the veins and vessels will tell me if I have diabetes. Of course I do. Of course I have it. I'm fat. And no doctor, not even Dr. Pence, would use that word around me if he wasn't 100 percent sure.

"Are you thirsty a lot?" Mom asks again.

"I only drink liquids when I'm tired or need to stay awake," I answer with little thought. I'm on autopilot right now.

"Do you drink water or coffee?" Dr. Pence asks.

"Water," I say.

"Kari, could you leave us alone for a second?"

"No, I want to hear this," Mom says through a hand now pressed against her face.

"Okay. Henry, when we met last time, you told me that your favorite beverage was Mountain Dew and I told you that you needed to drink healthier liquids. Are you still drinking Mountain Dew or other sugar-based sodas?"

"Sometimes," I say.

Dr. Pence gets up and walks to the front of his oak desk. With his shoulders curled and his hands clasped, he stares right into my eyes. "Henry, I need you to be honest. This isn't a game. Do you drink pop in the morning, during school? Do you drink pop at lunch, for dinner, before you go to bed, or whenever you body craves it? Do you drink sugary pops?"

"Most days, I drink five twenty-ounce Mountain Dews."

"That's one hundred ounces of pop," he says to Mom as if she couldn't calculate the answer herself.

I look at Mom, but she looks away, crying. I hate this man. I hate everything about him. He's an asshole. Fuck him and his dumb questions. He should have forced Mom to leave the room before this inquisition.

"But I haven't had a Mountain Dew in days." I try to save the situation and stop the crying. "All I drink is water and juice. I'm in training."

Dr. Pence gets a box of tissues for Mom. "Henry, come in

Monday for the test. You will need to fast for six hours before. Kari, if the results come back positive, we'll have to meet again and talk about treatment."

Mom blows her nose and nods.

"Henry, I truly hope the results come back negative and this training you're talking about works," he says. "I'm going to tell you what I tell every one of my obese young patients."

"What's that?"

"The last thing I want to do is attend your funeral."

CHAPTER 12
STIPULATIONS

It's weird when someone discusses your death. Sitting at the convenience store, all I can think about is diabetes.

Although I don't feel sick, I decide to not eat any junk food and I'm only drinking bottled water. There is nothing to get you off the Dew like hearing your gray-haired doctor say he will be going to *your* funeral.

As I start to feel completely depressed at my unraveling life, a bright light walks into the store: Annabelle. She skipped school today, so this is the first time I've seen her since she accepted my follow request at three in the morning. So even though I've known her since I was five and have been in love with her since I was twelve, this is the first time we've officially been friends.

She grabs her Lo-Carb Monster drink and picks up a Kit Kat. I guess she's going to buy it. My boss would hate that I'm bummed she doesn't steal anymore. It was our thing. She drops the junk food on the counter.

"Three twenty-five," I say, breaking my routine of not saying the total out loud. She pulls out a five and I count out her change. I should say something. We're online friends now. I should ask her about her day, her clothes, working at Molly's, something. She takes the dollar bill and three quarters and puts them in her small purse, black with a red flower, cuter than the massive tub-sized one she carries sometimes. Time's running out. I need to say something. What are friends if they don't talk to one another? I don't know, but they aren't friends. *Biggie, say something.*

"I was surprised you were up." That's what my head came up with. I'm an academic genius, and what my wonderful and well-disciplined brain told my lips to say is *I was surprised you were up.* Wow! I hope she walks out the door.

"What?" She turns and looks at me confused. Annabelle must have come in here a hundred times and never heard a word of small talk, so I don't blame her for wondering what the hell is going on today.

"You accepted my follow request at three in the morning," I say. "I guess I thought you would be asleep."

She leans back against the glass, placing enough pressure to open the door a sliver. "I wasn't feeling well and couldn't sleep. That's why I wasn't in school."

"Well, thanks for approving me," I say.

Just when I think she's going to walk out and head off to work, she steps forward.

Stand up straight and look her in the eye. She wants to talk. We've practiced this.

"Does your house really have an indoor baseball field?" she asks.

Oh. She wants to chat about Mom's house. I release a breath of both relief and disappointment. "Well, it's really just a baseball diamond under a tall roof. You only have to hit the ball one hundred twenty feet to reach the wall."

"Wow, that's cool," she says. "Can I get a tour?"

"What?"

"My aunt is teaching me all about the family business and she wants me to write some practice listings and you live in the most interesting house in town."

"It's not that interesting," I say.

"Whatever, it must be the only house in Iowa with its own indoor baseball field."

"I guess."

"I would love to see your house, get a tour," she says, still waiting for an answer.

I'm in the middle of the best conversation I've ever had. Not only am I talking to her, but she wants to hang out. What do I do? Do I quit while I'm ahead and invite her over for a tour or do I push it? Should I see if she'll agree to something else? Heck, I might have adult-onset diabetes at age seventeen, so I'm due for some good luck. Maybe, but I chicken out and say, "Sure, come over anytime."

"Cool. Thanks, Biggie."

She heads for the door and I close my eyes, open my mouth, press the heels of my hands to the counter, clear my head, and speak. "How about Friday and we get some food first?"

I'm not going to lie. Annabelle's face turns pale and her freckles disappear. I wait and wonder if she's going to yell "Gross." Time ticks away, while Annabelle stares at my wide-open mouth and eyes. My hands clasp together, expanding veins and arteries to the point where they almost break through my skin.

"I'm not going on a date with you," she says, something I figured out a few seconds back. "I just wanted to see the indoor baseball field."

"No, no, no," I say. "I just have a gift certificate for two to McKellen's and I don't want to be a loser and take my mom. That's all. Not a date. I won't tell anyone, I swear. I saw you with Mike. Remember?"

I'm relying on my email surveillance. I know she loves McKellen's but getting caught with me would be a disaster to her reputation.

She stands there, one hand holding open the glass door. "Well, Mike's a cheating asshole," she says, "so I'm not with him. But just because we broke up doesn't mean I'm going out with you. I don't even know you that well."

I nod violently. The excitement of her breakup with Mike only makes my blood race faster through my diabetes-filled body.

"Pick me up from Molly's at five on Saturday," she says.

"What?" I say, "So you'll go to McKellen's?"

"It's not a date," she says. "I just like the popovers. Don't tell anyone about this, you got it?"

"I don't talk," I remind her.

"And I swear if you tweet that we're going out or that you're my boyfriend, I'll never talk to you again."

CHAPTER 13
SMALL-TOWN HICKS

I have spent the last four years getting ready for this night. I must have read a hundred Annabelle emails and written twenty pages of notes and time lines in my green binder. I know some people would call me a stalker or a voyeur, but without that information, I have no shot with a girl like Annabelle.

Yesterday, before I mentioned the certificates, she gave me a look that screamed, "You're a weirdo," but by releasing a little bit of the intel I have gathered over the years, I'm two minutes from picking her up for a date. Okay, she doesn't think it's a date, but I put together an online survey with some of my Reddit buddies and forty-five of the sixty-seven people I explained the situation to say it's a date. So, I say it's a date.

As I park at Molly's in my newly washed Chevy Silverado, I hope that Annabelle changes after work. I'm sure she looks cute in the navy-and-tan work outfit, but I would love her to put on something tight and short. I want to see her legs and cleavage. She has amazing legs that I can't wait to touch.

She bolts out of the side employee door, wearing a bulky red Iowa State T-shirt and jeans. Better than the uniform, but nothing like Mike got.

Annabelle opens the door and climbs in the cab. "Nice truck," she says. "My uncle has a truck like this."

"Thanks," I say. I don't say *I bought it to impress girls*, but I did after reading last year about her love of Silverado trucks.

If I can be honest, I have never been to McKellen's and there are no gift certificates. I meant to buy some online but kept forgetting. Hopefully Annabelle will forget that too.

Before today, I had no idea how to get there. Thank you, Google Maps. As we hit the interstate, I turn up Def Leppard's "Let's Get Rocked."

"I dig this song," I say. In reality the song is all right, but not as good as Leppard's early stuff. But I know that Annabelle loves the song. Her cousin just saw Def Leppard in Germany, and they were talking about when they used to do a dance number to it as kids. "Sometimes I feel like I'm the only kid at Finch that loves eighties stuff."

Annabelle gives me a weird look. She tilts her head like a confused dog. "How would you know?" she asks. "You never ask what anyone likes."

The freshly trimmed hair on my head starts to itch, my fingers tingle, and my lips dry.

"I hear things, see things," I say. "When you're not talking all the time, all your senses are heightened, kind of like a blind person hears and smells really well."

I peek at myself in the rearview mirror. I look clean-cut with just the right amount of chaos.

I sneak a glance at her. Annabelle doesn't seem interested in talking about music or even my lack of chitchat at Finch. She's gazing out the window as we pass combines harvesting October corn. After only ten minutes, Annabelle's bored.

The restaurant is dark, which bums me out because I can barely see Annabelle's green eyes. For some reason, elevator music plays overhead. The table has a small lit candle and a white tablecloth. The waitress brings us a basket of bread and butter. I'm not a big fan of bread and butter, which keeps me from embarrassing myself in front of Annabelle. I can be a messy eater when I'm hungry, and right now I'm starving after a day of skipped meals. I know a person can't lose twenty pounds by not eating one breakfast and one lunch, but I figure a day of fasting can't hurt.

Neither of us says anything, which is nice. I know it's weird to be on a date, especially a dinner date, where no one talks, but I feel comfortable in silence. If only I could do something about the clang of dishes and glasses or the small talk from surrounding tables about traffic, cold bread, and lack of water. Those noises start to bug me and I notice Annabelle holding in a yawn. I need to do something out of the ordinary and shake things up.

"So," I say, "do you come here often?"

Do you come here often? That's out of the ordinary. Am I in a singles bar? What's wrong with me? I'm super intelligent and I've planned for this night for years. Why can't I just be cool?

"Used to," she answers. "My family used to come here a lot when

I was younger, but then my two older brothers went to college, so we stopped coming. I guess my parents think it's too nice of a place for just the three of us to go."

"How many brothers do you have?"

"Just the two older ones," she says. "I'm the baby."

"I'm the oldest," I say. "My mom had me when she was in high school."

"Yeah, I know the story," she says.

"What story?"

"Are you kidding me?" she asks. "It's not every year that the star volleyball player and the star quarterback have a kid together. My mom still talks about how your mom got pregnant and cost the volleyball team a chance at a state title."

"I'm sure my mom's sorry," I say.

"Oh, it's not that big of deal," she backpedals. "Just letting you know that"—she searches for the words to finish the sentence—"I know some stuff about you."

"I like your pictures on Twitter," I change the subject. "They're fun."

I expect her to say thank you or that's nice of you, but instead, she asks, "Who are your friends?"

I sit there silently. Is she going to make fun of me right here in the middle of this steakhouse for not having friends? I should've just kept my mouth shut. This date is turning into a Monday morning at Finch High School.

"We go to a really small school," she continues, "and everyone has a friend or two or three or ten. I mean, when you go to a school this small, it's hard not to have a bunch of friends. But I used to think you didn't have any, which is fine, if that's what you want. If you want to live like a hermit or something, that's your God-given right, I guess."

I'm not a hermit. A hermit by definition is some old guy with a gray beard living in the mountains. I just don't like talking in school. Those are two completely different things.

"But," she continues, "then you asked me to follow you on Twitter and I looked at your feed and you have like four hundred followers—twice as many as I do. So apparently, you like people, just none of us."

Does she think I don't want friends? I'm not some weirdo. I don't hate people or live in a shack on some mountain. I just don't say a lot or care for the jocks who go to our school.

She stops and stares and waits. The ball's in my court. How do I respond to her accusations? Do I just tell her I'm not a hermit? Do I tell her that I like people online a lot more than the people I go to school with? I don't know. So, for lack of a better option, I go with the truth.

"Kids at our school are mean," I say. "It's seems like every time someone opens his mouth, someone else rips on him. Everyone just makes fun of everyone else all the time. If you say the wrong word or stutter or slip or make a weird noise, someone is always there to make fun of you or laugh at you. I don't put myself out there. I don't say anything. And then I don't get made fun of or laughed at. Those people on Twitter, they just wanna talk. They want someone to listen to them. And they don't make fun of me. They're not mean."

Calm comes over my body. Saying all that out loud feels very therapeutic and cleansing. The words didn't sound dumb out loud. It all made sense.

"Do you think I'm mean?" she asks. "I like to joke around, but I don't think I'm mean. I don't think most people at school are mean."

I know Annabelle's a nice person, but not from how she acts at school. She's a big smart-ass at Finch, just like everyone else. I know the real Annabelle. She's so nice to her cousin in her emails and she always has nice things to say about people when she writes about them, but I can't bring up the emails for obvious reasons. "You seem nice," I say. "You've always been nice to me."

"Well, I just think you shouldn't judge people," she says. "You shouldn't think you're better than us."

"I don't think I'm better than everyone," I say honestly.

"You so do. You've always thought you're too good for us," she says. "You look down on us. You're the smartest kid in school, living in the biggest house in the county, and we're all just a bunch of small-town hicks."

"I don't think that at all," I say. "I just sit in the back of the room. How does that make me stuck up?"

"I'm not saying it's true, but you never talk to anyone," she says. "You ignore everyone like you hate them. When I come into the store, you never say hi or anything. Would it kill you to just once say, 'Hi, Anna.' What am I supposed to think? I've wanted to ask you to give me a tour for months and months, but every time I try to talk to you, you just give me a mean look, just like you do to everybody."

Thankfully the waitress brings our food, which forces Annabelle to stop berating me. Although my eyes are closed and my neck is stiff, I can feel the eyes from surrounding tables looking at us.

"Forget I brought it up," she says. "Let's just eat."

Maybe it's the lack of food in my stomach, but this rib eye tastes like candy. I shove small squares of medium-well meat into my mouth like jelly beans. Once the steak disappears, I scoop up garlic mashed potatoes. My tongue struggles to keep up with the constant flipping of warm potatoes into my mouth.

The steakhouse doesn't have Mountain Dew, so instead I slurp down Mello Yello in the time it takes Annabelle to eat one forkful of her chicken salad. Chewing vegetables, she looks at me like I'm a bear at the zoo that just ripped apart and swallowed a fish. I can tell she's dying to say something about the way I engulfed the twenty-dollar dinner, so I speak first. "I'm joining the baseball team."

She swallows a crouton covered with French dressing. "About time."

"What?" I ask.

"I mean, Biggie, you live at a baseball field. You really should play baseball, right?"

"Yeah, I probably should."

CHAPTER 14
MR. CRAWFORD

For the past hour, I've listened to Annabelle talk. She told me about the teachers she likes and the teachers she hates. She complimented my truck. She even admitted to stealing a stop sign off West Valley Drive. I've said nothing. As Mom gave her an eighty-minute tour of our house, I thought of my next move.

I don't want her to go home. I want to spend the rest of the night with her. Ask her to go for a drive in the country, off the congested roads between Finch and Cedar Rapids.

As we reach Molly's, I go for it.

"Let's hang out more," I say. "I mean, I want to be nicer to you. I want to hang out some more."

It sounded horrible. Really, really horrible. The suggestion is nothing like what I practiced in my head, something about moonlight, blah, blah, blah. Okay, maybe what I wanted to say was awful too.

"Um," she mumbles, which instantly tears my heart in two. "I told Michelle that I would be at Killer's party by ten. I'm already late."

"Oh, okay. I just thought I would ask," I say.

"You can come with," she offers.

"To Killer's?"

"Yeah."

"I don't think he likes me," I say.

"Why would you think that?" Her face scrunches together as if she's smelling something vile.

"I don't know, but I know he doesn't want me at a party."

She straightens her face and says, "All right. See you at school." And she jumps out of my truck. As she walks away, every part of me wants to roll down the window and accept her offer.

Does Killer like me? No, not really. But I know the reason I'm not going isn't because it's at his house. It's because I don't want to go. I want to go to my bedroom and get on my computer. And although I know passing on a real party with real conversations for an online one is dumb, especially considering who invited me, I can't bring myself to lower the window.

I wake up exhausted. I have no idea how much sleep I got, but it wasn't a full night. As I sit up, I wonder if Annabelle emailed her cousin about our date. If she has, that's a sign that she feels it's a date, a real date. After screwing up last night, maybe I'll get a second chance.

I type in her password *annarocks* and wait. There it is: Re: Saw the indoor baseball field. She must have sent an email from her phone, and her cousin has already responded. There must be big news inside of it. She must have had a good time. I click on the email:

Hey Cuz.

Went out with kid from the gas station. His parents
have an amazing house on the edge of town with
an indoor baseball field. His mom's really cool. She
has tons of nice stuff. She even joked that if I'm
an agent and they want to move, I could sell the
house. Oh and he's a Def Leppard fan like you!

Well, I'm going to bed. This weekend call me!!! Mr.
Crawford has gotten worse. He won't take his gross
eyes off me. I don't know what to do, should I say
something? Call me!!!

Anna

Her cousin replies:

I can't call you until tonight, so it may be early
morning Iowa time, so stick by your phone. Can
you sit in the back of the room? I don't know.

Cool about the Leppard fan, my kind of guy! That
house sounds amazing. You're going to be a kick-
ass agent someday.

Mr. Crawford, a twenty-something math teacher at Finch, must
be staring at her boobs or something. I've never had him, but I've
seen him flirt with girls in the hall. Never Annabelle, but I'm not
surprised to read the email. The idea of Annabelle being nervous and

uncomfortable pisses me off. I need to solve this problem. But how? I can't tell her that I read her emails. I will need to be sly, bring the topic up under the radar. She should come into the store on Monday night, so I have two days to figure this out.

CHAPTER 15

WE DON'T MAKE FUN OF YOU BECAUSE YOU'RE FAT

Work has always been my time. There's no one here to bother me. There's plenty of food and drink. Over time, my best customers have realized that I hate talking, so they don't even attempt chitchat. I know it's just a glorified gas station, but I love it here.

Tonight has not been much fun. Like a kid brushing his teeth a hundred times before going to the dentist, I lay off the junk food. I haven't eaten any junk food since Dr. Pence told me I might have diabetes.

Dr. Pence thought I had diabetes once before. The previous diagnosis I knew was stupid. People just know when there's a disease walking around inside of them. This time, I'm starting to believe I have it. My skin itches all over as diabetes ravages my body. Dr. Pence warned me so I have only myself to blame. But for the hell of it, I'm laying off fried foods this weekend. It's probably too little too late, but what the hell.

So I'm chugging water bottles with reckless abandon. In the hour and a half I've been at the store, I've finished four bottles of water. I wait patiently and nervously for Annabelle. I know she works tonight and she always gets something before her five-hour shift. I want to find a way to bring up Mr. Crawford without making her suspicious that I have been reading her email.

Call me an idiot, but I think I should just tell her. Be honest. I hear girls at school complain about lying assholes all the time. Maybe if I tell her that I read a poem of hers back in seventh grade and I go into her email every now and then to read more of them; tell her I'm her biggest fan; tell her I don't read any other emails, she will blush and appreciate my honesty. Maybe if I'm honest, that will set her mind at ease, knowing it's a friend who's peeking.

I want Annabelle to have the perfect date and that's why I go into her email. What girl wouldn't want the perfect date? I know most guys are selfish and don't care about what their girlfriends think, but I'm different. I have to be. Big guys like me can't get by on our looks. Girls need to be impressed by our honesty and our caring nature.

No, this is stupid. I can't tell her. She'll overreact. Never mess with a teenage girl.

I hear a car door slam and I know it's Annabelle. Her Taurus door squeaks when she opens and closes it. That sound gets me excited in a B. F. Skinner kind of way. I struggle to find breath. For some strange reason, I stand up straight; I haven't voluntarily stood up at work since, well, ever.

She walks in without looking at me and heads to the coolers. We just hung out a few days ago, where's the hello?

She sets the energy drink down.

"Hey, Annabelle," I say. "How're you doing?"

"Okay, Biggie," she answers.

"No candy?"

"Nope," she snaps.

"Are you okay?" I ask.

"Fine," she takes the change from my hand.

Since the other night, things have changed between Annabelle and me. How do I know? I know because simply knowing things about her isn't enough anymore. For years, I was happy with insider information. Now if I know something, I have to do something. I can't just let her mope around.

I know I'm not her boyfriend, but I still feel like I have to solve this Mr. Crawford problem. From her latest email to her cousin, I know he's stalking her and she caught him driving up and down her street. I need to help.

"You know Mr. Crawford, right?" I ask.

She spins around with a confused look.

"He came in here and was a complete jerk to me," I lie. "I hate the guy and wish he would leave town."

"What did he do?" she asks.

"Just treated me like an idiot."

"Mr. Crawford's a nice guy to everyone," she says.

To be honest, I've never talked to Mr. Crawford. I'm learning that while he may be a pervert who loves to stare at girls' cleavage, he could also be a nice guy.

Annabelle walks toward me and sets the energy drink back on the counter. "Have you been talking to friends of mine about me?"

"No," I say. "Why?"

"I'm just going to say this one time and then I'm going to leave," she says. "Quit playing games. I don't know what you're doing, but please stop." She picks up the drink and heads for the door.

"You can tell me anything," I say to her back. "I don't talk to anyone, so every secret is safe with me."

Still facing the door, she repeats herself, "Quit playing games. I don't like it."

"I'm not playing games," I say. "I just want you to know."

She turns around. "Have you heard that I've been having issues with Mr. Crawford? Who told you?"

"No one said anything."

"Whatever, I know you're in AP math classes. He's not your teacher, and he lives in Waverly, so he wouldn't stop in here on a Saturday."

"Annabelle," I say.

"I'm just going to go, because, to be honest, I feel really uncomfortable right now."

"Don't leave," I say.

This could be a dream. My entire body feels hollow. I can't feel my heart beat, my blood flow, my lungs pump, my stomach churn, or my eyelids blink. This could be a dream. There is no noise. No one else is in the store on in the parking lot. Not a single car has flown by the store on Highway 3. Yes, this could be a dream.

"Fine," she says. "If you have something to say, I'm listening."

"I'm not playing games." A lump grows in my throat and I feel like I could suffocate any second. Knowing it's now or never, I keep my mouth open and force out the words. "I've just liked you forever, so I want to make you happy. You need to know that whatever I've ever done, it was to make you happy."

"Ever done?" she asks.

With no reservations, I blurt out, "I can read your emails. I know everything about the real Annabelle. You can be yourself. In fact, that's what I want."

She fires the Monster at my shoulder. Shocked, I don't move. The aluminum can bounces off my shoulder, sending a sharp pain down my arm.

"You hacked into my computer!"

"It was an accident." I squeeze the pain out of my arm, I hear a whistle behind me. As if someone shot a BB through the can, energy drink squirts out of the aluminum like Old Faithful. The broken can spins like a pinwheel in a hurricane, dancing all over the floor. Turning away from Annabelle, I corner the can like I'm chasing a chicken and snag it. Energy drink fills my palms and covers my forearms and T-shirt. I toss the can into the garbage and find that Annabelle's left the store. I race after her.

"Leave me alone," she yells, facing the highway.

"Annabelle," I say out of breath. When will the morning walks start helping? "Please, let me explain."

She turns and I stand there speechless. I have no idea where to start. I have two choices. I can go with the perfect dates or the poetry. I go with the perfect dates. "I just wanted to know what you like, so I could take you out on a perfect date."

She points her finger at me. "First off—and you fucking listen

96

to me!—we have never, ever, ever gone out on a date. And I swear to God that if you mention last night to anyone, I will tell the world that you got into my email like some pervert. Second, why are you so weird?"

"I'm not weird," I reply and notice that people at the pumps are watching Annabelle swing her head and hands, searching for words, like she's having an epileptic seizure.

"You're the weirdest person I know. You never talk, you never go out, and you never try to make friends. And then when you decide to hang out with someone, you break into their email to see what they like to do. That's weird, Biggie. You know what normal people do? They ask the person, 'What do you like to do?' But not you. You hack into people's computers."

She stops talking to catch her breath. Two carloads of people pull into the parking lot and decide to watch us instead of entering the store.

"I'm so sorry" is all I can come up with.

"You don't talk because you think people will make fun of what you say. That's weird," she says. "I know what you think. You think we make fun of you behind your back because you're fat, but we don't. I swear. We make fun of you because you're just so weird."

"Listen, please," I beg. "It was something I tried in seventh grade and it worked. I read some of your poetry. I just wanted to know about you, and I was too shy to ask."

"You read my poetry."

"Yeah," I say.

"Fuck you, Biggie. Fuck you."

"Why are you so mad? I'm coming clean. I'm being honest."

"It wasn't for you!" she screams. "I didn't want you or anybody else in this hick town to read my poems. Do you have any idea how embarrassed I am right now? I feel like an idiot!"

"Don't feel like an idiot. I'm the idiot."

"Stay away from me," she pleads. "I hate everything about you. I didn't think you could be any weirder." She gets into her car and slams the door.

CHAPTER 16
THIRD CHANCES

I sit outside Dr. Pence's office and wait for my tests to come back. I haven't eaten in ten hours, but I'm not hungry. I want to have diabetes. I want to die. Today in school, everyone stared at me. I know Annabelle told everyone what happened. Even if she didn't, word would have spread anyway. Finch is a small town, and a girl screaming at a guy in a parking lot is big news.

I'm now the fattest and weirdest kid in school, and it's only a matter of time before I'm arrested for illegal email surveillance or computer hacking.

I rub the small circular bandage on my arm where the nurse took my blood. The results from my blood glucose test should be finished any second now. My mom keeps telling me that everything's going to be all right, but I'm ignoring her. She's another female I've hurt in the past week. When did I become such a liar? When did I stop being a good person? My love of junk food made me fat and hurt everyone around me. I would rather die than look into either Mom's or Annabelle's eyes. If not for my perfect attendance, I would have skipped school today, got out of Laser's truck, and just walked all over town. People say that when times are tough, you should be around friends. I disagree. For me, when times are tough, I want to be alone. I'm happy only when I'm alone.

"Henry," Dr. Pence's secretary says. "Dr. Pence is ready to see you."

I get up with Mom, Laser, and Maddux.

"Sorry," the nurse says, "he only wants to see Henry. He'll call the rest of you in later."

I hate Dr. Pence. He thinks it's still 1950 and the world doesn't have WebMD or websites about being overweight. I don't need a doctor to tell me that I have to lose a hundred pounds. And I really don't need a doctor that loves to sit on the edge of his desk and look down on me. He's probably like my customers who eat potato chips and drink Mountain Dew and never gain an ounce of weight. How can everybody in town eat like me, but not look like me? Can you answer that, Doc?

"Hey, Henry," he says in his fatherly tone. "How do you feel?"

Really? That's what he's opening with? How do I feel? I haven't eaten for ten hours and I probably have diabetes, which, along with my high blood pressure, means I'm going to need medicine and constant healthcare for the rest of my life. So to be honest, Doc, I'm doing pretty shitty, but I know Mom wants me to be polite, and I've hurt her enough this week, so I keep my thoughts to myself. "Okay," I lie.

"I asked you in here alone so we could talk about a few things," he goes on with his dry, I'm-the-smartest person-in-the-room tone. I'm sure he uses it everywhere. I bet his kids hate him too.

"Do you remember when I saw you in February?"

I nod.

"We tested you then for diabetes and it came back negative," he reminds me. "So I told you that you were given a second chance. With your parents we came up with a healthy eating plan. Do you remember?"

I nod again.

"Well, I'm going to ask you if you and your family did what I asked, and you can be honest. Whatever's said in here will stay in here. No one will know."

"Thank you," I say.

"Do you remember telling me that you were going to start exercising regularly?"

Of course I remember. I remember everything, I'm a straight-*A* student. *Can you just tell me what I need to do?* I think to myself, but out loud I say, "Yes."

"Henry, your mom wrote out your weekly diet for me." He holds up a piece of paper. "It looks like a lot of good food, healthy vegetables in moderation." He puts the piece of paper in front of me. It's a monthly calendar that Mom puts together. Every day it has what she plans to make for our family. "Is that what she makes for you?" Dr. Pence asks.

"Yes," I say.

"After breakfast, do you ever get something else before school?"

I nod. Last week, I would have lied, but suddenly I'm tired of lying.

"When?" he asks.

I say nothing. I just hang my head.

"Henry, I need you to be honest with me so I can help you. How many days a week do you eat on your way to school?"

"Most days."

He nods, disappointed.

"After you eat the lunch your mom packs for you every day, how often do you get more food in the cafeteria?"

"Most days."

"And after dinner, how often do you get more food?"

"Just on nights I work, but I haven't recently."

"How recently?"

"The last week."

"Henry, your mom said she found a note you forged to get out of gym class. Have you been going like she asked?"

"Yeah, I'm going to gym this year."

"What about last year?"

I just shake my head.

"Why, Henry? Why did you treat your body like that, knowing what you know? You have high blood pressure and are a hundred pounds overweight. Why don't you do something about these health problems while you're still young and capable of change?"

"I don't know."

"I want you to know that I appreciate your honesty and I'm not going to tell your mom about all the extra eating you have done. Even if I did, she wouldn't care as much about the lying as she would about the fact that you're slowly killing yourself."

"Do I have diabetes or not?" I stand up and look him in the eye. I'm so sick of his judgment. He's like 180 pounds, ripped. He doesn't know what it's like to be three hundred pounds. He doesn't know what it's like to live my life. I don't want a lecture. I just want to know if I need to start taking diabetes medication.

"No, Henry, you don't have diabetes," he says. "God wants you to have a third chance."

"What?" I start to cry right there in his office.

"You don't have diabetes. It came back negative."

I put my face in my hands and cry harder than when my grandma died. I can't stop. I have no control. I can feel the tears roll down my cheeks.

Dr. Pence reaches for a box of Kleenex. "Listen, Henry, I don't mean to be insensitive because I know this is very emotional, but you haven't beaten it, not yet. You have to change your life now. You have to quit lying and sneaking around and let the people that love you help you."

"For the past week, I've been exercising, getting up at five a.m., to run with Laser," I say with the tears falling onto my tongue. "He's been driving me to school so I won't get food. I have started to change my life, and I think that's why I'm okay." I wipe the tears from my face and breathe slowly to stop crying.

"You're only okay for now, and you still have high blood pressure."

"I know, but I swear, Doctor, I'm going to change, change everything."

"Good. Now go through that door there and clean up," he says. "It's my personal bathroom. No one will be in it."

I keep wiping tears off my cheek as I walk into the small bathroom. I turn on the sink and try to wash the puffy out of my cheeks. I blow my nose and take choppy breaths. My face feels frostbitten and my fists are clenched.

I look at my face, and I look so fat. The red, puffy cheeks only emphasize what people see when they look at me. I'm fat. I stare at my rounded shoulders and bloated chest. Not even the XXL T-shirt can hide my colossal gut. I've never really looked at myself like this before. I'm studying. It's not a quick glance while I comb my hair. This is an inspection.

Dr. Pence said God wants me to have a third chance, and I know most people don't get that. I'm going to finish all the goals I've set for myself. I'm not going to be fat anymore. I'm going to weigh two hundred pounds. I'm going to be in shape. I'm going to throw a perfect game for the Yellow Jackets. I'm going to be valedictorian. I'm going to continue my perfect attendance. And no matter what happened this weekend, Annabelle is going to be my girlfriend. I'm going to kiss her, hold her, and have sex with her. We will go out to eat, to movies, to concerts. We will text all day long at school and talk on the phone late into the night. To accomplish these goals, I have to set another one. One so important, I stand up straight, suck in my gut, and confidently say it out loud.

"I'm not going to be weird anymore."

CHAPTER 17
THE COOL GROUP

I need to show Annabelle that I can be just like everyone else—a "brick in the wall" as Pink Floyd sang. To do this I will need to make friends, tell jokes, and be social—all things I don't normally do at Finch High School.

But what do I say? Which students do I talk to? When do I say these things? Days keep crawling by and I'm still just sitting in the back of the classroom, listening to teachers, taking notes, and preparing for quizzes and tests, all the while saying nothing and doing the things Annabelle finds really, really weird. For years, she would sneak a peek at me now and then. The glances weren't followed by any real facial expressions, but there were glances. I didn't imagine them.

Now she never looks at me when she walks into class, so I know she's really angry. Not surprisingly, the Gmail account that gave me access to her secrets has been closed. She sent me a three-word direct message: *Turned Gmail off!* Worse, she hasn't stopped in the convenience store since the night she called me weird.

Days pass, and instead of opening my mouth, I think about Annabelle in the parking lot. I can't shake the memory of her scarlet cheeks and dilated eyes. I still can hear the slamming car door and whispers from the nosy people watching in the parking lot.

After two weeks, I've decided to give up. I will not be able to talk in class. It's impossible. I need a new plan—one without potential panic attacks.

Instead, like an undercover narc, I start to listen to everyone to collect information and formulate a plan to become popular. Since the parking lot incident, I've started following every classmate on Twitter and Instagram to see what people are doing and saying. I've taken a break from long-distance relationships and started solely focusing on Finch High School.

Slowly but surely, the plan comes together. Rather than taking notes in trigonometry, I craft how to fix things between Annabelle and me. Just like a five-star general, I plot the perfect path to win her heart. As I put my plan to paper, the tip of my black pen races over the white sheet. I now have the time line from sweaty student to Annabelle's make-out partner. As perfect as my scheme is, the first step sucks. I, the disappointing son of a school legend, need to ask Coach Phillips for a favor.

Sitting inside Coach Phillips's office, I look out the window and see students walking, running, talking, and hanging out. There are plenty of people at Finch who would love to be my friend. Heck, I could hang out with any freshman I want, but that doesn't help me with Annabelle. She needs to see me out and about, chitchatting with fellow students. Hanging out with kids outside of the cool group won't change her mind about me being a weirdo hermit.

I spin around in a squeaky old vinyl chair and try to remember the last time I asked anyone for help. I'm pretty self-sufficient—a huge job requirement for shy guys who prefer silence to small talk. I always have plenty of good-working pens and clear, crisp sheets of paper for class. I wear a watch so I will always know what time it is. And I have mastered simple truck and computer repairs. Unless something crazy happens, I should never have to ask anyone for help. With these skills, my life has been perfectly calm until Annabelle went all crazy in the convenience-store parking lot.

I have been completely out of sorts in the three weeks since our fight. My note-taking has fallen off so much that in the last week, I have ripped apart three assignments with a *B* scribbled at the top. I toss and turn every night in bed because of a bad mixture of headaches and stomach pains that just won't disappear. I'm desperate, which is the only reason I'm trying to sit still in this crappy chair in Coach Phillips's office.

Since he's nowhere to be found, I reread my plan's five steps, starting from the last step and working backward to the first. The final step puts Annabelle Rivers in my arms. She will be my girlfriend and we will kiss, sneak into each other's bedroom windows at night, go to homecoming and prom together, and pass notes in class. We will be full-fledged—no doubt about it—boyfriend and girlfriend.

The other steps are to become friends with Michelle and Becky. Before that I will become friends with Killer and Jet, and before that I will become friends with Kyle Reddick by helping him with his homework, which he will think is Coach Phillips's idea.

Becoming friends with Kyle shouldn't be too hard. We are locker mates and he usually keeps his mouth shut. With the exception of everyday greetings like "Hey" or "What's up?" or "How's is it going?" we never talk and I think he likes that setup as much as I do. He grew up in Chicago and spent two years in Des Moines before moving here in ninth grade, which makes him an outsider, a horrible thing to be in small-town Iowa. He might as well wear a big *O* on his shirt.

Outsiders are never truly accepted. Everyone assumes their parents have come to town to steal jobs, and their kids have come to the tiny high school to steal girlfriends and starting spots on sports teams. Towns like Finch are like some bad sci-fi movie where a kid is given his job in kindergarten and there's no going back. Everyone's fate is set. If someone comes to town late and throws those initial plans out of whack, they are assholes and must be destroyed.

Well, Kyle's family has yet to be destroyed, although I think his parents split a while back when his dad couldn't find work. I guess Kyle's dad found out the hard way that it's tough to find a job when you're an outsider.

Kyle showed up two years ago standing six feet tall and weighing almost two hundred pounds without an ounce of fat. He's ripped and has sandy blond hair and a small smile that's always accompanied by a couple of head shakes—sort of like a human bobblehead doll. Unlike most kids at Finch, he doesn't have a nickname. Nicknames tend to be handed out on the elementary school playground and since he was hundreds of miles away when I became Biggie, he's just Kyle.

All the girls went crazy when he showed up. He was like Justin Timberlake. Girls just stood in the hall like zombies and watched him walk past.

There's an urban legend that a junior girl, two years older than Kyle, dropped her books as he walked by. When he, a lowly freshman, handed them back to her, she fainted. I'm not saying it's true, but that's the story.

Somewhere between the fainting and today, Michelle tamed him. The class's most energetic and fun-loving person fell for the school's second-most shy kid. The two started dating as sophomores. Since there was no way that Michelle's parents were going to let her go to the movies with an outsider, she asked Annabelle and Becky to go with them to the theater. Killer and Jet saw that Kyle had a couple extra girls and they sat down and introduced themselves to the outsider. Before the previews were over, Finch had its cool group.

To become the group's first new member in twenty-four months, I need Coach Phillips to help me, which he won't be thrilled to do. I can't prove he hates me, but his cold, emotionless stares remind me how frustrated he is with me. He thinks I have wasted my legacy. Instead of coaching the offspring of Aaron Abbott, he has had to deal with a fat ass bringing I-don't-want-to-play notes from made-up, out-of-town doctors.

"Biggie, how can I help you?" Coach finally walks into the room.

I clear my throat and wait for him to file a couple papers into a drawer. After clearing a big enough space in the middle of his desk for his elbows, he rubs his goateed chin with his thumbnails. "Did you bring a note?" he asks.

"What?"

"A note to get out of gym class."

"No," I say. "I'm not getting any notes this year."

He leans back as I grip the aluminum handles on my chair, squeezing them so tight I expect the nails to pop out any second.

"Then why are you here?"

"Is it true that Kyle may be suspended a couple of football games to get his grades up?" I ask.

Coach just stares at me, and my breathing slows to a point where warm air feels like a wool blanket on my tongue.

"I can't talk about football players, Biggie," he says.

"Well, I'm his locker partner and I heard him telling Jet that you might sit him out a couple of games to make sure he passes all of his classes this quarter," I say deliberately. "You said you didn't want a repeat of last year when Kyle failed two classes and didn't play in the playoffs."

"I can't talk about it, Biggie," he repeats. "Anything else?"

"I'll tutor him, teach him study skills," I say. "I can help him."

"Are you looking for a job?" he asks. "Because I can't pay you."

"I'll do it for free," I say. "I just want to help out."

Coach rocks back and forth in his chair, making a creaking noise like a cricket chirping. "What are you up to?" he asks.

I run my tongue across my lips and chew on my bottom one for a few seconds before answering. "Kyle's nice, nice to me, and I want to help him. If I work with him, can he still play on Friday? I mean it's only Monday. There must be stuff we can do before Friday night, right?"

Coach sits back up and looks at me. I feel like I should say something, but I just look back. He's reading me. Coach knows I'm up to something, and I am, but nothing diabolical. I really do want to help Kyle.

He finally leans back and says, "There's a quiz in my geometry class tomorrow. If he gets a *B* on it, the entire football team will be thrilled."

"So no suspension?"

"Biggie, can't talk about suspensions with you, but let's just say everyone will be happy, including Kyle, if you can help him get a *B*."

"Cool," I reply. "So you'll say something to him?"

"Excuse me?" Phillips asks.

"You'll tell him that he needs to study with me?"

He laughs. I'm not sure what's so funny, but I smile back anyway.

"Sure, I'll tell him to come to your place at seven thirty tonight."

"Thank you, Coach." I get up.

"Biggie, are you still throwing with your step-dad?" He snaps open a cold aluminum can of Diet Coke and takes a long drink.

"Yes, sir," I say.

"Good. Keep me up to date on how that's going. We could use a big left-hander who's in baseball shape."

I nod.

* * *

Kyle's late, which only makes me more nervous. I know it's stupid, actually idiotic, to be nervous about a kid I see everyday coming to my house to study, an activity I've mastered. While I should feel comfortable, instead I'm very, very nervous. I should call and cancel; erase this five-point plan, this overreaching attempt to solve my Annabelle problem, as a foolish idea. Ever since she called me a weirdo, I haven't been able to think about anything else. When I run in the morning, I think about her yelling at me. I can't study, not well, because her voice constantly rattles in my head.

"You're so weird," I hear over and over and over.

I need to change her mind before I lose my mind.

Forty minutes later, Kyle knocks on my door.

"Don't screw this up," I whisper to myself, while I walk to the front door.

"What's up, Biggie?"

"Nothin'," I say.

"Kyle, great game last week." Maddux pops in from the kitchen. "Three touchdowns—and the third one, running over those four guys. Awesome!"

"I don't think it was four," he says.

"This week, remember to hold on to the ball. The Lions love to strip it from you."

"Maddux, get out of here," I say. "Kyle's not here to talk football. He's here to talk about math."

"Nobody cares about math," Maddux says. "Football's king."

"Actually, little guy, I need to care about math or I won't be playing on Friday." Kyle high-fives my brother and Maddux looks like he's going to faint right there, just like that junior girl two years ago.

"Are you serious?" Maddux asks as Kyle messes up his hair. "Coach can't kick you off. You're our ground game."

"Maddux, get out of here!" I repeat.

"But," Maddux protests.

"I'm taking care of it," I say. "Now go!"

He mopes off into his bedroom, and Kyle and I set up shop at the breakfast table in the kitchen.

He opens his book and pulls out a small green pencil. I've never seen such a weird-looking writing utensil. He wraps his hands around it and then scratches letters like a three-year-old would color in a cartoon dog.

"Here." I hand him a real, freshly sharpened No. 2 pencil. "You won't be able to write legibly with that."

He takes the pencil and twirls it around, inspecting it. "Are we writing tonight? I thought we were doing math."

Before I can answer, his phone vibrates on the table.

"Damn, I forgot to call Michelle," he says as he types something on his phone.

"Is she mad?" I ask.

He sets the phone back down. "No, not really. She's getting pizza with Annabelle."

Every inch of my body wants to ask him if we can join them, but we need to study. If I don't keep Kyle from being suspended, he won't want to be my friend. Tonight's about work. Hanging out with Annabelle comes later. I need to be patient.

"So where do we start?" he asks.

"Has Annabelle ever said anything to you or Michelle about me?"

I can't resist asking. It's only eight o'clock, and math can wait a few minutes.

"What do you mean?"

"Do you know about our fight in the parking lot of the convenience store?"

"No," he says. "All I know is that you stood her up at Killer's party a couple of weeks ago."

My body goes numb. I need all the strength in my neck to keep my head from falling face-first onto the wooden tabletop. I feel hollow inside like I'm in a dream, which might be a nightmare. "What?"

"She said you asked to hang out with her, and then she told you to come to Killer's party and you were a no-show. I don't know about a fight. I didn't even know you two hung out."

I just sit there and ask the same question over and over in my head. Why didn't I go to that party? I'm an idiot. She must like me or why would she tell people she agreed to hang out with me. *Pull yourself together, Biggie. You can do this. You can fix things. She likes you. This isn't a setback. This is good news.*

"All right, man, let's get you a *B*."

CHAPTER 18
MY BIG BUTT

On Thursday night, I open my front door and find Kyle standing there without a math textbook and his hands deep inside his pockets.

"How do you like me now?" He pulls out a quiz with a *B+* written in red ink in the upper right-hand corner. "Can you believe it? I got them all right, except for this one, which I forgot to fill in." He points to the question with his forefinger and then shows it to me again. "Here's the crazy thing—I knew the answer. I just got so pumped that I knew all the answers that I skipped right over it."

I have no idea what to say. I'm happy for him, I guess. In reality, if I had gotten a *B* because I missed a question, I would have been seriously depressed. The ice cream in my house would not be safe.

"You, me, party, tonight," he says. "Now that I'm back on the team, Killer's throwing me a party and I told him I'm only coming if Biggie can come too.'"

"It's Thursday night," I say.

"So we won't be out late," he replies. "We sit around a bonfire and then Michelle"—he peers over my shoulder to make sure the living room behind me is empty—"is going to bring some beer. C'mon, let's celebrate." He lifts the quiz a third time.

"Will Annabelle be there?"

"I can have Michelle convince her to come."

I lose my breath. I am minutes away from talking to her. In just four days, I've accomplished three of the five steps, and tonight I might conquer step four: becoming friends with Michelle, Becky, and Annabelle. All that's left is to get Annabelle to go out with me again. Hell, I might ask her out tonight. We could drive around and drink Honey Weiss. I have never executed a plan so well, so quickly before.

"Okay I'll go, but we need to stop at the convenience store first."

I can feel the heat from the fire before we even get out of the truck. It's sixty-eight degrees out, warm for October in Iowa, so a fire isn't really needed, but it adds ambiance. Jet, holding a Mountain Dew, stands next to Killer as he tosses chopped wood onto the roaring flames.

Jet's the smallest kid in our class at five-foot-six, 155 pounds. Although he's tiny, he's fast and strong. Just last week, he was our weekly paper's Athlete of the Week after he caught ten passes for 220 yards and four touchdowns in Finch's fifth football win of the season. He has long brown hair and the worst five-o'clock shadow in school. Only a handful of hairs grow out of his face and none of them are close together.

"Biggie, what's up?" Jet asks.

"Nothing." From my backseat, I grab a twelve-pack of Bud Light for the guys and a twelve-pack of Honey Weiss for Annabelle and me. Another perk of working alone at a convenience store is the easy access to alcohol. On my first day at the convenience store, Joe, my half-ass trainer, only taught me one thing—how to steal beer.

"There aren't any cameras in the store room so just make sure the tray's right and don't get pulled over and you're good," Joe said.

You don't need to read Annabelle's emails to know she loves Honey Weiss. Whenever I've overheard Michelle bring up a party, Annabelle always answers, "There better be Honey Weiss."

Each of my hands holds a twelve-pack of beer, which makes me Jet's best friend for the night.

"You brought beer!" he cheers.

"I did," I say. "I grabbed it out of the storeroom and put the money in the cash register. It all adds up at the end of the night."

"So you can get us beer whenever?"

"If my boss isn't there," I say.

"Interesting," Killer says. "Well, let me welcome you to the gang." He snaps his fingers and gives me a thumbs-up, which makes me very uncomfortable. Am I supposed to give him a thumbs-up? Or a nod? I go with the nod and some type of crooked grin.

"So, Biggie, what have you been up to?" Killer asks.

"He's training with Laser," Kyle informs him. "He's going out for ball next summer."

Ball, in some towns, means football or basketball, but in Finch, it's baseball. Baseball's our game. Everyone knows it, especially the football and basketball coaches.

"You sure it's good for your health to play ball?" Killer asks but doesn't wait for answer. "We don't need someone having a heart attack in the fifth inning."

The guys laugh so loud no one hears me say, "I'm losing weight," so I have to say it louder. "I'm losing weight!"

"Really?" Killer asks. His head is still bouncing from laughing at his own joke.

"Yeah, I'm less than three hundred pounds now, and I can now walk two miles without passing out."

"Damn, I didn't even know you weighed three hundred pounds," Kyle says.

"I was three sixteen or maybe three twenty, but I'm training with Laser and Maddux now," I brag.

I have no idea if I'm less than three hundred pounds. I have to be close, with the workouts and Mom's healthy menu. And the two-mile claim, it's true, but that doesn't mean I don't want to pass out and die during the final stretch.

I'm amazed at how much I'm talking. I really thought I would be standing behind everyone else—a fly on the wall. But I'm doing okay, and it felt good to scream *I'm losing weight.*

"How the hell does someone lose twenty pounds and no one can tell?" Jet jokes. "I'm just playing with you, Biggie. Good for you."

The guys all follow Killer to the fire, which sits inside of a circle of a few nylon folding chairs.

I take a drink of beer. The guys seem to down their beers while

I nurse mine. I don't seem to like beer like they do. The aftertaste doesn't go away as I walk closer to the fire. Maybe if you chug it, there isn't as much of an aftertaste. I wrap my lips around the top of the bottle and just drink. I can feel the beer zigzagging down my throat before falling into my stomach. I drink until the bottle's empty. Nope, there's still aftertaste. Suddenly I crave water, but the only things on this gravel driveway are beer and fire. I wonder if the Honey Weiss would taste better, but I also wonder if it's a girl's beer. I don't want to get made fun of, so I stick with the harsh Bud Light.

"Hey, Biggie, I don't mean to be rude, but you can't sit on those chairs. There's a weight limit and you are way over it," Killer says. "No offense."

"They'll hold him," Jet says.

"They're my mom's and she'll be pissed if one breaks," Killer says. "I got a blanket in my car you can sit on."

Killer walks to his Ford Mustang, opens the trunk, and pulls out a blanket. I don't even want to know how many girls he's had sex with on that thing. There's no way I'm sitting on it.

"I'll just stand. It's okay," I say.

"Just let him sit in the chair," Kyle commands.

"He'll break it," Killer whines again.

"I'll sit on the blanket," I say. "It's all right."

Killer sets the blanket on the ground, and like a two-year-old, I sit on it. I feel like an idiot.

"Hey, Biggie, pull your truck up," Kyle says. "You can sit on your tailgate."

CHAPTER 19
ALL GIRLS, NONE FROM IOWA

My back aches as I sit on my tailgate. It's better than sitting on a blanket on the ground, but those chairs look really comfortable. The guys are leaning back, stretching their shoulders and legs, and I'm sitting on a cold, hard tailgate, alone—the outsider.

I feel silly. I thought coming to this party would change my life. Everyone would be talking to me, staring at me, ripping on me. I'd feel like an idiot, at least until Annabelle accepts my apology and gets into my truck. I really thought I would have to sacrifice my autonomy, my life in the shadows. I was wrong. I'm still invisible. The cool kids are sitting around the fire, and I'm hiding on a tailgate. It's like math class, only with mosquitoes.

My pocket vibrates. I have a message from Maddy, my photographer friend in Colorado. We had a chat date for eight and my phone tells me it's 8:05. "Crap," I whisper under my breath. I text back, Sorry, can't talk. With friends. Chat in 2 hours?

She types out a colon and left parenthesis for a digital sad face.

Sorry. Can't wait to talk, I text back.

Cool, she texts back.

Before I even snap my phone shut, I'm sure Maddy has probably contacted another guy, another lonely soul looking for a Thursday chat date. By the time I get home, Maddy and this new guy she's probably typing Sure, I would love to chat to right now will be best friends, and I will just be a guy who stood her up. A shy, fat kid who thought he could have it all—online and real-life friends.

I want to go home. No one is talking to me here. Annabelle's friends sit in a circle of comfortable chairs talking about the basketball coach, who doesn't teach at Finch, so I have no idea who he is. I could laugh when they laugh, but they wouldn't notice. I consider saying "Good one" when Killer tells a story about Jet throwing the ball in the wrong direction and hitting the coach's twelve-year-old daughter, but I keep silent. That's me, the silent one. Whoever said real life is better than fantasy never gave a fantasy life a real shot.

Before I can slip my phone back into my pocket, it vibrates again. This time it's Brianna from Michigan. We didn't have anything planned, but she loves to chat on bad days. What's up, Henry? she texts.

Nada, just with friends, I text back.

"Who are you talking to?" Kyle peeks over at me.

"No one." I quickly put the phone back into my pocket.

The phone vibrates again. Apparently Brianna has more to say, including I didn't know you had any friends in town. I like to come across as a loner and love to tell people that no one in this crappy town is as cool as them. Girls like that. I put my hands on the outside of my pants as the phone continues to vibrate, massaging my palm through the denim.

Even sitting a few feet away, Kyle hears the buzzing sounds.

"You can get that," he says. "We don't care."

I just sit there on the tailgate. I don't say a word while I press down on my pockets, believing the pressure will deactivate the phone. As it keeps dancing in my pocket, I flash a small please-leave-me-alone smile. Seconds pass without a tickle from my pants and I know all is okay.

The guys walk over and suddenly there's a semicircle around me.

"Who was that?" Kyle asks again.

"My mom," I say.

"No one texts with their mom," Killer says.

"My mom loves to text," I say. "She's really computer savvy."

The phone vibrates again. If bees filled the truck bed, the buzzing noise wouldn't be as loud. I could just ignore it, but all three of them are staring at my pocket, which looks like it's trapped a hummingbird. Plus I'm curious who is calling. Three calls in ten minutes is sort of a record for me.

I decide I'll stick with the mom lie, which seems to be working or at least buying me time. I figure it will take less than a second to pull the phone out, see who called, and jam it back into my pocket. If I do it fast enough, the guys won't see anything. I look out at the harvested cornfield and wait for the guys to follow my eyes. When I see all three give in and look to their right, I pull the phone out. Before I can read the name, Kyle, with his massive, fishing-net hands, steals the phone.

"Kyle, what the hell?" I ask.

"It's Maddy," Kyle says. "Is she your girlfriend?"

"No, she isn't. Just give me back my phone."

Killer and Jet lean over to get a better look at the phone. "Ask her who she is," Jet says. "See if she's Biggie's girl."

"She called Biggie; he wouldn't ask if they are boyfriend and girlfriend," Kyle says.

"I got it," Killer says. "Tell her Biggie's in the bathroom and he left his phone. We're his friends and we're curious who she is."

"Okay," Kyle says and starts to type. "Is this okay, Biggie?"

What can I say? I could tell them to give me the phone back or someone's going to get hurt, but these are three highly trained athletes. I could cry and beg for the phone back, but then my nickname will change from Biggie to Crybaby. With no options, I just sit on the cold tailgate and pray that Maddy's phone explodes at this very moment, keeping her from reading their questions.

"She said she's his Indiana girlfriend," Kyle reads.

Surprisingly, they don't chuckle, even though hearing "Indiana girlfriend" out loud sounds ridiculous, absurd, and loserish. I figured it was Maddy from Colorado texting back to set up a time later to chat. I actually have three online girlfriends named Maddy. Not to brag, but three isn't even my record. I'm friends with six Jennifers.

"Ask for a pic," Killer says.

"Guys, don't," I say.

"'Can we have a picture of you?'" Kyle ignores me and just types away.

"Awesome," Jet says.

"She says, 'Is a G-rated one okay?'" Kyle reads. "Do you sext with these girls?"

I just sit there and say nothing. Sweat fills the palms of my hands and my breaths get caught in my throat. I wipe the sweat off my hands on my jeans and feel my keys. I should just forget the phone, jump off the tailgate, get into the truck, and speed home. I should have just stayed in my room and kept my chat date with Maddy from Colorado.

"'That's fine,'" Kyle says out loud while typing. "'But a sexy one would be awesome.'"

Time slows down and no one says a word. I feel like a cancer patient in a doctor's office waiting for test results with his family, only these guys aren't my family. They are three strangers holding my phone hostage. I miss my computer chair so much.

The phone vibrates as a blanket of warm vomit slowly covers my tongue.

"Holy shit, Biggie," Kyle says.

For whatever reason, Killer and Jet start laughing and dancing. It looks like Jet might throw up before me, he's laughing so hard.

"This girl is so hot," Kyle says.

In the picture, Maddy has on a pink bikini top and her brown hair is soaking wet. She doesn't smile, but, instead, bites her lower lip in a please-drive-over-here-and-grab-me look.

"I'm sorry for laughing," Jet says, trying to get his breath back. "I just can't believe how fast she sent us a picture back."

"Of course she sent a pic," Kyle says. "She's smokin'. Here's another text. Wait, this one's from Felicia. 'Husband's an asshole, wanna talk?'" Damn, Biggie, these texts just keep coming."

"Get a pic," Jet hops up and down like a five-year-old high on sugar.

"'Hey, Felicia, sorry about your guy problems, but this isn't Biggie, it's a friend. He's in the bathroom. How did you meet?'" Kyle talks and types.

For a kid who keeps getting suspended because of bad grades and who recently skipped a question on a test, Kyle sure can think fast when it comes to girls.

My eyes start to water and turn red. I turn away and grit my teeth, hoping that holds the tears in. I'm able to hold in the puke, but my stomach feels like it's full of watery bile and at any moment the vomit, like a tsunami, will rocket up my throat and mix with the gravel below my feet. As I sit there, rocking back and forth, trying not to throw up, the guys continue to play with my phone and my online girlfriends.

"Here it comes," Kyle says. "Wait. She wants to know who Biggie is? Crap, anyone know Biggie's first name?"

Now I know they've forgotten about me. I'm a foot from Kyle but he doesn't ask me what my name is. Plus, we're locker neighbors and I'm his tutor. How could he not know?

"Dude, it's Henry," Jet says. "Henry Abbott. Man, now I know you're not from here if you don't know who Aaron Abbott's kid is."

"'Henry. His nickname is Biggie,'" Kyle's still talking as he types.

"Hope you didn't lie about being a fat ass," Killer says, "because the truth's out now."

I want to smirk and say ha-ha, but my face is paralyzed from holding in tears and puke.

The phone vibrates again. "She says, 'We're chat buddies. What are you guys up to?'"

"Get a pic." Jet hops higher and faster. His face turns red and his mouth hangs open. He's so excited, you would assume any second now Ed McMahon is going to hand him an oversized million-dollar check.

"'Can we have a pic?'" Kyle types.

The phone vibrates again. "'Trade only.'"

"She wants a pic," Jet says.

"Of Biggie?" Killer asks.

"I don't know," Kyle says. "Of Biggie. Wait, should I type 'Henry or Biggie'? I better type 'Henry,' no confusion." He clears the screen. "'Of Henry.' Where's the question mark on this thing?"

"You don't need a question mark. Just send it," Killer commands.

The phone vibrates. "'Of you,' and a smiley face," Kyle says. "This married chick is hitting on me."

"I'm telling Michelle," Jet warns.

"Oh, Michelle would want me to get this pic. Trust me," Kyle says. "Biggie, come take my picture," he says.

Here's my chance. He has to hand me the phone to take the picture. Once I get it, I'll take off—get in my truck and just drive. But as he hands me the phone, I don't want to go. Maybe it's because if I leave, I have no chance of being friends with Kyle and zero chance of being a boyfriend to Annabelle. What's weirder than running away from friends? Plus I've never seen a picture of Felicia. I'm curious about what she looks like. So instead of bolting, I hold up the phone and take a picture of the dumb smile on Kyle's face.

"Wait, I should take my shirt off," he says. "That way maybe she'll send a naked one." He rips off his shirt, showing off his hairless chest and ripped abs. Man, I would have to work out for twenty years to have ribs poke out like that.

"Hey, quit staring, weirdo, and take the pic," Killer orders.

They all stand around me and wait for Felicia's picture. The phone vibrates and the picture appears. Needless to say, Felicia isn't as hot as Maddy. She's overweight and has a crooked, lips-sealed-shut smile and a sloppy haircut. Felicia's smart and has gone through some tough times, so I feel bad for her when the guys quickly delete the photo.

I want to tell the guys that she's a nice person and they are being jerks, but I keep quiet. Most nights when we talk online or text, I feel like Felicia's marriage counselor, and some nights, I really feel like I turn her bad days into good ones. I should stand up for her but instead I listen as the guys shoot insults.

"There are, like, two hundred girls in your contacts." Kyle tosses me my phone.

"Any of these girls from around here?" Jet asks. "From Iowa?"

I shake my head.

CHAPTER 20
I LOVE THAT SWEATSHIRT

I owe Felicia one. Her not-so-appealing picture gets me my phone back. The guys lose interest. Kyle turns away from me and asks, "Where are Michelle and the girls?"

"No kidding. Biggie's entertaining and all, but Becky said she might be bringing her older sister," Jet says.

"No college girl is going to talk to you," Kyle says.

"They're all drinking at Annabelle's," Killer says. "Her parents drove to the city to see a movie. I invited them, but they said they're hanging out where it's warm until her folks get home. Oh, and Jet, the cousin didn't come down. If you want to hook up tonight, it's going to have to be Becky."

"Whatever. I would go for the Belle before Becky," Jet says.

"Annabelle belongs to Big," Kyle says very surprisingly. "Biggie's trying to hook up with her."

What was that? My heart stops. It doesn't skip a beat—it stops. I'm having a heart attack, with chills, arm pain, and loss of breath. All the color in my face disappears. I feel frozen despite sitting five feet from a roaring bonfire on a sixty-degree night.

"You like Annabelle?" Killer asks.

"She's okay." Each word causes a dull pain in my throat. All the saliva in my mouth disappears. I could sand a piece of wood with my tongue.

"That's really interesting," he says. "Biggie and Annabelle. Doesn't really have a ring to it, but let's see how things play out."

"Hey, let's go over there," Kyle says, changing the subject.

"No, I built a fire and I hate her parents," Killer says. "Her dad thinks I'm an idiot for rooting for Notre Dame. I don't want any crap about last Saturday's loss."

"Why do you root for them? You're not even Catholic," Jet says.

Killer ignores Jet and fiddles with his iPhone. "Biggie, I just dialed Annabelle. Ask her to come over."

He reaches forward and the phone is up against my chest. I look down and see *Anna* and her phone number. It's ringing and I'm frozen.

"Shit, you'll never ask her out."

"Hey, Belle," Killer talks into his phone. "Things are boring over here. Why don't you guys come over?"

There's a long pause. Killer listens and we all stare. No one wants this bonfire to be an all-guy affair. I don't know how long Annabelle talks on the other line, but it feels like an hour. Finally Killer says, "Cool. See you then. Oh, and good news, I got Honey Weiss here."

"They're coming?" Jet asks.

"Eventually," Killer says.

"Sweet," Jet says.

"Oh, Jet, you don't get to stay. No one makes fun of *Rudy*," Killer says in a stern voice.

"Oh, you try and make me leave." Jet holds his ground, despite being six inches shorter and seventy pounds lighter than Killer.

"Just admit it's the best movie ever, and I'll let you stay," Killer says.

"Um, guys," I interrupt. "Can we not tell the girls about my online friends? You know the girls on my phone? The pictures?"

The trio of star athletes looks at me like I'm the biggest nerd, loser, weirdo ever to walk on the gravel roads of Finch. I produce a little smile and hope for kindness or, at the very least, pity.

"Why don't you want us to tell them?" Jet asks. "That one girl was hot."

"I just want to keep it a secret," I say.

"Press conference." Kyle jumps in. "We'll keep our mouth shut if you gives us a ten-minute press conference. We get to ask you anything and you have to be completely honest. If we think you're lying, we'll tell Annabelle that you're an online sex god."

"Yeah, that sounds cool," Jet jumps in. "We get to ask you anything."

For millions of people, a press conference would be fun, but not for me. I'm a very secretive person who doesn't like to talk, much less admit embarrassing things. But I'm not on Killer's gravel driveway to impress him. I'm here for another reason. I left my comfort zone to impress Annabelle, so I would rather say dumb stuff to these guys than her. "Okay," I finally say through a lump deep in my throat.

"Cool," Kyle says.

"Question number one. Why don't you talk at school?" Killer asks.

I'm speechless. Who cares why I don't talk? Who cares what I have to say? I'm the kid in the back that doesn't take an ounce of attention away from the kids who thrive on it. I'm nobody's problem, nobody's enemy.

I thought for sure the first question would be *Why are you out here?* But no one seems to care about that. And if they had asked that, I would've lied because I'm not telling these loudmouths that I love Annabelle.

So why don't I talk? Well, that's an easy question to answer. "Because at our school when people talk, they're made fun of and I don't like being made fun of. It's nice to be the only kid at school that isn't picked on."

They all erupt laughing. "Are you kidding me?" Killer says through maroon cheeks. "No one gets made fun of more than you. We call you Biggie, for Christ sake."

"What do you make fun of?" I ask.

"Lots of things," Killer says. "For one, last winter you wore the same Memphis Tigers sweatshirt all the time. We counted that you wore it twelve straight days."

"What's wrong with that?" I ask.

"You're seriously asking what's wrong with not changing your clothes for two weeks?" Jet asks.

"I washed it every night," I say. "It was comfortable."

It was also the only sweatshirt that wasn't tight on me.

"And who roots for Memphis in Finch, Iowa?" Killer asks.

"You cheer for Notre Dame," I say. "It's in Indiana."

"Don't you dare bring up the Irish, the number one sports team in America," Killer says. "When Memphis starts playing football games on NBC, you can root for them."

I see headlights coming toward us.

"They're here," Killer says.

Even I'm floored by how quickly I got here on a gravel driveway with Annabelle. It took me only one week of tutoring Kyle to figure out the social-mathematical equation: two hours with the cool kids equals precious time with the cool girls, which include Annabelle.

She's stopped coming to the convenience store and sitting next to me in class, so I really haven't spent any time near her lately.

Her presence feels like home being just two feet away. If I wanted to, I could just reach out and pull on her brown wool sweater. I could run my hand up and down her curvy hips or massage her back.

Obviously I can't do those things, but I'm getting closer. I know it. For now, I just need to show her the real me and make her forget about the emails.

She looks around the group, and I can see happiness on her face. She normally has a serious, the-world-could-end-at-any-minute look. But between Killer and Jet, she glows. I love her smile. She has this openmouthed grin. The tips of her front teeth just touch her bottom lip. Her smile is so nonchalant that it's not a dead giveaway that she's happy.

A person needs to look into her green eyes to find out. She has the biggest eyes when she's happy. Most people don't turn their oval eyes into circles unless they're terrified or surprised. Annabelle does it when she's happy. She laughs with her eyes. The funnier the joke or prank or pitfall, the wider her eyes open. They say if a guy can get snot to roll out of another guy's nose, he has told a pretty funny joke. For Annabelle, if she thinks something's really funny, her eyes open so far they look like green dinner plates with a white trim border. They're hypnotic.

Michelle runs up and gives Kyle a kiss on the cheek. "Hey, sweetie," she says. "I'm so proud of my smart boy."

"Thank Biggie. He told me what to do. I knew every answer."

Michelle spins around and sees me still sitting on the tailgate, left hand squeezing my suddenly still phone.

"Well, thank you, Biggie." She offers me a high five.

I clap her hand, which is hung high above her freckled face, and she says, "It's so good that you can come out with us." I feel like she thinks I'm mentally handicapped or something. "Good that you can come out with us." What does that mean?

I see Annabelle walk up laughing at her friend. As Michelle walks away, I keep my hand up and wave to the girl of my dreams. She returns only what's left from her laugh, a small smile, before looking at Kyle, who has already launched a Honey Weiss at her.

"Honey Weiss, awesome," she says.

"Biggie brought it," Kyle says.

Annabelle, still furious, says nothing. There's still work to do, but I feel like I'm making progress.

Unfortunately the girls don't add anything new to the conversation. They love to talk about sports too, just in a different manner. Six days after the last game, the girls still talk about the big win and how well the guys played. After twenty minutes of football talk, the girls start talking about clothes. They tell Killer how cool his torn jeans are or tell Jet how funny his shirt is. He loves to wear short-sleeved T-shirts that say things like *I used to jog five miles a day. Then I found a shortcut.* Or *I fart, therefore I am,* the one he's wearing tonight.

I barely listen. Instead I think about getting a big bear hug from Annabelle with her in that brown, two-sizes-too-short sweater.

Annabelle doesn't say much. She sips on beer, looks around, and smiles. I know why she isn't talking—because, like me, she thinks everyone is an idiot. No one really cares about sports or clothes.

When we talked at the steakhouse, the dialogue was interesting. We spent two hours talking about eighties hair metal and popovers. The time flew by. Out here, time moves slowly, even when Annabelle's around, drinking her Honey Weiss beer and laughing with her big green eyes.

"Love that Nike sweatshirt." Michelle notices that I'm outside of the recently created circle of popular kids. "It looks like a tent on you; you're losing so much weight."

"Thank you," I say.

"How much have you lost?"

"Twenty pounds."

"Good for you." Michelle says.

She tugs on my sweatshirt, and reflex makes me smack her hand. "Sorry," I say. "You can touch it if you want."

"Touch what?" She giggles.

"What?"

"Biggie, you are so cute," Michelle, ever the politician, says. "You need to always hang out with us."

As Michelle flirts with me, Killer and Annabelle wander off into the harvested cornfield, high-stepping around cornstalk stems. Michelle notices where my eyes are looking and turns. She leans in, her painted red lips an inch from my ear.

"Killer's asking her out," she whispers.

The words burn my ears like she's poured battery acid into them instead of warm breath.

"He asked me today in school what I thought about it, and I said go for it," she continues, now at safe a distance from me. "Hey, Biggie, can you open this?"

She breaks my sight line to Killer and Annabelle in the field with her bottle of Honey Weiss. I rip it out of her hands and use my boiling anger to easily spin off the cap.

"Thanks, Biggie," Michelle says. "You're so awesome. I've always thought you were really cool and smart."

I hear Michelle speaking, but I don't listen. My full concentration is on Killer stealing my girl.

From ten yards away with only moonlight helping me, I see it. Annabelle's eyes are as big as the full moon above. She's happy.

"Do you think he asked her yet?" Michelle asks.

"Yeah and she said yes," I reply.

"For sure?"

"Yeah, for sure."

"How do you know? Can you read lips?" she asks.

"Nope. Eyes."

CHAPTER 21
DAMSELS IN DISTRESS

Three weeks have passed since Annabelle and Killer became the school's power couple. So far, he has been on his best behavior. He's always at her locker to carry her books and to say something witty to make her laugh. I hate that laugh now—half giggle, half chuckle.

"He-he-he," she laughs every afternoon as I place my books in my bag.

The good news is that Kyle, Jet, and Killer still ask me to hang out, which keeps me near Annabelle. She still doesn't talk to me, which makes things awkward when the gang's all together, but I put up with it just to be near her.

* * *

With my truck traveling sixty miles an hour down a two-lane highway, the guys share highlights from tonight's football playoff game. Kyle had two rushing touchdowns, including a 57-yarder on the first play. He grabs the Bud Light box and grips it between his toned forearms, turning the cardboard into a makeshift football. The two remaining bottles clink, forcing me to quickly examine the cardboard for spilled beer falling toward my newly polished leather. No flood yet, but the clinking continues as Kyle sways back and forth in the front seat, reminding the guys how he dodged and juked defenders. I try to ignore the sliding and colliding bottles and keep my eyes on the road.

Killer brags about three touchdown passes. In a dramatic reenactment, he flips a twelve-ounce aluminum can to Jet after chanting, "Hut, hut, hike."

Jet snares the cans out of the air, shouting, "Touchdown!"

It's a weird feeling being the shy one in a group. Part of me is relieved to be left alone and left out. Another part of me would like to join the conversation. On the tip of my tongue are questions like, "So who's your next opponent?" or "Was that team even any good?"

I could jump in, but I stay silent and watch vehicles pass us. Every now and then, I fear a cop car is going toward us in the other lane, but it's just a car with a luggage rack. Although no alcohol has touched my lips, I'm pretty sure it's a crime to be in the same truck with three high school juniors downing beers like M&M's.

"What do you have on this iPod?" Killer asks.

"So what does Biggie like for music?" Killer spins through the menu. "Damn you love the eighties. These are all hair metal bands."

"Is there any Guns N' Roses on there?" Jet asks. "They are the only decent band from the nineteen-eighties."

Killer searching my playlists, but I already know he won't find anything. I grip the steering wheel and wait for the razzing to start.

"Shockingly, there's no Guns N' Roses." Killer says out loud what I already know. "There's plenty of Def Leppard. You have like every single song they have ever put out."

"Def Leppard's not horrible," Kyle says. "'Pour Some Sugar on Me' is a cool tune."

"Not true," Killer says. "The first twenty seconds of 'Sugar' is cool. The rest of the song sucks."

Jet starts singing, "'Love me like a bomb, bomb, bomb.' I fucking love that part."

"The rest of the song just sucks," Killer says. "I don't mean to be a jerk, Biggie, but you only have twenty seconds of decent music on this entire iPod."

"That's cold," Jet says.

From the backseat, Killer reaches forward and grips my shoulder. "I know you get some online action, but if you want a real girlfriend, you're going to need some decent music. No hot girl is going to fuck you with this crappy iPod."

I want to tell him that Annabelle loves my music and I could care less what any other girl thinks, but I keep quiet, hoping that everyone will start to ignore me again.

"I'll tell you what," Killer says. "I'll take your iPod home tonight and fill it with some good music, music from this millennium."

"Whoa, those are girls on the side of the road," Kyle interrupts Killer.

Up ahead are three girls standing around a green Chevy Cavalier lying grill-first in a ditch.

"Those are college girls," Jet says.

"How do you know?" Kyle asks.

"I have college-girl radar," Jet brags.

I have only been hanging out with Jet for a couple of weeks but I already know he's obsessed with college girls. Every time the guys talk about weekend plans, he says we should go to the University of Iowa or the University of Northern Iowa and just hang out. He's thankfully ignored.

"Damn, I wish I owned a tow truck right now," Jet says as we fly past them.

"There's a tow cable in back," I say. They're the first words to leave my lips since we left Finch an hour ago.

"What?" the three guys shout in unison.

"We can pull them out?" Jet asks.

"I've never used it, but my uncle left it in the truck when I bought it," I say. "He said, 'Chevy trucks were built to pull Toyotas out of the ditch.'"

"Have you ever pulled a car out of a ditch?" Kyle asks.

"No," I admit.

"How hard can it be? Let's do it," Jet pleads. "You have to go back. We can seriously save them, save the damsels in distress."

I don't know if it's the mocking of my iPod catalog or the constant bragging about football dominance, but I feel the need to be, well, cool. The idea of saving those three college girls makes me not only smile, but glow. The hair on my arm stands up and my fingers feel weightless on the steering wheel. I press down on the brakes.

"Let's save some college girls," I say.

"I can't believe I'm going to have sex with a college girl," Jet says.

CHAPTER 22
COBB SALAD

We hop out and I reach into a large red tool box in the bed of the truck. Even though I've had the truck for more than a year, I've never opened my uncle's old tool box. The only time before tonight that I've even moved it was to hose out the truck bed.

Sitting right on top is a thick, silver cord with two worn metal hooks on each side. The cord is surprisingly heavy, causing me to grunt a little when I pull it out. The three guys, two with girlfriends, chit-chat with the three girls as I fiddle with the towline, which is only a couple of feet long.

"I need to back up the truck to the car," I say.

No one responds with words. Instead, they shuffle their feet close to the road. One of the girls mimes with her arms, most likely retelling the sad story about how they ended up in the ditch.

After backing the truck within a couple feet of the small, green Chevy Cavalier, I am forced to make a decision. To attach the hook, I have do what all fat people hate to do—lie down on the ground.

The only way I can safely attach the far hook to the Cavalier is to get down on the cold ditch grass and secure it. This will do two things. One, I become the hero. The guy who saved the girls from massive tow bills and lost time spent shivering in twenty-degree temperatures on the side of the highway.

Two, it forces me to push myself back up. While it's easy for a fat ass to fall, it's not so easy for someone big like me to get back up. I have to do it in shifts. First, I use my arms to pull my chest off the ground. Then, I swing back and forth, trying hard to get my belly off the ground. Eventually as sweat swims all over my body, I get to my knees. This will allow a moment to catch my breath. Then, I kneel for a few seconds. Finally, I push hard on the ground and lift up a knee.

If I can keep my balance, I should be able to reach my feet in one attempt, but nothing is guaranteed. Best-case scenario, I secure the latch and get up in a minute. While sixty seconds in real time isn't much time, sixty seconds in fat-guy-getting-up-off-the-ground time measures out to approximately ten hours.

I could easily avoid this situation by handing the tow cable to Kyle or Killer and let them get the credit.

"You want me to latch that?" Killer asks.

"No," I say. "I can do it."

Everyone circles around me in silence. All I can hear as I drop to my knees are cars flying past on the highway. The "vroom" noises are accompanied by shots of chilly mid-November wind. Like an infant, I crawl, pulling the tow cable. As I near the bumper, I drop my head counter-clockwise and slide it under the backside of the compact car.

It's not hot or even warm, which makes me think the girls have been stuck for awhile. I see a metal loop and latch the hook. The good news is that I am able to stay on my knees, which should save me several steps in the fat-guy-getting-up process.

Like pistons, my knees rotate backward and I pull my head out. I grab the bumper and pull myself up, holding my breath to avoid any weird grunts or pants. I push down hard on the bumper and pull my knees back, which lift my head, shoulders, and spine. Standing straight up, I look over the car at nothing. In front of me are only dark, empty Iowa fields. I must be able to see for miles. It's while staring that I notice the tow cord is not in my hand, but on the ground next to my tennis shoe. Crap! Here we go again. I close my eyes and begin to bend my knees.

"I got it," a voice says.

I turn around and one of the girls is locking the other hook onto my truck. "Can I pull it out? It's my car," she says. "My dad has a truck just like this."

While I focus, my head nods "yes" without any internal debate. In the dark of a half-moon night, I see she's short. Not midget short, but she would be lucky to convince someone that she's five-foot-three. Despite being height-challenged, she leaps right into the truck, bouncing off the running boards like a gymnast. Through the back window, I can barely see her brown hair. There's a pause, which means she's screwing with my power seat. It's going to take me five minutes to get it back into the perfect spot.

"Biggie, move or you are going to get hit," Kyle says.

I step back and watch the small car roll out of the ditch.

"Hey, who wants midnight pancakes?" Jet asks.

"I could eat," says one of the girls.

Although Friday has turned into Saturday, Perkins has few open tables. The hostess seats the seven of us at a rectangle table in the middle of the restaurant. One by one, a boy sits across from a girl until I sit down across from no one. All three of the girls are pretty in their own way. Each one of them is clean cut with straight hair surrounding makeup-covered faces. They each smile at witty and smart-ass comments. None of them is tall. The one on the far end across from Jet might be the tallest, but she's no basketball player.

The Cavalier owner is the shortest of the three and is not really fat, but suffers in comparison to her two friends, who look like animated twigs. She looks like she could be younger than her thinner friends too. Because I was grabbing the tow cord and not involved in the initial chitchat, I don't know their names. I'm sure if I just brought that fact up, they would repeat them, but I keep quiet. Instead of joining the conversation, I sip on the room-temperature water and search for our waitress.

"What's your name?" a girl asks.

"Oh, shit," Kyle says. "We never introduced Biggie. Biggie, this is Jenna, Amanda, and Courtney—she's the one that drove your truck."

"Hey," I say.

"What's your real name?" Courtney asks.

"Henry," I mutter and quickly take a drink.

"We call him Biggie for reasons you guys can see," Killer says.

"He's a big boy." Killer stretches out 'boy' with a low baritone voice.

"Nice to meet you, Henry," Courtney says.

Choking on water, I cough out, "Nice to meet you, Courtney."

"Down the wrong tube?" Jenna asks.

With a crooked smile, I say, "Yeah."

"You know I remember you." Jenna turns her attention back to Killer.

"You do, huh?" he responds.

"You hit the game-winning shot last year in a basketball game against Madison Lake. That three-pointer ended my little brother's high-school career," she says.

Crushing an ice cube with his teeth, Killer says, "If you want an apology, you're not going to get one."

She smiles and shrugs her shoulder. "I'm just saying I remember you, that's all."

"Hey, I scored twenty-two points in that game," Jet adds. "You should be dreaming about me."

"You scored twenty-two, but where were you in crunch time?" Killer asks.

"Driving the lane and kicking out a perfect pass," Jet claims.

"I don't remember that." Jenna smiles so big that I can't tell if she is lying to flirt with Jet or really doesn't remember what led up to the game-winning shot.

The waitress, a short, pudgy old lady with two pens slid into her silver-and-black ratty hair, asks us, "What can I get you?"

The guys each order breakfast platters full of pancakes, eggs, bacon, and toast. The girls decide to split a massive plate of fries. It isn't on the menu, but the waitress, with Harriet on her name tag, says she can throw something together.

After Killer told everyone my name was Biggie for reasons everyone can see, I decide against ordering pancakes or fries or meat of any kind. With words that taste like vinegar coming out of my mouth, I say something I never thought I would say in a million years.

"I will take a Cobb salad with French dressing on the side and a large glass of ice water."

"Biggie, you don't get a salad at midnight at Perkins," Killer informs me. "It's midnight pancakes. It's a tradition. He's new to our group," Killer tells the girls. "He's kind of on a trial basis."

Screw you, I think to myself. I don't even want to be here. If he doesn't want me to sit here and listen to him talk about how great a football and basketball player he is, I can happily leave. Good luck finding a ride home.

"Biggie tells really funny jokes," Kyle says as Harriet sets down drinks.

My crappy small glass of water is replaced by a big crappy one, still no ice. Everyone else sips Mountain Dew, Diet Pepsi, or coffee.

"Tell us a joke," Courtney says. "I love jokes."

My joke telling doesn't come naturally. It takes hours of research on more than a dozen websites to find a handful of funny jokes for Kyle. I normally do the research on Sunday afternoon. I find three or four good ones and share them at the locker. By Thursday, I'm out of good material.

"Tell the one about the butler. I like that one," Kyle says.

I gulp enough warm tap water to refresh a marathon runner and stare ahead into the eyes of the six-person crowd. They look at me with complete concentration. Three girls, two that probably go to college, and three popular kids from my school, including one who may or may not be screwing the girl of my dreams, wait patiently for a joke that I'm struggling to remember.

There's no turning back now. They are going to keep looking right at me like I'm Dane Cook on a Vegas stage until I say something, so I open my mouth.

"There's this rich couple and they are going to a party on the other side of town, so they tell their butler, Jeeves, that they will be gone all night and he's to watch the house."

For reasons I can't explain, a couple of people start to smile. Their cheeks get a little red and their eyes light up. The beginning of the joke isn't funny, but they must just be excited with the expectation of laughter.

I continue, "Well, the party is all business talk and cigar smoke, so the wife tells her husband she's going to take a cab ride home.

"When she gets home, the lights are all out and Jeeves is sitting in a chair in the living room. She tells Jeeves to follow her upstairs to her bedroom. She closes the windows and drapes and tells Jeeves to take off her dress."

The girls look at each other, likely expecting this joke to turn dirty with some hardcore sex action. The giggles under their breaths give me a little confidence and I finish the joke.

"So he takes off her dress. She says, 'Take off my stockings,' so he takes off her stockings. She says, 'Take off my bra and panties,' and so he takes off her bra and panties." Courtney takes a long drink of her Diet Pepsi as I get to the punch line.

"She then looks at him and says, 'If I ever catch you wearing my clothes again, you're fired.'"

Everyone at the table starts to laugh. Kyle even pounds the table. Courtney laughs, but not into the air. She laughs into the ice cubes buried inside her drink. This causes her to hop in her chair and bobble the glass. She avoids spilling the syrupy brown liquid on the table, but she can't keep pop from getting stuck in her nose. With both hands she covers her nose and coughs like a long-time smoker.

"There's pop coming out of her nose," Kyle points out. "You know it's a good one, Biggie, when you get pop to come out of a girl's nose."

While my joke brought some ha-has and chuckles, people are grabbing their sides and laughing hysterically at Courtney's coughing and red face.

Under the table, I pump my fist. As the guys keep hitting on the girls, I look around the restaurant. I can't believe I'm in a Perkin's at 1 a.m. I never thought it could happen with these guys, but it has. The gallons of tap water force me to hit the bathroom. While listening to the various noises one hears in a men's bathroom, I imagine the distance between this urinal and my bedroom.

I am four miles from Cedar Falls, which is fifteen miles from Finch. Twenty miles. Feels farther. I flush the urinal and head over to the sink. As I wash my hands, I sneak a peek at the mirror. My thoughts drift back to Dr. Pence's office, and my goals: the weight loss, the perfect game, Annabelle.

"I have a lot of work to do," I whisper and head back to our table.

The chairs are empty. The table remains filled with half-empty glasses, sullied spoons, grimy forks, disheveled napkins, and plates filled with leftover pancakes, toast, and scrambled eggs. While the dishes are there, the gang is gone.

"They said you're the rich kid who was going to pay for this." The pudgy waitress returns.

"I'm not rich. I work at a convenience store," I mumble.

She sticks the bill in my face. In large red ink, she wrote $62.18.

"You gonna pay the bill or do we have a problem?" she asks, obviously angry about another all-night shift.

Outside, Jet, Kyle, and Killer surround my truck, chatting about God knows what. My blood boils and my nose huffs and puffs like a Spanish bull. I want to grab their shirts, slam them against the truck and scream, "You owe me sixty bucks," but instead I say, "Where did you go?" An idiotic question which I already have an answer to. I apparently have no spine.

"Out here," Killer answers anyway. "Kyle, give him the paper."

Kyle lifts his elbow to showcase a slip of paper wedged between two fingers.

"After you look at that paper, you won't be mad about paying for grub," Jet claims.

I snag the strip and unfold it. It's a phone number. As if I'm trying to dumb myself down for these guys, I ask another dumb question.

"What is this?"

"It's the combination to the girls' gold safe," Jet says. "What do you think? We got Courtney's number. She's single like you."

I have hundreds of girls' numbers in my phone and black binder, so having a girl give me her number is nothing new, but for some reason this sheet of paper feels slippery and fake. The area code, 319, is right. I count ten numbers, all single digits.

"She just gave this to you?" Finally, I ask a question without an apparent answer.

"I told her you liked her and wanted her number," Kyle says. "I knew you would pussy out."

None of that is true. I can ask a girl for a number if I want one.

"I mean, we get a guy a number and he complains," Killer says to Kyle.

What am I supposed to do with this? Should I text her?

"It's funny, Jet," Killer says. "Now, you're the only one without a girlfriend in the group."

"Did you say I would text her?" I whisper.

"I have options," Jet says. "Don't worry about me. Just figuring stuff out."

"Guys, should I call her?" I say a little louder, but my words are still being drowned out by their worthless chatter.

"Jet, are you talking about Becky?" Killer asks. "She wants nothing to do with you."

"SHOULD I TEXT HER OR SOMETHING!"

Everyone in the Perkins parking lot, even the twenty-something married couple thirty feet away, freezes in silence. I just breathe and wonder when the last time was that I screamed in public. I'm not sure I ever have.

"Yeah, you should text her," Kyle says. "This is a good night, Biggie. You saved a girl and she gave you her number."

"This is how we work," Killer says. "Drive us around, buy us Perkins, buy us beer, and we get you a girlfriend."

"I didn't ask for one." My voice returns to a whisper.

CHAPTER 23
A TEXT

"You need to throw up," Killer says. "Do you know how to do that?"

I really don't, so I shake my head as a cop car pulls into the driveway.

"Craig won't arrest us because we play football, but he will take your license," Killer continues. "He always makes examples of the non-athletes. Go behind your truck by the tailgate, bend over, and stick your finger deep down your throat. Dude, you have like three seconds go. We'll distract him."

I can't get busted for drinking. Mom would kill me. *Damn, Henry, why do you drink with these guys? Okay, calm down and just put your finger in your throat.* It won't be that bad. I bend down behind my truck and stick my finger into my mouth.

"What are you guys up to?" the officer asks the guys off in the distance.

"Nothing, sir, just standing by a fire," Jet says. "Isn't it a nice night, officer?"

As I start to hear the officer walking toward me, I bend over, stick my finger down my throat, and choke. Reflex pulls my finger out of my mouth. Two deep breaths and I stick my finger down again, farther this time. My knuckle passes my two front teeth, my shoulders bounce, and my eyes water, blurring my vision. Once again, nothing comes up.

"I hear something," the officer says. "Is someone behind the truck?"

I start to shake. I have to do this. As I hear footsteps, I put two fingers in my throat as far as I can. My spine comes alive and tries to escape the ribs and skin on my back. I feel liquid slither on the bottom of my hand. It's surprisingly hot, almost burning my cold hand. I pull out the two fingers and bile follows all over the frozen gravel.

"Awesome," Kyle says.

I look up and he's holding Jet's camera phone in the back of my truck bed. He must have sneaked in there while I was talking to Killer.

"I can't believe you actually threw up," he said.

Kyle leaps out of the truck like the bed's on fire. To show off in front of his friends, he hurdles the side of the truck bed and, after a five-foot drop, lands awkwardly on the gravel. He uses his free hand to balance himself, but he still slips on the gravel driveway. Kyle wiping out brings more laughs from Killer and Matt, along with the officer who Kyle said could arrest me for drinking.

The officer is a guy named Craig. He's about five-foot-seven, maybe, and a durable two hundred pounds, probably a former wrestler. He looks old with his face beat up from zit scars. The stubble on his chin tells me he hasn't shaved for a day or two. He opens a pack of Marlboros and lights a cigarette. He takes a long puff and blows the smoke out over the flames of the bonfire.

Kyle makes the guys forget about his fall by pushing Play on my video—a fat kid hiding behind a truck with one, then two fingers down his throat. He has everything—the running behind the truck, the bending over, the failed attempt when I start to cry, and finally the puke flying out of my mouth like I am part of an exorcism.

The guys erupt with laughter. Craig grabs the phone to get a better look.

"I can't believe you finally got someone to believe you, Killer," Craig says. "I never thought you would pull this plan off."

Let me translate what Craig's saying: I can't believe you found someone so stupid.

I wipe puke leftovers from my chin. I grip my jeans with both hands and clean as much puke off my hands as I can as I walk closer to the guys and the cop. Jet has long since retrieved the beer from the empty field, and although none of guys are drinking, the beer sits right next to his leg.

"Are you all right?" Kyle asks. "No hard feelings. We wouldn't have tried it if we didn't know that you're always up for a good joke. Everybody is going to think this video is hilarious."

I don't say I'm fine or that I'm not. I just stand there, rubbing vomit onto my jeans. My mouth and throat hurt with a sharp dentist pain. My cheeks are soft from the cold and the tears, and my eyes itch, like someone waved pollen right in front of me. My hair sticks straight up from frozen sweat. I stumble when I walk. The bitter taste of bile on my tongue forces me to spit, but the more I do, the stronger the taste of vomit is in my mouth.

Kyle grabs a beer and hands it to me. I don't want it. I need bottled water, not beer, but I take it anyway. He tells me it will help. It doesn't. The beer mixes with the bile and I bend over the frozen ground and throw up again. The bottle slips out of my trembling fingers, and beer escapes and slips and slides around small pieces of gravel. The smell churns my beat-up stomach and if I had anything left in my stomach, I would upchuck that too.

"You need a doctor?" Craig, the officer, asks.

"No," I say. "I'm okay. I just need some water."

"I've got some in my squad car," Craig says. "I'll grab you a bottle of water."

Kyle offers me a hand and then pulls me up. Upright, I use the top of my sweatshirt to wipe off even more vomit residue from my chin and lips. Kyle and I walk over to the other guys, who are still watching the video. Their foreheads are red from laughing so hard. They are probably watching it for the tenth time, while I continue to clean myself up.

"You threw up a lot," Craig says. "I got a cold hamburger from Molly's in my squad car. You can have it."

It's been two months since I've been to Molly's. To be honest, I'm shocked the place is still open without my daily food purchases. Since I have stopped running with Laser, I'm relying solely on healthy eating to lose weight.

"No, the water's fine." I rip open a bottle of generic water. With bile still on my tongue, the water tastes dirty, almost like it was sitting in a bucket of pebbles before going in the clear, plastic bottle. The more I drink, the better it tastes. As I finish the sixteen-ounces, I feel all right.

"Biggie's losing weight," Kyle says. "He's lost like twenty-five pounds." Kyle rubs my shoulder like he's my dad. "He's going out for the baseball team."

"Your dad's Aaron Abbott?" Craig asks.

I always answer yes to that question, even though it's not true. Aaron signed away his rights to me before leaving for college. He legally said he wanted nothing to do with me, but I still tell people he's my father. I guess because the alternative means admitting I was abandoned. That's a story I don't want to tell.

"When's the last time you saw him?" Craig asks.

"I've never seen him," I say.

The entire group gives me a weird, confused look.

"How is it in a small town like this, you've never seen Aaron Abbott? He's at like every big sporting event."

"Biggie's never been to a sporting event," Jet says accurately. "That probably explains why."

"You're just like him," Killer interrupts.

"Yeah. People always say we look alike," I reply.

"No, you act just like him. He never says anything. He just stands there and stares."

"Shut up," Kyle says. "I can't believe you're still mad that he ignored you after the state title game."

"Oh, he didn't ignore me. He looked at me, just glared, like it was all my fault." Like a stern father, Killer points his finger at all of us before saying, "I pitch a decent game. You guys know it."

"I don't know. He shook my hand. It thought he was alright that night," Kyle says.

"Of course, he shook your hand. You hit a three-run blast," Killer says. "He thought you played a good game, but me, he just stared at me. Every time, I've ever seen him, he's just stood in the back, said nothing, and judged everyone. Just like Biggie."

The words shock my system. I feel myself leap out of my body.

"I don't do that," I defend myself.

Killer takes a long drink and says, "Whatever. I don't like him."

My phone chimes. It's a text message from Courtney. She can't be in a ditch again. The text reads, We are partying at my sis's. You should come with friends. Thank you for other night.

Wow, I kind of thought Courtney didn't like me. I followed Killer's advice and texted her, but out chats were boring, and she often disappeared after a text or two. After a couple nights of staring at my phone waiting for her to respond to some stupid question, I gave up.

Courtney was nice in person. She called me Henry and laughed at my joke, but my goal still is to date Annabelle. All of my hard work is for her, not some girl who goes to Waverly-Shell Rock High School, which is thirty miles away from Finch. If I wanted a long-distance relationship, I'd stick with my online girlfriends.

As I go to erase the message, I taste leftover vomit in my mouth. I just threw up, on purpose, and they have it on video. Plus, I think Killer's mad at me because of Aaron. I need to look cool again, and what's cooler than hooking up with a girl? Here goes nothing.

"Anybody want to party with the ditch girls?"

I hold up my phone.

Jet grabs my vomit-juice-filled sweatshirt and does his best to swing me back and forth. Because I weigh twice what he does, he does more tugging than shoving.

"College girls!" he yells to the starry sky.

CHAPTER 24
ARE YOU DISAPPOINTED?

Texting with Courtney, I am able to find out some basic information. The girls are actually at her older sister's Jenna's house. Jenna's nineteen, two years older than Courtney, and a student at Coe College in Cedar Rapids. It's pretty impressive to live in a house as a college freshman, a feat Jenna pulls off by working full-time at a cell phone store.

The house is small, probably built in the 1950s. Not much to see in the front, just a rectangular picture window and a few shoveled cement steps leading to an aluminum screen door that Jet pounds on several times.

Jenna opens the door, yells, "The party's here," and releases a strong whiff of alcohol. Apparently, the party has been going on for awhile.

Jenna looks like a skinnier version of Courtney. She also has shorter black hair and brown eyes instead of green. She's wearing a navy blue Northern Iowa Panthers T-shirt and jeans with just soft blue socks on her tiny, square feet.

It's easy to see that three girls live here. Every piece of furniture—from the coffee table to the two end tables to the leather couch—shines in the absence of dust. As I walk through the front door, I see into a kitchen that could probably fit a breakfast table and two chairs, but the girls left the linoleum floor bare. There are two microwaves, black and white, and a wine rack filled with empty bottles.

We take our shoes off and set foot on the carpet, thin and apartment beige. The room fills with the sound of a man singing country music, but I can't see a stereo. I assume somewhere hidden are an iPod and a pair of tiny, but potent speakers.

Courtney walks in, and I recognize her smile, but little else. She's bigger than I remember. Not taller, just bigger. She's perfectly round, not one part of her body an hourglass. But she knows what works for her. The guys' eyes go right for her low-cut red shirt, which she must have spent an hour squeezing into. It's tight, but not as tight as her dark black jeans. She's wearing white tennis shoes with blue laces.

"Hey, Henry," she says and circles her arms for me to come in for a hug, which I do. I squeeze just enough to feel her D cups press against me.

"Henry." Killer laughs. "Only his mom calls him Henry. We call the fat bastard Biggie or Big."

"You already said that joke at Perkins, Brian," she remembers accurately.

"Any of the college girls single?" Jet wastes little time.

"Nope, I'm the only single one in the bunch," Courtney says, "although one of the roommates is with a cheating asshole."

"Let me know when she arrives," Jet says.

Courtney and I sit on the couch in complete silence. I'm speechless. I don't know what to talk about. All I really want to talk about is the red shirt. I practically have to grit my teeth to keep my eyes on Courtney's face and not on her big boobs. As I look into her eyes, I can't think of anything to say.

"Why aren't you talking to me?" She pulls me out of my daydream.

Earlier this week when Courtney didn't answer one of my texts, I was pissed. Now, the tables are turned and she's waiting for me to talk. I'm tempted to pull out my phone and just send her a text, but knowing that would be very weird, I just grin back.

"Are you disappointed?" she asks. Her back's straight. The smiling and hunching has ended.

"No, why would I be?"

"I don't know," she answers. "You're just dozing off."

"I'm sorry," I say. "I like your shirt."

Oh my God! I basically just told her I love her boobs. I'm screwed. She's going to slap me, and we're going to have to leave.

"Thanks, it's new." Her smile reappears. "I saw the shirt at the mall yesterday and just had to have it."

She has hypnotic eyes and an amazing smile, and, of course, the boobs, but I wish she looked more like Annabelle. Courtney has her tongue pierced, which is hot, but Annabelle has her nose pierced—a little silver stud, hardly even visible, but so sexy. *Stop thinking about her. She's with Killer.*

"Do you think it looks good on me?" she asks.

While I should just say, "Yes," I go blank. My eyes focus on her face.

Courtney's cheeks are dark with no life. Annabelle has freckles, not many, maybe a dozen, but I love how red they shined when she yelled at me outside the convenience store. All I really want to say is, "Courtney, you're nice, but you're no Annabelle," but I can't say that, so I'm moving on.

"Henry." She tries again to force a response. "Why did you come here if you aren't going to talk to me?"

"Courtney," I say. "I'm shy."

"Oh," she says, stunned. "You seemed to say a lot when we were texting."

Over her shoulder, I see Kyle tapping his phone on the way to the bathroom. "I have to pee, one sec." I jump up and follow Kyle into the bathroom.

"Dude," Kyle says. "There's only one toilet, so give a man some privacy."

I ignore his command. "I need you to help me."

"I ain't holding shit," he jokes.

"No! Really! Why would I want? Never mind," I go on, flustered, running words together without pauses. "I'm speechless. I can't talk to her."

"Turn around, so I can take a leak," Kyle commands.

I follow orders. Now facing a pink bathrobe hanging on the bathroom door, I continue, "We're just sitting there, not saying anything." I rattle off the words as a hard, steady stream of piss enters the toilet bowl. "Now, she wants to know if I think she's ugly. She thinks I'm disappointed."

The stream stops and next I hear a zipper connecting. "Do you?"

I turn around as Kyle pulls the sink lever for hot and then rubs his hands under the water like he's trying to start a fire. "Do I what?" I ask.

"Do you think she's ugly?"

"No."

"Well, tell her that," Kyle says. "That's a good icebreaker. I don't think you're ugly."

"I'm seriously speechless. It's like writer's block."

"Listen, Big." Kyle starts a pep talk. "Where are we?"

"A bathroom."

"No, what town?"

"Marion."

"And why are we here?"

"She invited us."

"This chick likes you. Okay, this isn't some online thing. She has seen you, talked to you, and likes you."

It seems like Kyle likes Courtney more than I do. I can't explain it but I have no desire to sit and talk to her. All I want to do is stare at her partially unbuttoned red shirt.

"Can you just come and talk to her?" I beg. "I'm just really uncomfortable sitting with her."

Kyle turns off the water. "You're uncomfortable because you like her. I was the same way early on with Michelle. Thankfully, she talked so much that I could just sit there."

"No," I argue. "I don't think she's for me. Don't tell anyone, but I'm just going to wait and see what happens with Killer and Annabelle."

Shaking his hands dry, Kyle says, "Dude, do not, I repeat do not, wait for Annabelle. She's not that great."

"You don't know her like I do," I say.

"Oh, I know her. She and Michelle have been best friends since kindergarten, so I have hung out with Annabelle a million times. She's not that great. She loves to throw around insults. I mean, she's kind of bitchy. And, she doesn't put out at all."

Kyle rubs his hands on his jeans to finish the drying process. "Why would you want to go out with a girl who is going to be mean to you and won't let you touch her? This girl, I mean look at that shirt. She's going to let you touch her. Hell, probably a lot more, and she's nicer."

"If Annabelle's so bad, why is Killer dating her?"

Kyle just smiles and releases a slow, cocky laugh. "I told him something, something Michelle told me."

"What?"

"Annabelle says she's waiting for marriage," he says. "So Killer thinks he can get her to"—he stops for a second, tilts his head, and squints his eyes, before snapping his fingers—"break her vow. That's what he said. He wants to be the first guy she screws. They don't date. They don't go out to dinner. Well, nowhere but Molly's. They don't go to movies. All they do is hang out inside while Killer makes one move after another."

"What an asshole," I say.

Kyle opens the door. "C'mon, I'll help you talk to her."

Courtney is still sitting on the couch, alone. She finishes taking a drink from a green glass with blue and red flowers painted on the side.

"Courtney, you know Kyle," I say, so relieved to no longer be in a one-on-one situation.

"Of course," she says.

"I was just curious what's in the glass, Mrs. I-love-cocktails-more-than-beer," Kyle says with complete comfort, probably because he has a hot girlfriend.

"Oh, I call it a Courtney." She laughs without hunching over, tilting her back. "It's part Bacardi, part Red Bull, and part Mountain Dew."

My first reaction is, hey if we're ever out of gas, that's the strongest combination of caffeine ever. While I'm thinking about how long Courtney will be awake, Kyle keeps on talking for me.

"So, did you invent that?"

"Well, no, it's probably not a Courtney, but I love it, so I gave it my name. A guy made it for me at a party last summer."

"Nice," Kyle says. "Can I have a little sip?"

While Kyle innocently flirts with Courtney, Killer not so innocently flirts with Jenna. She's leaning up against the refrigerator and he's leaning toward her, using his outstretched arm to balance himself against the fridge and keep a little distance from Jenna's body. She's wearing a smile that looks voluntary. I draw a small smile when I watch them walk into a bedroom and shut the door behind them.

"Kyle"—I break up their discussion of booze and Cedar Rapids's parties—"looks like Killer's not waiting for Annabelle anymore."

"Probably not," Kyle says. "He can't control himself."

"Dammit, I don't need this tonight," Courtney says.

Her disappointment is quickly followed by the sounds of car doors closing out front.

"This is just perfect." Courtney hops up to talk to her sister. As Courtney knocks on the bedroom door, three guys, none much bigger than Jet, walk through the door and shake snow off their clothes.

"Who are you guys?" one asks. Kyle and I are about to introduce ourselves when Courtney races back to the living room and stands between us and the new guys.

"Hey, Ben. Good to see you." Courtney hugs Ben, who I can only assume is Jenna's boyfriend.

"Where's Jenna?"

"Holy shit, Biggie," Kyle whispers.

"She must be in her bedroom, Ben," Courtney says. "She'll be right out."

I rarely talk. That isn't a lie. I have literally gone days without speaking, so even I'm surprised when I let "Awesome" slip out.

Now everyone is looking at me. By speaking up, I appear to know something. I seem to have information for Ben. He takes a few steps toward me, and I straighten my back and lift my shoulders.

"What's going on, Court?" Ben asks her but is staring me down. His face glows like a roaring fire. He starts to look rougher, tougher, slightly bigger and stronger. His muscles expand and, I'm not lying, he grows and his brown hair somehow transforms from a gentleman's part to a thug's crew cut.

"Who are these guys?" he asks.

"They pulled me out of the ditch. Remember, I told you about them," Courtney says. "Ben, nothing's going on. This is my good friend Henry and his friends Kyle and Jet. Oh, I don't know your real name, I'm sorry. They came down from Finch."

Ben barely listens. Now his eyes are focused on the kitchen. He slips past Courtney, who unsuccessfully steps in front of him. He disappears into the kitchen. We can hear him pound on what I'm guessing is Jenna's bedroom door. The door rattles so hard that I can almost feel the floor move, like we're on a boat.

"Baby, let me in!" Ben screams in between punches to the door.

"Have you ever been in a fight?" Kyle whispers.

I can't take my eyes off the kitchen or my ears off the pounding. I don't answer Kyle's question and he continues, "You're a big guy. If things go bad, just get in the way. Nobody's going to mess with a giant like you."

"Ben, calm the hell down," Jenna screams, still out of sight.

"Who the fuck is he?" Ben returns her scream even louder.

"No one calls the cops," Kyle says as Courtney and Ben's two friends run into the kitchen. "Big, we got to get Killer and get him out of here. If the cops come and see us and all of this alcohol, we're suspended for this weekend's playoff game."

"I was simply showing him my gymnastics trophies," Jenna says. "He wanted to see them."

"With the door locked? I'm not an idiot," Ben says.

Kyle grabs the top of my sweatshirt, like a mother of a two-year-old, and pulls me into the kitchen. "C'mon, Biggie. You need to scare the shit out of this guy."

We get into the kitchen and Jenna has all ten of her fingers clenched around Ben's shirt. She's pushing him away from her door like she's trying to keep a couch from falling down steps. He pulls on Jenna's hair so hard she falls to the ground. Killer just stands there and zips up his jeans, which destroys the gymnastic trophy theory.

"It's time, Big," Kyle says.

Kyle's wrong. It isn't time—it's already too late because Ben decks Killer. As Killer falls, Ben's two friends grab and hold him back up. Kyle runs into the kitchen while Ben punches Killer again. This time, his knuckles cut open Killer's cheek. Kyle grabs Ben's arm and attempts to throw him up against the wall. Ben knees him in the leg, and as Kyle bends down, Ben throws his elbow up against Kyle's forehead.

"Stop it!" I yell.

"You next, fat ass?" Ben walks up to me, rubbing his right elbow with his left palm. "I've already kicked the shit out of two of your friends and my whore girlfriend. Are you next, fat ass?"

In my life, I have never gotten into a fight. Oh, there have been situations where I could have stood up for myself and I walked away, but I have never been punched, kicked, or thrown down. I assume it's because I keep to myself and because I'm three hundred pounds. As Ben closes in on me, I know that streak is going to come to an end. He's going to throw a punch. I smell his stale vulgar breath, and I know there's only one way for me to keep from getting my ass kicked.

In one motion, I reach forward, lift him off the ground by his winter coat, and flatten him against the refrigerator door. Magnets, coupons, and photos go flying in all directions. He retaliates with a punch to my ear. It doesn't hurt. All I feel is a tingling in my hair. With my left hand, I squeeze his throat and lift. "Call me fat ass again. Do it!" His boots kick my shins, which only makes me squeeze harder.

"Let him go!" Jenna screams.

His fingernails slice my wrists, leaving rivers of white lines on winter-dried skin.

"Let him go!" Jenna punches my shoulder as hard as she can and I drop Ben. He drops to his knees, and Jenna punches my shoulder again as my friends and Ben's friends just watch. After the second punch, I turn to tell Jenna to quit it, and before I can speak, she punches me right in the nose. The pain shoots throughout my head before I can touch my nose. I'm light-headed, off balance, and blind. Okay, not blind, but I can't see clearly and end up walking into a wall headfirst.

"Everyone, get the fuck out!" Jenna yells.

Ben regains his balance and pulls himself up with the help of the countertop. He tries to soothe his girlfriend. "Baby, calm down."

"Fuck you," she says. "I told you, no more fighting in here. Now get out, everyone."

All of us walk out slowly. When we get outside, Ben turns to Killer. "You can have her, but she'll cheat on you too."

Our group ignores Ben and walks toward the truck. "What were you doing?" Jet asks Killer.

Killer just grins and says, "I love college girls."

As we get to my truck, I feel blood on my tongue. My nose is bleeding all over my mouth, lips, and chin. As I look for something to plug my nose, I hear Courtney.

"Hey, guys! Here are your coats." Courtney runs out of the house. "Is your nose bleeding?"

Assuming she doesn't need an answer, I say nothing. It would have been hard for me to talk anyway with my fingers squeezing my nose shut.

"I'm really sorry, guys," she says. "Jenna and Ben are kind of toxic sometimes."

She offers a little grin as I take my coat. "Next time, no crazy boyfriends, I promise."

I don't say it, but I know it. There won't be a next time.

CHAPTER 25
THE BATHROOM STATUE

A handful of Kleenex stops the bloody nose, but my right eye, which ten minutes ago collided with a wall, is bugging the hell out of me. A puddle of tears sits on my cheekbone. My eye, surely black and blue, throbs to the vibrations of the truck's tires on the interstate. Lucky for me, the midnight sky fails to light even the smallest area in the truck. The tears from the punch from a girl and the collision with the wall are a secret from the other three guys.

"I know we all want to talk about it, so I'll say it. Did Biggie almost kill someone?" Jet asks.

"He was a foot off the ground," Kyle says.

"Thanks for stepping in, guys," Killer says. "That guy's fists were so fast."

"Well, you were making out with his girlfriend," Kyle reminds him.

"Whatever, he's crazy and she's dumping him," Killer says. "We didn't just fool around, we talked, too."

They chatter on about the fight and Jenna and Courtney. I really should be listening to find out exactly what happened behind the locked bedroom door, but all of my energy is focused on holding in tears and staying on the suddenly icy road. My fingers are trembling and can barely hang on to the steering wheel. My eyes keep trying to close.

I notice a sign for a rest area, two miles away. A grin soothes me. If I could just clean myself up, wipe off the tears, and get this Kleenex out of my nose, I would be okay. The rest area delivers just what it advertises—rest, a break from this truck, from these guys. I don't want to hear about Jenna's punch or her ability to kiss.

I head to the men's room, which is perfect: clean and empty. I plant my palms on the white porcelain sink and stare at myself in the mirror. My hair reaches for the ceiling in a million different directions. My cheeks are puffy from tears and my lips look chapped. The corner of my eye is red, but it's hard to tell if it's from the punch or the crying. It's not blue, like I feared, but maroon. Slowly, I stretch out the thin facial tissue and then breathe hard through my nose. No blood. Thank God for small victories.

I sit on a toilet and close the door. Suddenly, I'm safe. No one can come in here; no one can bother me, hit me, make fun of me or call me weird in here. This will be my new home, my safe place from a world that I never wanted to be a part of in the first place. Everything was awesome before I admitted to Annabelle about the email surveillance. We went out, an actual date. I shouldn't have said anything about Mr. Crawford. Whoever said that honesty is best policy should see me now.

Two months of trying to be normal have led me here, a toilet stall at an interstate rest area. I'm not in the stall because I have to use it. No, I'm in here because I just got punched in the face by a girl as I tried to protect Killer, who stole the girl of my dreams only to cheat on her.

How is that not weird? How does my old life seem normal all of the sudden? People don't drive thirty minutes to get in a fight; they stay at home and sit on Reddit all night. Annabelle had it wrong. I'm normal; it's everyone else in my two-bit town that is weird. I just want to go home to my bedroom and lie down in my bed.

I walk out of the stall just as Killer walks up to a urinal. He unzips his pants and leans forward, staring at a wall of advertisements for snow machines, real estate agents, and limousine drivers.

"Hell of a night," Killer says over the sound of his propelling piss.

I say nothing and wash my hands.

"Thanks for standing up for me," he continues. "That was a cheap shot. Jenna told me that her boyfriend was a jealous asshole, and I guess she was right."

I stay quiet, just using the brown paper towels to rub the water off my hands.

"She was pretty cute," Killer goes on. "No offense, but she's a lot hotter than Courtney. Not that you shouldn't keep dating her, but you have to admit that Jenna's the better-looking sister."

I finally speak, "I know why you're with her."

"Who, Jenna?" Killer walks to the sink and turns on the water. "Why? Because she's in college and really, really hot? And it's not just her looks. She's smart."

"You know who I'm talking about." I just stand there, right in the center of the bathroom. Not a bone in my body has moved. My hands aren't shaking, my legs aren't twitching, and my eyes forget to blink. I'm a massive, seventeen-year-old bathroom statue.

Killer gives me a dumb what-are-you-talking-about glare, causing rage to run throughout my body with the same velocity as the pain did a half hour ago in Jenna's kitchen.

"Anna?" Killer asks for clarification.

I nod and he continues to quickly wipe water off his hands with a paper towel.

"Biggie, when Kyle brought you to my house, I was skeptical. I mean, you were a weird duck. But, now that I've gotten to know you and hang out with you, I feel like you're a good guy. I can't believe I'm saying this, but I'm happy to be friends with you. And because we're friends, I haven't told a soul about your hacking into Anna's computer. I could tell everyone you're a pervert, but we're friends, so I keep it to myself."

He rips off a sheet of brown paper towel and starts to rub his hands dry. Looking right at me for the first time since he walked into the bathroom, he continues, "You see, friends don't make life difficult for friends. Friends make life comfortable. And since we are friends, I'm not going to make your life difficult by saying anything."

I remain a statue. Perfectly still in between the stalls and sinks. Two feet in front of Killer, whose face turns red with the fear that I will rat him out to Annabelle.

"You think I care what people think of me?" I calmly answer. "For another shot at Annabelle, I would take all the laughs. Tell everyone. She knows I'm not a pervert. They were just harmless emails."

He stops and takes a deep breath. "You don't get it." He starts to poke his chest with his finger. "Anna loves me. Hell, she has since she knew what love was. Go ahead and tell her. All I have to do, then, is go to her doorstep, cry a few tears, tell her that I'm so, so sorry, and she'll take me back. She loves me."

I don't say anything because I can't think of anything. My mind's blank. He just goes on and on, like he's the future valedictorian and I'm the dumb jock.

"Biggie, I like Jenna and when she punched you in the nose, that only made me like her more. Who knows? Maybe things with us will work out. If they do, I'll cut Anna lose and you can be Prince Charming. You can be the shoulder she runs to. But if you say anything, if you do what friends don't do to friends, then I will, out of spite, keep her around until we graduate.

"You can judge me all you want, but the simple fact is that I'm Brian Burke and you're the strange kid who sits in the back of the room and peeks into girls' computers. She loves me for who I am—the quarterback, the power forward, and the starting pitcher. And she hates you because why not. What does she need you for? That's why she'll forgive me and never forgive you."

He turns back around and shoves the paper towel in the garbage can. The metal top swings back and forth from the force of his dried hands.

"Don't get me wrong," he says. "I like you, Biggie. I know you'll always be a good friend."

He leaves and the bathroom door closes behind him. I still stand there, perfectly still. All I can think about is what Kyle said. All I can picture is Annabelle giving in and losing her virginity to that asshole. I squint hard to erase the image of them in the backseat of his Mustang. He said she loves him because he's Brian Burke, star athlete. I honestly believed I could win her heart by getting close to her, showing her that I'm the nice guy. I'm a fool.

* * *

When I get home, I quickly take off my jeans and bloody shirt, and put on my running clothes. I walk down the steps and sit in a chair in the living room. Calmly, I slide on the tennis shoes and tie the laces. Finally, I lean back, stare down the hallway, and wait.

Forty-five minutes later, the hallway light powers on. Laser, barefoot and still in the shorts and T-shirt he slept in, appears with his palms rubbing life into his eyes.

"Biggie"—he seems startled—"you're up early."

"I need to say something." I lean forward and allow a deep breath to give me confidence. "I started working out because I wanted to throw a perfect game. I wanted to take my magic pitch and baffle twenty-one straight hitters. But, now I want something else. Now, I want to be like you, like Aaron, like Maddux. I want to be…" I stop and search for the perfect word. Laser, still probably half asleep, waits quietly. "I want to be the best, the best baseball player in town."

"It's going take work," he says.

"I will work as hard as I have to." I stand up. "I want you to train me like you do Maddux. You see him as the best player of his time. I need you to see me like that. And I'm willing to do whatever it takes. Train me like you train him. Make me the best baseball player at my school."

Laser walks up to me. His hair disheveled and his eyes a little bloodshot. "I love this attitude, but you need to slow down. One step at a time. You make the team and then we look at the next step. All this talk about being the best is just talk, and to be honest, you're not ready to talk like this."

I lean down and place my eyes inches from his. "Don't underestimate me. I'm serious. Stop thinking of me as a lazy fat ass and start looking at me like you do Maddux."

"What's this about?"

"I'm tired of it. I'm so tired of other guys getting what they want and I just stand there. I'm tired of standing on the sidelines and watching other people find happiness. It's time for her to stop ignoring me and start cheering for me."

"Her?" He catches the slip. "Who are you talking about?"

CHAPTER 26
REPETITION

For the past six months, my life has been in a state of repetition. Every day is just like the previous one. I wake up at 5 a.m., work out with Laser or Mom, go to school, and stare at Killer and Annabelle. Then, I head home and throw pitches to Maddux or Kyle. After a healthy dinner, I study for a couple of hours, hop on the computer to solve some girl's problems, and then go to bed around 1 a.m.

The only real break from the monotony comes on the first Tuesday of every month—doctor day. After school, I ride with Mom to Dr. Pence's office. We always get there early and pass time reading outdated magazines. She flips through *US Weekly*, and I read month-old copies of *ESPN the Magazine*.

Either nurse Janet or Phyllis—I prefer Janet because of her sly grin of a smile—will call me back, measure my height, write down my weight, take my blood pressure, and withdraw a vile of blood.

When they're done, I wait roughly fifteen minutes for Dr. Pence. While I wait, I slip into a drafty gown. Eventually, Dr. Pence pokes and prods me. When we're done, he tells me, "It's harder to keep your weight down than it is to lose it."

I was dropping weight like the Cubs lose baseball games. In December, I lost twenty-six pounds. In January, I dropped another fifteen. Although I had only twenty-eight days, I lost twenty-one pounds in February. On March 1, I weighed 248 pounds. When Laser and I went running in the morning, we did just that: run. On March 22, I ran two miles in seventeen minutes, fourteen seconds.

Then, I just stopped losing weight. In April, I actually put on four pounds. Maddux said it's because Laser upped my weight training. Mom said it was because my workouts were no longer strenuous. I believed them.

Now, it's May and with the Iowa High School baseball season starting in a few weeks, Dr. Pence wants to see everyone. As I sit in the waiting room, I feel exhausted. Instead of looking at a magazine, I reread diabetes symptoms on my phone. It says diabetes can affect vision, which leads me to stare at the clock on the far wall. Is it blurry? Could I see it better last time?

This is ridiculous. If I didn't have diabetes at 317 pounds, I'm not going to catch it at 250.

"Kari, Henry, the doctor can see you now," Phyllis says.

Where's Janet? She's my lucky nurse.

"Good luck, Biggie," Laser says as Mom and I walk toward the nurse.

We walk past the patient rooms and turn left into his office. He's already there, planted on the corner of his desk. As he stands up to greet us, I see a freshly opened box of Kleenex. Seeing the tissues takes my breath away. Is that for me? My mom? *Calm down*, I tell myself. *There was a box last time too, and you didn't have diabetes. Get yourself together.*

We all sit in the same spots as we did eight months ago after Laser busted me for sneaking junk food before school. It seems like yesterday.

"Henry, how are you?" Dr. Pence asks.

I want to respond, "You tell me. You have all the answers. You took my blood and ran tests." But like always, I suppress my anger. "Fine," I say instead.

"Well, I just brought you here today to say, Kari, you have a healthy son," Dr. Pence says. "He's still about forty pounds overweight, but his tests look good overall and I don't think he needs to come here next month."

"That's wonderful," Mom says.

What a fucking asshole. Really, I'm healthy. That can't be said in a phone call or in an email? *You have to leave me hanging for twenty-four hours? I thought I had diabetes. I thought I was sick. I didn't sleep a wink last night.* I wanted to jump up, grab his white coat, and throw him up against the wall like I did that asshole in Marion. I can just see him planted above his desk, legs flailing, saying he's sorry with the little breath he has left.

"Biggie"—Moms brings me back to reality—"isn't that good news?"

"He couldn't have told us on the phone?" I mumble.

CHAPTER 27
NONEXISTENT AND AVERAGE

It has been written that someone must do an activity ten thousand times to master it. I used to believe that whoever wrote that must have never seen a five-year-old play piano or an eleven-year-old like Maddux hit three home runs in a game. For most of my life, I thought it was a dumb saying.

Yeah, I have sucked at sports most of my life. Why? Because I was an out-of-shape slug with no motivation. I sucked, by choice. To slip into the shadows, I had to erase thoughts of, "Biggie could help my fill-in-the-blank team" from the heads of Finch coaches. While I was packing on the pounds and watching coaches turn away from me in disappointment, I believed that at any time I could turn things around. Lose a few pounds, practice my craft awhile, and I would be a better athlete than Killer or Jet or Kyle.

Despite my improved health, my athletic abilities in gym class are somewhere between nonexistent and average. The high from my perfect game in Wiffle ball was sobered by chest pains and dropped passes when we moved on to flag football. While football made me want to die, it wasn't anywhere near the torture of volleyball. At least in football, I had an idea where the ball would be going. In volleyball, the ball flew all over the place. During one twenty-minute volleyball game, I got hit in the face seven times, three of which bounced off my arms first.

While volleyball incurred the most bumps and bruises, basketball provided the most laughs. The basket seemed the size of a hula hoop when Killer or Jet shot the ball. But for me, getting the basketball through the orange aluminum rim was like threading the eye of a needle. I lost count of how many balls bounced, clanked, or skimmed the rim before one, thankfully, dropped through. I would have celebrated, but I was gassed from running up and down the court defending classmates who moved ten times faster than me, even while dribbling a ball.

So many sports were periods of embarrassment. Bowling, lacrosse, golf, floor hockey, dodgeball, and tennis were exercises in bobbling, falling, slipping, and sliding. I started to hate gym once again. The memory of the perfect game faded. It had been months since I, one-by-one, set down every kid in my class, some twice.

Coach Phillips's announcement that "on Tuesday, we will play Wiffle ball" has kept me awake for days. All of the ridicule and embarrassment of gutter balls, unintentionally launched tennis balls, swinging and missing golf balls have led to this day.

Nearly nine months ago I threw a perfect game. I did it while I was massively obese. I did it hating gym. I did it under a burning sun and over boiling concrete. I did it with zero confidence and little knowledge about Wiffle ball. The fact that on September 4, I could possibly get a Wiffle ball from the pitching mound—well, it's more of a spot—to a bat would be deemed impossible by any athletic academic. Yet, it happened. It happened, and no one reached base.

Is it dumb for me to look at that thirty minutes as the greatest half hour of my life? Maybe, but I do. My perfect game is my favorite memory, from Jet's groundout to Michelle rubbing my shoulders to Annabelle telling Coach to put me on the baseball team.

As I return to the makeshift Wiffle ball field in the school's parking lot, I can't wait to hold that plastic ball again. My fingers tingle as they wait for the openings on the white globe. I can only imagine the future as I walk to the field. I am now seventy pounds lighter than the last time I did this. Over the past nine months, I have thrown hundreds and hundreds of pitches, mastering fastballs and changeups. Then, there's the Wiffle ball—a slider-curve-knuckleball, which Maddux says is unhittable. If I can make a baseball dance in midair, imagine what I could do to a real Wiffle ball, a toy build specifically to flutter.

I calmly ask Coach if I can be all-time pitcher again. He nods and places a yellow plastic ball in my hand. What happened to real Wiffle balls? The yellow ball feels smaller and slimier. It feels cheap and flimsy. This ball feels fragile, like an egg—like one flex of my wrist and the ball will shatter as confetti of yellow plastic floats in the air.

I take the mound with 100 percent confidence. Yellow ball or no, Wiffle ball is my game. Michelle steps to the plate and I look her in the eye. My teeth and lips are locked, and my eyes squint to see her wave her bat and shoulders like a metronome. She seems at ease. Oh, this girl has no idea what's coming at her.

Just like the white one did months ago, the yellow ball hovers, slices, dives, and floats. However, she swings the bat and the ball loops to right field. Kyle runs out and Becky runs in, neither giving the kind of effort I would like to see. The ball bounces between them and then high into the air. Becky bobbles it like a hot potato, and Michelle runs to second.

What was that? I think to myself. Kyle easily could have caught that, but he had to let his girlfriend get a hit. Damn chivalry.

Up next is Ben, a short kid who specializes in cross country. He doesn't play baseball, so I feel at ease. I snap off a pitch and the ball moves like a firefly. Ben swings and drives the ball to center field. Annabelle runs under it and catches it.

"That's my girl," I say out loud. Now I'm back on track.

Up next is Jet, Finch's best hitter. Like the first day of school, he taps the concrete with his bat and licks the humid spring air.

I quick pitch him. No glance, no long, deep breath, no windup. I just throw. He swings and pulls the ball to left field. The ball slices air like a bullet. It doesn't soar. It doesn't drop. It just speeds past us like a Roman candle before bouncing off the mud brick of Finch school.

"Home run!" Jet screams. He runs around the bases like it's a victory lap.

"What's happening?" I question.

CHAPTER 28
SIGNATURES

How did Jet rocket my magic pitch over the school's brick wall? Something doesn't feel right and I don't know what it is. In desperation, I have started to stare at my hands, more specifically my fingers. They aren't skinny, like the digits on a skeleton, but they aren't casings of sausages anymore either. I have no idea how much of the seventy pounds I lost came out of my fingers, but some must have. It's also possible that my fingers look the same now as they did last fall. I have no idea. I've never really stared at my fingers before.

Why my infatuation with my appendages? Well, a week after getting lit up by classmates during a Wiffle ball game, I'm still puzzled, confused, and speechless about what happened. I don't really believe in bad days. Somehow, the game has changed. The variables of my and Maddux's perfect game plan have changed. The theory is that if I can throw a perfect game with a lot of extra pounds and little baseball knowledge, I can also, in turn, get everyone out after losing weight, gaining strength, and acquiring knowledge. Yet, almost nine months after Maddux and I scratched out his plan to shock the Finch baseball world, I'm not able to make people look silly in the box. And tryouts are twenty hours away.

In desperation, I have turned to staring at my fingers. After hours and hours of twisting and turning my wrist, after days and days of playing peekaboo with my palm, I have only one hypothesis: It is easier to throw a Wiffle ball perfect game with fat fingers. Do the plump tips of fat fingers make the ball dance with more vigor than skinny ones? Maybe. Maybe not.

I don't know, but I better come up with an answer quick. If I get roughed up tomorrow on the diamond like I did last week on the playground, my yearlong quest to throw a perfect game will end before I even put on a uniform. My goal is to do something Aaron never did, and I don't mean getting cut from the baseball team.

"Biggie!" Kyle catches me staring at my palms and fingertips before I place my textbooks into our locker.

"You working tonight?" Kyle asks.

"Yeah. Till eight," I say.

He leans in to share a secret. "Get off tonight. We're going to Cedar Rapids, and we need you to drive."

"Kyle, I work in four hours. There's not enough time," I claim.

"Biggie, are you going to play ball or not?"

"Yeah," I say with little confidence. He apparently has forgotten my horrific performance in Wiffle ball.

"Well, there's a tradition here at Finch. Before the first game, players pound a few beers, head down to the opponent's field, and piss our names in the infield."

"Sounds fun, but I really have to work." I walk away before Kyle makes one last attempt to get me to drive them an hour south.

"Courtney will be there," he screams down the hall.

I hadn't spoken with Courtney since the fight. I lost any desire to remain friends with her the second her older sister coldcocked me in the face. Plus, she's really bad at texting. After the fight, she called my phone, but my rule with girls hasn't changed. Don't call me ever.

"C'mon, you want to see Courtney. She's cute." Kyle continues his sales pitch.

"I don't know. Her sister did sucker punch me."

"Really, did that girl hurt you? You have like a hundred fifty pounds on her," Kyle says. "I promise you that she won't hit you tonight."

My eyes open so big that they almost fall out. A grin lights up my face, and I ask a very, very, very important question.

"Will Jenna be there?"

"That's the rumor," Kyle says. "Don't you dare say anything to Annabelle or even Michelle, but they ran into each other at a George Strait concert and they've been talking every day. He just told me about it yesterday."

I almost want to scream "Yes!" at the top of my lungs. Killer said at the rest stop if things worked out between him and the Coe College sophomore, he would dump Annabelle. Changing Annabelle's relationship status would be worth an ass-chewing from my boss.

✳ ✳ ✳

The guys are drunk. In the eight months we have been hanging out, I have seen them pretty tipsy, but tonight they are full-on drunk. Apparently Jet's older brother told him that you need to drink one bottle of beer for every letter of your name or you won't have enough stored piss to finish the signature. It's ridiculous, but the guys are having fun, so I let it go.

It's about 10:30 p.m. when we pull into the parking lot at Rapids South High School. The high school was just built in 2008, so even in the dark I can see the state-of-the-art, three-story glass and brick building.

For being new, the baseball stadium looks pretty blah. The stands can only hold a hundred people, and the outfield fence is a boring eight feet tall all the way around. Whoever the architect was, he didn't have much imagination.

Jet doesn't waste any time. He flips himself over the fence like he's a felon escaping a state penitentiary. He lands shoulder first on the ground, but bounces off the grass like it's a trampoline. As if he's stumbling through a hurricane, he finds his way to second base, unzips, and starts peeing. We can't hear him write, but we do hear, "Now, that's the stuff."

"You guys are really going to pee, huh?" a girl's voice asks.

Killer, Kyle, and I turn around and see Jenna and Courtney walking toward us. Both are in summer attire: tiny shorts, tight shirts, hair combed straight down to their shoulders.

Courtney is almost unrecognizable, especially with only the moonlight's help. In November, she seemed boxy with squared shoulders and a barrel of a body. Now, her body seems more of an hourglass. Jenna still looks like a pencil compared to her thick marker of a young sister, but Courtney has definitely lost a few pounds since the party.

"It's a tradition," Killer says.

"You boys." Jenna chuckles.

Kyle squeezes my shoulder, while saying, "Ladies, let me introduce you to the new Biggie."

"Wow!" Jenna walks around me like I'm a steer she's looking to purchase. "How much weight have you lost?"

"Well, I lost eighty-two pounds, but I've recently put some weight back on while training for baseball, so, I don't know, seventy-something," I say.

"Are you guys going to pee or not?" Jet screams from first base.

With the girls hanging back, we scale the fence and find a spot on the infield. I pick the pitcher's mound, but I really don't have to pee. Unlike the guys, who were emptying beer bottles like there was no tomorrow, I was sipping on a twenty-ounce Diet Mountain Dew.

There is no way I'm going to be able to pee Henry or Biggie, so I just plan to pee my initials. As I reach down for the top of my zipper, Killer screams, "Lights!"

With one hand on my penis, I fall awkwardly off the pitching mound and cheek-first to the grass infield with my little guy half inside my pants and half inside beads of grass. So cold! Lifting my hips, my hand skims the grass to shove it back in.

As we regroup by my truck, Jenna smiles and stares at Killer. I just don't get it. Her violent tendencies aside, she really is cute and out of Killer's league.

As the unlikely couple takes off for a walk, Kyle says, "Hey, Jet and I are going down the road to Taco Bell. You want some tacos?"

"Can't we come?" I say.

"Nah, Jet's got some personal stuff he needs to talk about. It's all hush-hush," Kyle says. "Hang here."

As I watch Kyle and Jet stumble off to hopefully get me some tacos, Courtney stands just under my shoulder. If I turn my neck at all, I will be looking at her. Even staring at the guys, I know her eyes are on me. She has to be thinking, *Is he going to look at me?*

Am I? Not really sure. My neck tightens and stiffens. One slight twist and a rush of uneasiness will shoot down my spine and scatter throughout my body.

"Hey," she says.

I look at her. There she is, just looking at me. Her eyes wide open. Her lips curled slightly. I can't tell if the fruity smell is shampoo or perfume.

"You don't talk much." She pulls me out of my internal shampoo-perfume discussion.

"No, not really," I reply. "I'm sorry."

"What are you thinking about?"

That's a good question. I'm not sure. I guess, I'm thinking about how uncomfortable I am, yet I have zero desire to run away. What would I type online? If a girl said I wasn't talking enough, what would my response be?

"I'm really just a listener. I'm different that way." Oh, I like this. "If you want to talk about something, I'll listen."

"Oh! You're the strong and silent type."

"Yeah, I am." I stand up straighter, stretching farther away from her glowing nose ring and shimmering smile.

"We could talk about how much I hate Taco Bell," she says.

"I don't think they took our order."

"It's okay. Their food is gross. Have you ever been to Chipotle?"

"No," I answer.

"I love Chipotle," she says. "If you want to make me happy, get me a chicken burrito from Chipotle. Yum!"

"All of this talk about Mexican is making me hungry," I say.

"Sorry," she says. "I could talk about how much I hate Jenna and Brian hanging out all the time."

All the time? "Yeah, I would love to hear about that."

※ ※ ※

Kyle is passed out when we pull into his driveway. I rattle his shoulder to wake him up. He squints his eyes and moans a little.

"What time is it?" he mumbles.

"Three thirty," I say.

"You ready for tryouts tomorrow?" he asks.

"I think so," I say. "I'm a little worried about my best pitch, but what are you going to do?"

"Well, good luck." He starts to climb out of the truck.

"I don't mean to be a jerk, but I think we should say something to Annabelle about Jenna."

He hops down, but leaves the door wide open. "She knows." He rubs a little more life into his bloodshot eyes.

"She doesn't know," I say.

"Yeah, she knows. Maybe not about tonight, but she does."

"How could she know, and I wouldn't?"

Kyle exhales a deep breath and balances himself by placing his hand on my shoulder.

"Biggie, Killer swore me to secrecy. You can't tell anyone this."

"Okay," I say.

"After the fight at Jenna's house, Killer kept seeing her. Maybe for a few weeks. Then, he told Annabelle about Jenna. He told her everything and broke up with her. Annabelle wouldn't have it. She fought for the relationship. She forgave him, and they got back together."

"Yeah, but she won't forgive again," I say.

"Maybe not. Maybe she'll dump him. Maybe she'll go out with you. But she'll always be in love with him. They're neighbors. When they were kids, they practiced kissing. She loves him. You understand? Annabelle may someday be your girlfriend, but she'll never be your girl."

Kyle's words don't shock me. Deep down I knew she loved him. After all, they flirt with each other by my locker every day. At the moment, I feel bad for Annabelle. She deserves better.

"Biggie, you need your own girl—someone who will love you like she loves him."

CHAPTER 29
1,000 FRIENDS

As I log into Twitter, I still debate whether to rat Killer out. When I pull up Annabelle's page, there she is squeezing Killer's torso in her profile picture. I scan throughout her recent pictures, and I see one after another of her and Killer hanging out, hugging, smiling, and laughing. There must dozens of them.

I grab my lamp and try and throw it at my wall, but the cord stays plugged into the outlet, and the lamp only falls off the desk and hangs there, swinging by its cord. If I had a bat, I would smash the shit out of it, but I just stare at it swinging. Without a bat, I just calmly reposition it on my desk.

When I lean back in my chair, my butt almost slides off. My eyes, half closed from a night on the road, barely focus through the closing slits. I scroll through her photos until I see one after another captioned *Prom Night*.

In every picture, and there must be a hundred of them, Annabelle smiles or grins or laughs or makes some type of funny face. How can she be happy? Why isn't she pissed off at him? He cheated on her, dumped her.

I used to think she was so tough. If a guy pissed her off, she dumped him. When we had dinner, she called me out for being a recluse. In that parking lot, she ripped me a new one for peeking at her poetry. But she's not tough. A tough girl would have kicked Killer in the balls and gone with someone who would treat her right.

I can't count the nights I have sat up and talked online to some girl in some state who was mistreated by her boyfriend or husband or "live-in lover," a term I learned from Patty in Michigan.

Those girls are my friends, but I never fully respected them. I would tell them how wonderful they were and how they deserved better, but they never left the jerk. They, instead, talked to me.

As I flip through the prom photos, I think off all the conversation I had with Felicia about her husband. I remember how Karissa's boyfriend would leave for an entire weekend and not call to let her know he was safe or even where he was. Carolyn, an eighteen-year-old from next-door Illinois, became a home wrecker when she fell for a married twenty-seven-year-old, who in the span of seven months dumped her, took her back, and then went back to his wife, who actually took him back. Some guys can do whatever they want. It doesn't matter. Not guys like me. I'm a guy who can't get a girl, not a guy who no matter how hard he tries, can't get rid of one.

Even Lucy took back her meth head of a boyfriend and then the asshole had her stop talking to me because good girlfriends don't do that. Well, good boyfriends don't get high all the time, I wanted to text back, but I didn't. I still imagine my phone ringing in the middle of the night.

When did Annabelle become like all of these girls? Why can't she tell Killer she deserves better or at least quit smiling in every goddamn prom photo?

I create a direct message prompt and type:

It sucks that I will never stop loving you, and you'll never start loving me. Enjoy getting cheated on!

I want to push Send. I want to throw my monitor. Punch it. Spit on it. My fingers seize the black plastic framing the screen. They don't move as I huff and puff. Then, I let go. Sliding the mouse, I select the message and hit Delete.

Before logging off, I look through my notifications that include a few retweets and one follow request from Courtney. Her profile picture is of her and someone I don't know at the beach making silly faces—tongues out, heads tilted, and eyes bugging. That sort of thing.

I make my own funny face when I click on her page. She has 999 followers. When I follow her I'll be number one thousand. Awesome! It's sad to admit, but it might be the coolest thing that has ever happened to me.

Plus, how did she get to one thousand? I thought I was super popular with 457. One thousand friends. I start a direct message and type, "Hey, it's Mr. 1,000."

Well, that's dumb. I quickly erase and replace with, "Thanks for the follow. I love that I'm 1,000."

What if being one thousand isn't that cool? She will probably think I'm weird for noticing it. Finch is small. She goes to Waverly-Shell

Rock, a lot bigger school. It's possible that kids at a school that big have two thousand Twitter followers.

I erase the message and stop to stare at the screen. Maybe I should just text her. I excel at text messaging. Excel. I should try being straightforward. I pick up my phone and start typing.

"We need to get…"

What was the name of the place? She said it had good burritos. I go to Google and search "Good burritos in Iowa," and get Bandit Burrito, Mr. Burrito, the Fighting Burrito, and there it is—Chipotle.

I finish my message with, "some Chipotle sometime."

I hit Send and a gush of air rockets up my throat.

"This could be bad," I tell myself.

CHAPTER 30
SLIP AND SLIDE

My lucky blue Nike T-shirt now hangs off me like a rain poncho. Losing seventy pounds has left me with few clothes, lucky ones, anyway. To most, it's a plain shirt, just blue and not even a unique blue like navy blue or midnight blue or baby blue. It's just blue with a small Nike swoosh on it. Mom bought the shirt for me last year for, like, four dollars, but it's my lucky shirt. I wear it on test days under a sweatshirt in the winter and all alone in the spring, and it's never let me down.

Sitting on a bench in the Finch locker room, I pull my shoes from my bag. When I got them in October, the shoes were a size too small. They were extremely tight. I felt like I was walking around in a vice, but I figured at the time that weight loss would also mean smaller shoe sizes. It doesn't. The shoes are even tighter now, but I live with that because the overly tight shoes help me plant better on the pitching mound.

I slip on the other shoe, gritting my teeth. I can almost hear a snapping sound when my ankle touches the sole. As I walk onto the field, there must be thirty kids running around. Players toss, flip, and fire baseballs at one another. Are they all trying out?

"Biggie, let's go," Coach Phillips screams.

It's not nervousness, but a love of math that makes me count the steps to the mound. In my head, I count five steps, ten, fifteen, twenty, twenty-three steps for me to get to the mound.

"Biggie," Coach Phillips says. "Let me just say I'm proud of you. Jim tells me you've lost almost seventy pounds. If this quest you've been on the past few months has helped you get in shape, well, you should be very proud of yourself."

I climb up on the mound. "Thank you, Coach."

"Now, Biggie, I just want you to throw warm-up speed," Laser says. It's his first official day as Finch assistant baseball coach. "Concentrate on mechanics, and keep it slow."

I reach into a white bucket next to the mound and pull out a baseball. Twirling the white ball with red stitches, I inspect it. It's a baseball, all right. I set my feet parallel to my shoulders, bend my elbows to ninety degrees, and set my glove directly in front of my nose. I place the ball in the web and look down at Kyle, who is crouched over and pounding his fist into his glove.

I step back, creating a triangle with my feet and my crotch. I lift my right leg and twirl my left foot. The ball leaves the webbing and stays in my two forefingers while my left hand moves slowly behind my back. Just when the ball disappears from Kyle's sight, I drop my right foot, plant it in the dirt, shift all 250 pounds of weight to my left leg and push off from the mound.

I curl my back and allow the weight to climb up my leg, my spine, my shoulder, my left arm, and finally two forefingers. Right as the ball passes my ear, I release it. Normally, these steps should take place faster, move violently, but this is a warm-up pitch, so it's about perfection, not power. The ball flies through the air and lands right in the glove. He barely moves.

Nothing is said, which angers me. I do it again and again and again. Five minutes pass, and I have thrown fifteen pitches, all just fast enough to reach Kyle's mitt, which hovers two feet off the ground, ninety feet away.

I throw another one, perfect; then another one, perfect; and another one, perfect.

"Hell of a job, Jim," Coach says. "I must admit I thought this was going to be a sideshow when you called. I never imagined this."

"Are you ready for the exclamation point?" Laser asks.

"There's more?"

Laser walks up to the bucket and pulls out a baseball. "Biggie, go get it." He rolls the ball on the ground, and I chase after it. The ball rolls toward left field. Like a boy chasing a chicken, I race after the ball. I have never run so fast in my life. My legs and arms chug like pistons on a race car. Just as the ball gets ready to leave the infield, I reach down with my bare hand and grab it. I plant my leg and fire the ball to Laser, who is standing at first base. I try to throw the ball hard, not accurately, but the ball still finds its way to Laser's glove. He snags it out of the air.

"Take your places!" Coach Phillips screams.

The players scatter all over. Killer and Jet head for the dugout.

"Biggie, we're going to scrimmage," Phillips says. "You have our eighth-grade team behind you, and Kyle behind the plate. Let's see how you do against real-life hitters, okay?"

As players scatter behind me, I see Maddux in the stands holding up three fingers.

Number 3 is one of several names for the pitch that is going to help me reach baseball perfection. Over the past year, the pitch has had several names: the magic pitch; the slurve, because it's a slider and curve; the knuckler, because it acts like a knuckle ball; and even the slip and slide. While it's been called a lot of things over the past seven months, its main name is the Wiffle ball.

It's called that because when I throw the baseball properly, the collection of red yarn, dark cork, and white cowhide will magically turn into a globe of plastic populated with connect-the-dots holes. If my arm travels at the right speed, if I release the ball as it passes my left ear, and if my fingers apply just the right amount of pressure, the baseball will not only zig, zag, hop, dive, and flutter, it will do what all unhittable breaking pitches do—hover in midair.

Technically, the Wiffle ball travels at a speed of sixty miles per hour. From the time the baseball leaves my hand to the time it crosses home plate, half a second will have elapsed, so most people will laugh when I tell them that during its journey, the ball will, again if thrown perfectly, hover and spin in midair. How long does the ball hang there? A split of a split second. Just long enough for a batter to squeeze the bat handle, to flinch, to blink or lose concentration.

The ball's lull sets the batter off balance and out of whack. Now, he only has a snap of my fingers to regroup and reload. There is not enough time to find the ball and place his bat on it. And even if he could somehow reach out and slap the ball, the ground ball or pop-up would be easily corralled by one of the eight fielders chosen to help me. Today, right now, Jet, Killer, all of the varsity players are going to see the Wiffle ball in action.

First up is tenth-grader Shawn Christensen. Despite being fifteen, he is tall at six-foot-four and very fast. He is part of Finch's small-school state champion 400-meter relay team. Rumor has it that his dad held him off the varsity last year so he could attend camps all over the South, building a name for himself.

Deep breath and I throw a pitch right into Kyle's glove. No one is umpiring, but it's a strike. I wind up and throw another fastball. Christensen smashes the pitch right back at me. I duck out of the way, and it flies into center field.

"You've got to catch those," Coach Phillips tells me.

Next up is Jet. With a runner on base, I have to pitch from the stretch, which is going to slow down my fastball. I decide it's time to throw the Wiffle ball.

I place my fingers in the proper spots and squeeze the right amount of pressure. Kyle pounds his glove twice, and I wind up and release the pitch. The ball starts high and darts straight downward. That's a good one.

Jet drops his bat and slaps the ball up the right-field line.

Christensen easily scores from first as some eighth-grader lobs the ball back into the infield. Jet dances on second. I'm failing. I have no idea what to do next.

＊ ＊ ＊

I sit in Coach Phillips's office and wait for the ruling. During my first scrimmage, I faced fifteen hitters and allowed five runs and eight hits. I did strike out three guys, but all in all, it was a disaster. An entire school year of work flushed right down the drain. How did this happen? I need to stop asking myself that. And I really need to quit staring at my worthless skinny fingers.

Phillips and Laser walk in. I hear the door softly close. Ah, the closed door, a sure sign of bad news. Or is it? Bad news, I mean. It's pretty apparent to anyone who watched today's tryout that I suck. I don't think I fooled anyone with my off-speed pitches, and my magic pitch might as well have started on top of a kid's tee. I'm just relieved that it happened in secret, in practice, in front of just the baseball players. No one else knows, not Annabelle, not Courtney, and not Aaron.

"How are you?" Coach Phillips asks.

"Fine," I lie.

Normally when I sit in Phillips's office, he fiddles with papers before finally getting around to the point. Today, he jumps right in. "I like your fastball. You're off-speed stuff doesn't really work, but it will. For right now, I think you should be our closer. You come in and throw the final couple of innings, save some wear and tear on Killer and Aargo. I can see it now. You come in all six-foot-four, 250 of you and scare the hell out of the batter. The poor kid won't stand a chance."

My stomach churns and my eyes itch. It's over. The dream is

201

dead. Phillips just benched me after the first practice. I may not know tons about baseball, but I know closers in the majors pitch the ninth inning and high school ball ends after seven frames. When Phillips says he wants me to close, I translate his words to mean, I don't want you to pitch at all. With Laser as my step-dad, I'll be on the roster. Heck, I may even pitch in a blowout or two, but those two assumptions don't change the fact that everything I worked for, including the perfect game, is dead. I plant my palms on the chair and prepare to push myself up.

"So, do you think you can help us?" Coach Phillips asks.

"Today was the first time I pitched," I say. My mind's clear and the words come pouring out with little thought. "I really thought I would love it out there, but I didn't. I didn't like it at all. I know it sounds stupid, but I started pitching to throw a perfect game, and maybe to help me get a girl. Since neither will happen, no, I don't want to do it. It's not fun."

In one motion, I climb out of the chair and reach for the door. Three steps later, I'm clear. The outside is only another three steps away. I shuffle my feet like I'm on a bed of hot coals until I'm free, outside, in the fresh air. I stand there and wait for the locker room door to slam behind me. It never does.

"Biggie," Laser says. "What's going on?"

I spin around and look at him eye to eye. Slouched and broken, I stand in front of him like a bum asking for loose change.

"I wanted to throw a perfect game," I say. "I'm not even a starter. I'm no better than some pinch-runner or something."

"It's a start," he says.

"A start?" I ask. "Last year was the start. This is the finish line, where the rubber meets the road. I'm supposed to be our best pitcher. I'm supposed to be able to pitch a perfect game."

I shake my head, which allows me to scan the field. Although I'm on the sidewalk next to it, the diamond feels miles away. I feel like an idiot for believing I could be a baseball star.

"Everything you told me was lies," I continue. "You told me that I had talent, that I could be a great pitcher. You made me think I could be a star baseball player like you, but it was all lies, all lies. And I know why. I know why you kept feeding me bullshit. No matter how bad I looked, you wanted—no, you needed me on this team. And why? Because you have no idea how to be a father unless your son's a baseball player."

The allegations roll off my tongue with ease, which can only mean that I believe every word of it. There is an ever-expanding part of me that knew from the start that it was a joke. *Biggie on a baseball team? It just sounds ridiculous*, I think to myself as I wait for Laser's reaction.

"Are you about finished?" he asks.

"Yeah."

"Biggie, it's just a game," he starts in a calm, relaxed almost whisper. "That's all. It's just a game. You can play it without carrying the weight of this town on your shoulders. It's fun. It's you and a group of your friends playing some other guy and his friends. You play hard. You run. You catch the ball. You hit. You sweat, and at the end of the game, win or lose, you're happy you got up that morning. It's just a game. Fine, maybe I said a few things that I shouldn't have to get you out of your room and onto the street, but look at you. Look at what you've accomplished. And listen to me right now because this is gospel. The kids on this team are really, really good, and it's a great team, but with you, this team behind us can be historic. That's truth."

"It sounds like more lies to me," I contend.

His mouth tightens and his eyes pulse. He's holding something in, but I don't know what. Does he want to yell at me? I have no idea. I'm sure most people would bow their heads and walk back into the locker room, do what their parents say. Right now, I feel genuine relief. A huge weight has been lifted off my shoulders.

Deep down, I hate sports and I always have. And even deeper down, I know and have known for months that a perfect game is impossible, and the last few weeks have only reinforced the fact. From Annabelle picking a cheating asshole over me to the Wiffle ball home run to the barrage of base hits during today's tryout, I've been following through on a fool's paradise.

My arm, which is still sore from firing fastballs, trembles under a heavy duffel bag dangling between Laser and me. I lift the bag as high as possible, but Laser ignores me.

"Keep the bag," he says. "Go home. Be mad. Be pissed that you're not starting the opener. You let that anger fuel you. Take a long run, clear your head of all the garbage inside, and then come back. I'm not going to force you, and I'll wait, but you come back. No matter what, just make sure you return to this team because we both know you're a ballplayer. Whether you're a good one or not remains to be seen, but we both know that you were born to play this game."

CHAPTER 31
CHIPOTLE

Many of my online girlfriends have up and vanished. Over the past fourteen days, I have sent messages to the 121 girls in my black binder and only twenty-six responded. There are still some good ones in that bunch. Micheala from Chicago is missing a hand, yet she's hilarious. Two nights ago, we had a joke-telling contest that lasted over an hour. I didn't even look up any jokes up on the Internet, didn't have to. I've memorized dozens of the jokes I told Kyle.

Danica from Florida ran away from home and lives with nine other girls in a five-bedroom house. Okay, I know she's full of it, but who cares. We talked last night about one of the girls at her house being a lesbian and did a pros-cons list on whether Danica, a self-proclaimed bisexual, should make a move. That was fantastical.

While I'm getting my online groove back, seeing Annabelle and Killer or Kyle and Michelle flirt in the hallways makes me feel alone. I find myself texting with Courtney at least once a day, and the conversations always drift to Killer and Jenna.

For the most part, I'm Annabelle free. No more staring at her juggling textbooks at her locker or twirling her hair with a pen. I never check her Twitter page or look for her car at Molly's when I drive by. Even last Sunday when I heard she and Killer broke up, I resisted the urge to stop into Molly's and see her. Kyle's right. She'll never be my girl.

I tell myself to not ask about Jenna when Courtney messages me because I know it's really an Annabelle question. When I ask about Jenna and Killer going out, I'm really getting affirmation that he's left Annabelle. I need to be strong and erase Annabelle from my thoughts, especially when chatting with Courtney. She's wonderful and the only girl who doesn't call me Biggie. I don't know why she calls me Henry. Courtney hears the guys call me Biggie, and I have never told her the nickname bothers me, so I wouldn't blame her if she joined the crowd. But she hasn't. I guess she just knows, maybe because she used to be a bigger girl too.

Courtney has been a big help in the last couple of weeks. Since I quit the team, I've gone underground. No chatting at school. No jokes at the locker. No driving the guys around on weekends. Seeing Kyle or Killer or Jet makes me think about the Finch baseball bag in my closet. They keep telling me that Coach would take me back as long as I agree to certain punishments. Every sales pitch increases the guilt, thick as a mudslide that continues to surge below my skin. I carry my family's disappointment around inside me in the same way I carry around my beating heart or pumping lungs.

At school, I'm more and more hiding in the back. At home, I creep up the stairs and tightly shut my bedroom door. I can't look at

Laser. He said he wouldn't push me and he hasn't, but I'm positive that Coach Phillips's alleged willingness to bring me back has 100 percent to do with Laser.

I know I let him down. Worse of all, Maddux doesn't even come up and play video games with me anymore. I let him down the most. I just couldn't perfect the "Wiffle ball."

Today was the final day of school and everyone got out at noon to go to Des Moines for the second day of the Principal Park Kickoff Classic, and as I lie on my bed, the Yellow Jackets—including Kyle, Killer, and Jet—are preparing to play Council Bluffs High School in Friday night's semifinals. Last night, Killer tossed a gem. He allowed only one run over nine innings. Finch and Rapids South played thirteen innings, almost two full high-school games, before the Yellow Jackets' lone senior, Curt Aargo, hit a game-winning two-run double in the bottom of the thirteenth. Finch won 4–2. All last night, I kept picturing Annabelle cheering Killer on, probably in some new low-cut shirt that says, "I love Killer," in big letters spread across her boobs. Hell, Jenna's probably there too.

I could have gone to the game with my family, but it would only remind me of my yearlong quest that ended in a complete failure.

By the time I get home from school, my house is, for a second straight night, empty. For most of my life, all alone was my favorite status. It's when I excelled. It's when I was at my best. Whether it was studying for a big test, chatting online, playing video games, or reading a book, I loved being alone. No one bothered me. No one made fun of me. No one got in my way.

My bedroom seems smaller than before. There used to be so much room to pace back and forth as I tried to create perfect responses. I could twirl my chair like a toddler's spinning top and my size fourteen feet wouldn't bump any furniture. After chatting all night with girls online, the early-morning stroll from bed to bathroom felt like a mile-long desert march. Now, it seems like a prison.

It's actually funny, but when I used to sit alone in my room, it was never quiet. There was the click of keys or the hiss of a fan. I trained my ears to hear female voices when girls typed messages. If anything, it was loud.

Now, it's quiet. Too quiet. I'm so alone…and hungry.

There's healthy food in the fridge, but now that I'm not playing baseball, turkey sandwiches on wheat bread sound like rubber inside two sheets of sandpaper. I could go to Molly's or the convenience store, but I feel like taking a drive. Maybe I'll try out that Mexican food place Courtney likes. A long drive with booming rock music sounds refreshing.

A couple weeks ago, I texted her about Chipotle and never got a response. Since then, we've texted back and forth a few times about various things, yet she's never brought up that first text message I sent. Nor have I for that matter. For someone who is so perfect at getting girls online to fall for him, I'm horrendous in person. I strike out when I don't swing, like with Annabelle, and I strike out when I do, like with Courtney.

I guess I can't say I struck out with Courtney; she just hasn't responded yet. For all I know she never saw the message. I mean she has a thousand followers on Twitter; maybe she gets hundreds of text messages every day.

I pick up my phone to text her again about getting burritos, but my fingers just linger away from the keyboard. They know that if I text her, and she says, "No," I won't leave this bedroom. And I need to get the hell out of here before I start banging my head against the wall. I slip the phone in my pocket and pick up my keys.

Showing up at Courtney's house unannounced sounds like a great idea until I see her green Cavalier parked in the driveway. I decide to park a block away and role-play our eventual discussion. Forty-two minutes later, I'm still sitting in my truck and watching the clock tick toward 6 p.m. An hour is almost gone, and I must have given myself a hundred ineffective pep talks.

I start my truck and like an eighty-year-old Sunday driver, I coast up her street. Tapping the gas and sliding my fingers up and down the wheel, I pull behind the Cavalier.

I consider honking or calling or backing up and going home, but those ideas are annoying, weird, and cowardly. Good or bad, it's too quiet living life all alone. I'm seventeen years old; it's time for me to have a girlfriend.

The truck door creaks as I open it. Normally, I hop out like a gymnast finishing a dismount, but today, I slide down. I use the same formula to get out of my truck that I use to put on jeans: one leg at a time.

Once the rubber soles of my shoes settle on the walk, there is no going back. Surely, someone has peeked out a window or heard my truck turn off. Everyone in that house knows I'm here.

As I reach for the bell, the front door opens. Some kid, likely Courtney's eleven-year-old freckled brother, checks me out.

"You the cowboy?" he asks.

"Um, what?" I answer, wondering if my red Nike T-shirt and tan shorts make me look like a cowboy.

"Are you the cowboy that is taking my sister out tonight?"

I really, really wish I would have called now. As I drove into Waverly, I felt spontaneous and impulsive. I thought for sure Courtney would love my spur-of-the-moment action. Plus, I wanted to put my life in the hands of fate. If I drove over here and she wasn't home, maybe God doesn't want us together. Her car sitting in the driveway looks like a big, old billboard sign saying, "She loves you. Come ask her out."

But now I'm stuck. I'm the guy who showed up unannounced while she was getting ready for her date with a cowboy.

"No, I'm not a cowboy," I tell the shaggy-haired little boy.

"Henry." Courtney appears from the side of the house.

"Henry," the boy says. "That's a dumb name."

"Hayden! Shut the door!" Courtney commands. "What are doing here?" she asks.

Head tilted slightly, Courtney stands near her green and very unreliable car wearing a black, baggy University of Iowa football shirt and tiny, tight white shorts, which cover about as much of her legs as her pale blue flip-flops cover her feet.

210

"I didn't know about the cowboy," I admit.

As she starts to laugh, a gust of wind blows her dark bangs away from her brown eyes.

"I really thought I could talk you into getting some Chipotle," I say as I watch her flip the hair out of her eyes. "I thought you would be impressed that I remembered you saying that you like their food."

She flips the stubborn bangs away from her eyes again and then motions me off the stoop and down to the driveway.

"You do get bonus points for remembering that, but I also have to take some away because you didn't do your homework."

"What?"

"There's no Chipotle here," she informs me. "The closest one is in Iowa City."

"You said you loved it."

"I do," she says. "My family goes to a lot of University of Iowa stuff. When we are there, we almost always go to Chipotle."

"Oh," I say, embarrassed. "Do you really have a date? Your brother said you're going out with a cowboy."

"Yeah, I do," she says.

"Okay," I say. "Well, lesson learned. I should've called. I'll go."

"He won't be here for an hour," she says. "Do you want to take a walk?"

I shrug my shoulders and look at the driver's door of my truck.

"Henry, do you want to talk to me or not?"

After walking in mostly silence for two blocks, Courtney detours into a park and plops down on a swing.

I follow and pick the swing next to her. While we are two

blocks away, I can still see an image that I know is my truck. Feeling awkward, stupid, and out-of-place, I just want to climb into it and drive. I need to go somewhere other than here, other than home. It's too quiet there. Hell, maybe I'll drive to Iowa City and get a burrito.

"You know, Henry, it's really immature of you to be mad at me right now," she says. "You didn't call or anything."

"I'm not mad," I say.

"You've said like three words."

"You're not talking either," I reply.

She flips herself off the swing and lands in a foot-made dirt hole. "If you're going to be a jerk, I'm going home."

Her untucked T-shirt covers her butt as she walks away. My mind's blank, and although my mouth hangs open, nothing comes out. A long, deep breath, a few blinks, and then, "Don't go out with him!"

She flips around, now probably twenty to thirty feet from me.

"Just call him and say you can't go!" I keep talking.

"He'll be here in an hour," she says. "What kind of girl do you think I am?"

As she waits for an answer to a question I have no intention of answering, I shrug off the swing and jog up to the sidewalk. Our yelling has caught the attention of the rest of the park's population, and I don't feel like putting on another show with another pissed-off girl.

"Just because we talk every night doesn't make us boyfriend and girlfriend," she says for only me to hear. "Henry, you have no idea how long ago I gave up on you," she says. "It was months ago when

I stopped wondering if you would ask me out or randomly show up at my door."

"Why?"

"That night at Perkins, I really thought you were nice, so I invited you to my party," she says. "You and your friends came, and then you just ignored me. Then, you start texting me, but it's just friends stuff, nothing serious."

"I don't understand what you're saying," I interject.

"I guess I'm saying you're not going to make me feel guilty for telling you no."

As things go further downhill, my thoughts become scattered as I stare into her green eyes. All I want to do is to put my sweaty palms on her cheeks and pull her lips to mine. Hold her tight and just kiss her. Allow my hands to fall through her hair. With 90 percent of my brain fantasizing about the taste of her lips and cheek and neck, my responses shorten.

"I like you," is all I can muster with the remaining 10 percent.

Her head falls as those three words paint a pinkish hue on her cheeks.

"More than Annabelle?" Her head rises for an answer.

"Annabelle? We're through," I say, actually believing it too.

"Because she's dating Brian?" she asks.

"They broke up, and that's not even it. I was done before that. Brian was cheating on her and she didn't even care," I say. "And because she doesn't like me. Whatever. But I'm done, Courtney. I promise if you go out with me tonight, I will be the best boyfriend. I will be so much better for you than this cowboy guy."

"Henry, I have to be honest with you," she says. "If you're asking me to pick, I will pick him. He's taking me horseback riding, and he's even bringing me a cowboy hat. And it's more than that. My date—he saw me at Dairy Queen a couple of weeks ago, and he walked past like four girls to talk to me. And in less than ten seconds, he asked me out. The way he looks at me I know he thinks I'm hot. When I look at you, all I can think about is how much you like what's-her-face."

"I meant it. Annabelle and I are done."

"Okay, maybe if things go poorly tonight, we can go out another night," she offers. "I'm not going to forget about you. We're late-night texting buddies."

Courtney's compromise is fair, all things considered, and I should just accept it and not go about sabotaging her date with the cowboy, but I'm alone tonight for a very shitty reason.

"Listen, you can go out with him some other time. And I'll compete for you. But I need you tonight. Let me have tonight."

"I'm sorry, Henry, but he'll be here soon, and I have to get ready."

"I've beat diabetes twice," I yell to the sky.

The left turn in the conversation puts a perplexed look on her face.

"Twice, hell, maybe more," I continue. "My mom thought I might still have had it up until a month ago."

"Well, that's good," she says. Or something like that. I'm ignoring her for the most part.

"Everyone assumed there was something wrong with me. No one could comprehend the fact that I was happy." The rant has begun. "Was I fat? Yes! So what? Was I sick? No! Was I unhealthy? Not really. I was happy. I wasn't delusional. I was happy."

I look over my shoulder back to the park and see a little girl swinging high up and down, and the sight of that girl enjoying this warm spring night pisses me off even more. I hate happy people.

"When my doctor told me last year that I beat diabetes again, I made some goals. Hell, I felt invincible, like I was special, unbreakable. I told myself that I was going to weigh two hundred pounds, date the girl of my dreams, and pitch a perfect game. Now, I seem to be putting on weight, the girl of my dreams is dating…I don't know, I guess my archenemy…and even though I threw hundreds, Courtney, hundreds of pitches, I still suck as a pitcher.

"My brother…"—although I'm on the verge of crying, I can't help but smile and let loose a short laugh—"told me he could teach me an unhittable pitch. It turns out that it's just a crappy curve ball. So two weeks ago, I found out that I'll never be the person I want to be; I'm stuck being the person I am. And I know I should be happy with what I have, but I'm not. I'm really, really sad all the time. And I know I'll be happy again.

"I'm not trying to be overly dramatic, but on the way over here, something dawned on me. Today, well, tonight actually, I was supposed to throw a perfect game. Killer, I always knew, would throw the opener, and I would pitch game two. I would be perfect, and my life would never be the same. Courtney, if you don't go out with me tonight, all I will think about is how I'm a failure. Everything I've done will lead to a night where the world is awake and I'm asleep."

She turns away and starts walking home. As I catch up with her, I use the tips of my fingers and I snag enough football shirt fabric to stop her.

"Courtney," I say.

"I said don't make me feel guilty, and what was that? My sister, who is my best friend by the way, is seeing your friend. I know you quit the baseball team."

"I didn't quit."

"Yes, you did. Brian said so."

"Okay, okay, okay." I'm mumbling. "I didn't quit, exactly. I tried out to be a starting pitcher and was told I wasn't good enough to be a starter, so depending on how you look at it, I was cut."

"Well, I'm sorry about that," she says. "I'm sorry you're alone tonight, but I really do have a date."

Once again, she's walking away from me, and I'm the creepo chasing her.

"If this guy is so wonderful, why don't I know anything about him? Why haven't you mentioned him?"

She spins around. "I didn't feel like it."

"This guy, is it serious? Your profile says you're single. It doesn't even say 'complicated.'"

As we reach her driveway, she says, "It's only been one date and it sucked. He invited me to his house to watch a movie, and he watched ten minutes of it before he reached for my clothes. There. Now you know about our date. He begged for a second chance. I said, "You better make it good," and tonight we're going horseback riding. You're all caught up now."

"His house? Is he in college?" I ask.

"No, he's twenty-four."

My head's going to explode. Twenty-four. I can't believe I lost one girl to a guy who sleeps around and another one to a pedophile. What is wrong with every girl in the world? I keep my thoughts buried by tongue rubbing the inside of my teeth and staring at the blue, cloud-free sky.

"Say it," she orders. "Tell me what you're thinking."

I need to keep quiet. I need to say *it's fine* but I don't. Instead, I blurt out, "You can't date a twenty-four-year-old. It's illegal."

"I knew I shouldn't have told you," she says. "And by the way, I can date him. I turn eighteen in three months."

"He's twenty-four. Courtney, wake up! He's using you for sex. He wants to have sex with a high-school girl one more time. He's never going to call you his girlfriend or introduce you to his parents. It's all about sex."

Before my accusations end, my eyes are shut and my face prepares for the slap. "I'm sorry," I say.

"Apology accepted because you're wrong."

Since my foot is already in my mouth, I add, "This whole thing has been a huge disappointment. I know that sounds mean, but honestly I can think of nothing else to say to you. I'm really disappointed."

For some reason, she's smiling at me. I can't tell if she's playing games with me or just trying to hold in a string of expletives.

"I have to go get ready," she says.

As I watch her walk up the steps, I feel like an asshole. Courtney is the nicest person I know, and I just yelled at her because I'm lonely and jealous. I grit my teeth and once again chase her.

I tap her shoulder and say, "Don't turn around. If you do, I'll get flustered and put my foot in my mouth again. I'm horrible at face-to-face conversations. Just listen. I'm sorry. You heard right. I quit the baseball team, so I had no right to bring that up. I'm such a mean person today, and you're so nice and so beautiful. In fact, I can't think of one thing about you that I don't like.

"Did you know that you're the only girl I know that doesn't call me Biggie? Don't answer that; let me finish. You don't disappoint me. I'm disappointed with myself. I wait too long. I think the worst, and then worst eventually happens. But that's my fault; I guess you know that, but I do, too. Have fun tonight."

She slowly turns around and glances at me, but says nothing. Her lips are locked and her cheeks are flat. She's holding everything inside.

"You can breathe," I say.

We both let out an awkward laugh. But it feels nice, as if we created our own cool breeze on this calm June Iowa night.

"Send me a picture of you in the cowboy hat, okay?" I say.

"Only if I look good in it."

CHAPTER 32
BIGGIE ISN'T A MEAN NICKNAME

For the past six hours, I have been maneuvering through a maze of highways, county roads, city streets, and gravel back roads. When I wanted to turn left, I turned left. When I felt an urge to go right, I spun the steering wheel clockwise. I listened to loud music by Poison, Kiss, Bon Jovi, and Def Leppard. I burned through all the playlists on my iPod.

I don't want to go home. The house feels empty, quiet, and cold. I've spent hundreds of nights alone in my bedroom and not felt the slightest sense of loneliness, yet my bedroom now seems like a consolation prize. I'm supposed to be in Des Moines, celebrating with my teammates after my perfect game or seventeen-strikeout performance, or making out with Courtney, rubbing my hands all over her new hourglass body. Heck, there's no reason why I couldn't have done both.

Yet, here I am alone: a failure, who couldn't figure out how to pitch or how to get a girl to go out with him. Life sucks. There is no other explanation as to how someone who has mastered trigonometry, physics, and British literature can't figure out baseball or girls.

With my tank running low, I pull into my driveway and notice Killer sitting on my front steps. What the hell? Why isn't he in Des Moines with the Finch baseball team?

I turn off the truck and climb down. For reasons I can't explain, I'm really nervous. Hair on my arms stands up and my steps are short and measured. I'm in no hurry to reach the front door.

"What's up?" he asks.

"Nothing," I say. "I heard on the radio that you guys are in the championship game."

He nods a couple of times, but says nothing. We just stand there silent, hands on hips, ears at attention, and eyes on each other.

"Cool," I say. Killer standing silent in my driveway is freaking me out.

"This tournament," he finally says, "means everything. We're competing against the big schools, and if we beat them, we can say we're state champs, regardless of class. The Des Moines paper does a poll of all schools and we could be ranked No. 1. Do you know what that means?"

I just shake my head, confused as to why I'm getting a history lesson.

"Whenever you hear someone talk about Finch baseball, they always say we're the best small-town team in Iowa. It's like a back-handed compliment. I want people to see us as the best team, period. That's why this is so important. You see that, right?"

"Yeah, I get that." I really don't, but Killer's face looks different.

He always portrayed power and strength, but now he looks weak and small. He's obviously nervous. He pulls a program out of his jeans and hands it to me.

"I circled it," he says.

It's dark, but I can still make it out. "Henry Abbott, pitcher."

"Like we've been saying, you can come back. Coach will still take you back."

Before I can speak, he lifts his hands and pleads, "Biggie, I threw nine innings Thursday. Aargo tossed seven tonight, and Kyle pitched three on Thursday. We are down to Jet, and he's not a good pitcher, not like us. I can't believe I'm saying this, but you throw really, really hard...even harder than me. You need to come back with me. You need to beg Coach to let you pitch tomorrow. We can win this. Our offense is on fire. We scored nine runs tonight against a future college pitcher. We're hitting everything, and St. John's used their two top pitchers against Waverly-Shell Rock. Hell, you could give up six runs, and we could still win."

"I'm not going to Des Moines and giving up six runs," I say. "No way. I'll be a laughingstock. And what if you don't score six runs? Then I'm the losing pitcher of what you're saying is the biggest game of all time."

Killer pulls on his hair and, as if he wants to pluck out my eyes, flashes his fingers at me. For a second I think he is going to claw me like a rabid stray cat.

"Don't be an asshole. I'm not saying you're going to give up six runs. I'm just saying you could and it wouldn't matter if you did. We would still win," Killer says.

Maybe it's because I'm on a step and he's on the sidewalk, but Killer seems so irrelevant. We're back in second grade and he's the smallest kid in school, not the star quarterback. His chin points to the ground, and his shoulders sag. He looks tired and beaten, distressed and worried.

I hover over him like a god. Helped by a step, I'm a foot taller. While his body slumps, I'm at attention. Standing tall, relaxed, and confident, with the flick of my finger, I could knock him over. He's a rag doll asking for a favor.

"No," I say. "I'm not helping you."

"It's not me, you idiot," he replies. "We're Finch. It's the town. Don't you care about your hometown?"

"Don't do that," I say.

"Don't do what? It's true. This is a baseball town. You know it. Everybody loves the Yellow Jackets, and I'm telling you that your town needs you."

"Killer, it's like the third game of the season. I really don't think everyone in town cares that much."

"I WANT TO WIN!" he yells.

Killer paces a little in front of his car, and I realize we're not in second grade anymore. He stands tall and looks right at me. "You think I wanted to be born in a town of thousand people? I'm not small town. I'm as good as any one of those players in Des Moines, Iowa City, or Cedar Rapids. I don't have a single Division I college offer yet.

Why? Because all of my stats have an asterisk. All of my hits are against small-town pitchers. I beg and I beg Coach Phillips to schedule games against bigger schools, but they won't play us. They're scared because they don't want to get beat by a small-town school. Well, we got in this tournament and they have to play us now. And I don't want to lose because we ran out of pitchers. We're not out of pitchers, Biggie. We still got you. Maybe you're right and this town doesn't really care, but I do. I need you to come back."

"Why would I help you?" I ask. "You stole Annabelle."

"Oh my fucking god, is this still about Annabelle? Dude, she's not going to date you. You hacked into her computer. Do you have any idea?"

"You gave me the horrible name Biggie! You're the reason everyone, even my little brother, calls me Biggie."

His face looks shocked and he shrugs his shoulders and twitches his face. "Biggie's a cool nickname. There's nothing wrong with it."

I raise my hands and draw an are-you-kidding-me look on my face. Completely stunned and almost speechless, I say, "It's cool if it's ironic, like let's call hundred-pound Johnny 'Biggie.' But if Johnny's fat, it's mean and awful."

"Fine, I'm a horrible person, a horrible boyfriend, but what about Kyle, Jet, Aargo? Hell, your stepfather is a coach. Your brother is the batboy. You can hate me, but still play a game with your friends tomorrow."

"It's not going to happen." I turn toward my front door.

"Biggie," he begs.

With my hand an inch from the doorknob, I decide against going inside and, for some idiotic reason, spin around and yell, "I don't want to give up eight runs and twelve hits! You're desperate. Don't you see that? I'm not your savior. I'm not a good pitcher."

As I turn to shove crooked metal into the keyhole, Killer says, "Annabelle was wrong about you."

My neck twists and my eyes watch him back up toward his Mustang.

"She said the reason you ignore all of us is because you think you're better than us with your brains, your big house, and your indoor baseball field. But you don't think you're better than us. You're scared. The biggest kid in school is scared of everything. Biggie is a little coward. We're through. This year didn't happen. The next time you see me we're sophomores again, and you don't talk to me and I don't give a shit." He jumps into his car and peels out of the driveway.

The inside of my house is dark, but I don't need any light to make my way to my room. Without taking off my shoes, I flop down on my bed and realize that sometime during my shouting match with Killer, I stuck the program in my pocket.

Despite what I said outside about being on the team, it feels kind of cool that my name is listed on the roster. I pull out my phone and use its light to read my name. It says I'm No. 9.

I sit up. That can't be right. No. 9 is retired. No. 9 was Laser's number.

I hop off my bed and dart toward my closet. I rip open the Finch duffel bag and pull out the jersey. My hand runs over the No. 9.

I set the shirt down and run down the steps, out the door, and down the street.

CHAPTER 33
RETIRED NUMBERS

With the Yellow Jackets in Des Moines, Finch is quiet. With the exception of an orange summer moon climbing over the water tower, running at 11:30 p.m. is just like running at 5 a.m. Every forty or so steps, I see a pair of headlights providing just enough of a glow to see a half-asleep driver. None of the shops on Second Avenue are open. The school is dark and empty. The wind is calm and warm and getting warmer with every step. Mike's Sports Bar is open, but only a rundown, rusty two-door Chevy and a conversion van with a paper sack covering a broken window sit in the parking lot.

And there are stars. In May, I can see Leo the lion, Virgo the maiden, and the Big Dipper. At 5 a.m., my eyes focus forward. Tonight, my neck twists and turns in all directions. The sky is amazing.

I stop running when the worn-out rubber on the soles of my shoes hits the asphalt of the parking lot of Finch Field. Slowly, methodically with purpose, I walk to the right-field fence and climb. When my chest reaches the top of the eight-foot chain-link fence, I pump my forearms and flip myself over, sticking my two-foot landing.

I remain focused and inattentive to any sounds. There may be crickets at my feet or bees swirling around my ears or frogs croaking in the creek behind the left-field wall, but I'm not listening. My eyes are locked on a gold "25" on a billboard attached to the left center-field wall. Above the 25, in blue letters, is the name Abbott. My father wore No. 25, and when I was in fifth-grade, the school retired the number. For the past six years, no Yellow Jacket has worn the number. It was the first number the school retired. Soon, billboards went up for 12, 22, 50, and Laser's No. 9.

I thought the grass would be wet or at least damp, but it's rough and crisp after two weeks of dry temps. With each step, I crush blades of grass with my tennis shoes.

Three feet from the wooden banner, I stop and release one long breath. My shoulders are at attention and my chin is squared. My hands hang free but don't sway. My shoes are a foot apart but lined perfectly. With the exception of my lungs pushing against my chest, I'm standing perfectly still.

Seconds tick away and minutes pass, but I say nothing. I just stare at the 25 and gather my thoughts. I have so much to say, but no idea where to start. After six minutes, I say, "I'm not a coward."

My eyes water and my breaths putter. I rub my nose, mouth, and chin to regain my composure.

"I was called a coward tonight," I continue, "and I'm not. Also tonight, I had to tell a girl, a girl that I like, that I'm a quitter. Nothing makes a girl fall for you like those three words: I'm a quitter."

Like a reflex, I chuckle and run my two front teeth over the tip of my bottom lip.

"I saw your Facebook page. I've looked at it for years. I saw you and your two boys hugging each other at the baseball field. They're probably pretty good with their dad being a former first-round draft pick. Do people in Tempe know you're a high-school legend? Do they know that No. 25 is retired, and you're in the Iowa High School Baseball Hall of Fame?

"When your two boys, I think their names are Justin and Matt"—I wait for the sign to verify the information, but the two-dimensional white, blue, and gold sign confirms nothing—"when they walk around, do people say, 'I thought he would be bigger, stronger, faster, better at baseball, football, basketball, better looking'? Do they have to deal with your legacy?

"You know I hate you?" I continue, cheeks warming and tightening. "I know I should hate you for what you did to my mother, but that's not why. It's not because you hired a lawyer and signed a paper saying you're not my dad anymore. It's because you knew I couldn't be average, ordinary, or normal. You knew expectations were going to be impossible for me to meet, and you didn't hang around to help me get through that. You just left and left me with the snickering, the whispering, and the looks of disappointment.

"I told this girl that I was going to play baseball and she said, 'Good.' She had no idea if I could even catch a baseball, but she said, 'Good.' When I asked why she said that, she said, 'Because you're Aaron Abbott's son.' That's what I live with, you selfish asshole.

"Yeah, I was going to play baseball. My brother and I were

working on this pitch. It was going to be unhittable, and I was going to throw a perfect game. I'm an idiot. All the pitch does is hang up there. I would be better off placing the baseball on a tee. When I found out that I didn't have a magic pitch, I quit. But now my friends need me, and I'm going to help them. I'm going to see if Coach can use me. I don't know what will happen. Coach could tell me to go home. I could pitch and do well. I could pitch and do horribly. But I can't worry about you. If I go there, I can't worry about you.

"I know that people tell you things. Finch is small, and people talk to you. I know that. And you probably know I'm smart. You probably know that I stay out of trouble. What you don't know is that I like pitching, and I truly believed I could have thrown a perfect game.

"After the celebration, someone would have called you and said, 'Go online. Henry pitched a perfect game.' You would have logged on, and maybe for a second, just maybe, you would have felt a little regret for leaving me. Maybe you would question what you did. Maybe you would look at your sons differently and worry that you picked the wrong ones."

My shoulders are now slouching, my back curled and feet shuffling. My fingers either rub my palms, my eyes, or my cheeks. I'm shrinking.

"I just came here tonight to say I'm done with you. I know you already split us up, but I think I should get a turn, a chance to say you're a nuisance to me. And you know what really sucks? In the movies when people split, someone throws a plate or breaks something. They find an object that the person gave to them, and they break or burn it. But you haven't given me anything. I have nothing to destroy or throw at this sign.

"All you have ever given me is my last name; something I can't rip, burn, spit on, piss on, or return."

I fiddle with my sweaty shirt, then expel a long breath and say, "Tomorrow, I'm going to pitch. And no matter what, my brother, my mom, and my step-dad are going to be proud of me."

I swallow the lump in my throat and raise my shoulders, lift my chin, and flex the muscles in my legs and arms. I have no intention of looking weak.

"If I do well, you can think whatever. If I do poorly, be happy. Be happy Matt and Justin are the sons you kept. I don't care. I'm so tired of giving a shit about what you think about me. I just want to stop being judged by someone I've never met. I'm tired of being called weird or scared or a quitter."

I massage a tear into my cheek and turn away. As I try to steady myself, I see Laser's sign with his retired No. 9.

I run back and stand close enough to Aaron's sign that my breath bounces off his last name.

"Tomorrow, I will be wearing No. 9. And when I'm done, Maddux will wear No. 9. And someday, my son will wear No. 9. No one will ever wear your number again. Not in this town. Someday, people will forget about you."

CHAPTER 34
CAN I HELP?

Wearing a Finch baseball hat and balancing a Finch baseball duffel bag on my shoulder makes it easy for me to sneak past security at Principal Field. Next, I have to find Coach Phillips, beg for a spot on the team, and then hope he doesn't want me to spit shine his shoes.

I pray that I won't run into Kyle, Jet, Mom, Dad, Maddux, or worst of all, Killer before I can talk to Coach. The game doesn't begin for ninety minutes, so I'm not 100 percent sure the team has arrived. With every step, Killer's idea becomes dumber and dumber. A poster on the wall lists all of the Kickoff Classic champions, a menu full of large schools in Iowa. Killer was right, a win tonight would put the Yellow Jackets on the map.

Huddled ahead are Coach Phillips and Laser. They scan a sheet of paper. If I hadn't just driven three hours, I probably would have turned around and ran, but here I am. I might as well see if I can get a seat in the dugout to one of the biggest regular-season games in Finch history.

I'm happy that Coach Phillips sees me first. He frightens me less than Laser, which makes no sense, seeing how Laser would do anything to get me on the team, and Phillips could care less. That being said, I'm glad Laser hasn't seen me yet.

"Biggie, good to see you." Phillips eyes my hat and duffel bag.

He's no genius, but I think he can put two and two together.

Laser turns and looks pale. It's been two weeks since he told me he didn't raise a quitter. I'm sure he had given up on me.

"Hello, Coach." I slowly pronounce my words. "I want to help the guys win this championship. Can I help?"

"I don't know," he says. "Come back in an hour, and I'll let you know."

"What?" I ask.

"Come back in an hour, and I'll let you know," he repeats himself. "I'm busy right now."

"Okay," I say.

For the next hour, I sit outside the locker room. People pass, but no one I recognize. Finally, after an hour, which felt like ten, Maddux tells me to come into the locker room and get ready.

As I slip on the jersey, which is a little baggy, Coach walks past, but remains silent. I've never felt more uncomfortable. Obviously, he's screwing with me. If he didn't want me here, he wouldn't have told me to get dressed, but I can't help but think an ass chewing is coming up soon.

Phillips, Laser, Maddux, and I walk to the bullpen. It's cloudy and the wind blows crisply onto my face. I look around and only see a handful of people searching for seats in the stands. The sky has zero blue, only shades of gray and black, like some old movie. It's cold, but it's not supposed to rain. As we walk to the bullpen, the scoreboard says that Council Bluffs beat Waverly-Shell Rock 5–1 in the third-place game.

I search the stands for Jenna and maybe even Courtney. I'm not sure how much they hang out or if Courtney is the kind of girl to travel two hours to see a baseball game, but it doesn't hurt to look. In between games, there are maybe a dozen people in the stands, and none look like Jenna or Courtney.

"Biggie," Coach Phillips finally speaks, "are you ready for this?"

I nod and take the ball. It's used, brown like soil, and the formally red seams are a dull maroon. Jet tosses baseballs on the far pitching mound. I only need to see two pitches to know Killer's right. He doesn't have a lot of stuff.

I decide to show Coach that I'm fine. I toss a strike to Laser, who's catching for me. Even at 70 percent, with no windup, I throw faster than Jet, who's moaning and groaning before each pitch. Slowly but surely, I ramp up the velocity. The snapping noise coming from Laser's catcher's mitt gets louder after each fastball. By my tenth pitch, I'm firing at full speed and making it look like Jet is playing egg toss with his younger sister.

I throw forty-two pitches, mostly fastballs, before Coach tells me to stop.

"Jet, head to the dugout," he says.

"Yes, Coach," Jet says, adding, "Hey, Biggie," as he walks by.

"Sit on the bench," Coach orders me.

He leans over; the smell of cigars fills my throat, almost causing me to gag.

"Biggie, you just sit here by yourself and watch the game," he says. "Watch every aspect of it. Watch every play, good or bad, we make."

"Am I going to pitch?"

"I'm not even sure if you're going to be allowed in the dugout at this point."

"I can't go in the dugout?"

"The dugout's for ballplayers, for people who love to play, for people who have fun, for people that don't skip two weeks of practice. You quit on me, son. I don't know what to think about you just showing up for a game."

I sit there in complete silence and think about what he said. Did I come down here because of the championship game? I don't know. Maybe I did want to help Kyle and Jet and maybe even Killer. Maybe I felt I owed Laser something for training me and giving me his number. Maybe seeing my name on that roster got to me. Hell, I don't know why I'm here, but I'm here.

Jet struggles from the start. He allows a run in the first and second innings and a three-run home run in the third. The good news is that Killer wasn't kidding about Finch's hitting. Kyle smacks a three-run triple in the bottom of the fourth, and Finch leads, 6–5. After shutting out St. John's in the fourth, Jet allows three hits and one run in the top of the fifth. I count every pitch. When a St. John's batter pops out to Killer for the final out of the fifth, Jet has thrown 102 pitches. Unfortunately for me, his arm is still attached.

Finch retakes the lead in the top of the fifth when Aargo doubles off the wall, scoring Kyle. Going into the top of the sixth, Finch leads 7–6. Killer said if I could have held St. John's to six runs, the Yellow Jackets would win. He was right.

Jet walks the first two batters of the sixth. He's now at 112 pitches, give or take a couple I may have missed because I was looking into the stands.

Laser and Maddux leap out of the dugout. Maddux carries a face mask and catcher's mitt. I stand up. Defying gravity, a lump climbs up my throat. I reach down and grab my cap and glove.

"Let's go, Biggie. You have to get warm," Laser says.

I throw seventeen pitches as Killer, Kyle, and Coach Phillips walk back and forth to the mound. When the umpire orders the meetings to end, Jet, with little effort, tries to pick off a base runner. Everyone knows he's done. I know he's done, which explains why I feel like I'm going to piss my pants.

After my eighteenth warm-up pitch, Phillips lifts his left arm. He's calling for me.

He's waiting for me.

He raises his arm again.

The moment freezes me. My throat feels sore, and my hands numb. Although I'm standing in a massive baseball stadium, I feel cornered, trapped, like to get to that mound, I'm going to have to crawl through a tight tunnel. I can't do it. I have to go. I have to get out of here. My pants feel itchy, and my cap feels too tight. I take the cap off and try to breathe.

"You have to go now," Maddux says.

I still stand there with my cap at my hip. Even when I hear

the announcer say, "Now coming in to pitch—No. 9 junior Henry Abbott.

"You have to go right now, Biggie," Maddux says firmly.

"Maddux, be quiet," Laser says before placing his hand on the No. 9. He rubs my back, which doesn't make me breathe any easier.

"They're quiet now, but they're going to cheer for you. You know that, right? They're going to stand, clap, and cheer your name. Not because of who your dad is or who I am. They aren't going to cheer because of the uniform you're wearing or because you're a star. They're going to yell your name because each and every one of them knows what you've done for their favorite team.

"Those people in the stands, they love Finch baseball, and they know all about your hard work. They saw you run up and down their streets. They've noticed all the weight you've lost. We live in a small town, Biggie, where everyone knows everything. Some will say that's a bad thing. But you're going to find out tonight that being from Finch is wonderful. Strikeout or walk, they're going to cheer your name, and you've earned that moment." He pushes me forward. "Now, go get six outs."

I stumble, but keep moving. I take four or five steps, but then I turn around.

"Hey, Laser, I just want to say—"

"You can thank me when the story ends. Today, all this, it's just the beginning. Go get six outs."

I step onto the grass and take small steps. I'm terrified.

"Biggie, you can't walk. You've got to run!" Maddux yells.

CHAPTER 35
FASTBALLS

The mound doesn't feel as high as I imagined. For some reason, I always believed that all of the other mounds that I practiced on would be lower, beaten down over time, but the mound in the middle of the Principal Park infield was the same height as the Laser-constructed mound in the dome. Straight ahead of me are rows of Finch fans, all wearing blue and gold. They stand in silence.

Although I'm surrounded by Coach Phillips and our infield, I know every eye is on me. I'm a car wreck that has to been seen. I'm the old lady who has slipped on ice. I'm an old man clutching his chest. People stare because they don't know how it happened and they don't how it will end up.

I'm too far away to hear the whispers of, "Is that Biggie?" or "Is he on the team?" or "Does Coach Phillips want to lose his job?" But I know that's what they're saying.

"When you tried out two weeks ago, I really loved your fastball," Phillips says. "Do you have confidence in it? Can you throw it for strikes?"

"Yes, sir," I say.

"Then do that," Phillips orders. "Throw one strike after another. Look at me. You will not—you hear me?—you will not get fancy. It's one fastball after another."

As everyone heads back to their spots, I turn around and see Jet stretching his legs in his favorite spot, center field. He's back in his comfort zone. I'm two hours away from mine.

I look up at the darkening sky and see zero stars, which differs from the perfect game fantasies I imagined as I jogged through Finch. Also above me are light towers releasing blocks of clear, white light. I count about eighty-two bulbs before Kyle attracts my attention and tells me the signs or, better yet, sign. One finger means bring the heat.

I can tell the baseball hasn't been used yet. The umpire must have handed it to Kyle before he walked out to the mound. It's the same size as every other baseball I have thrown since last September, but glossy. The ball's white, ideally white. There's hardly a smudge on it, just two sweaty fingerprints from Kyle's fingertips.

When I look down at Kyle, he seems a hundred miles away. For a moment, I wonder how I can get the ball that far. The fans are a hundred feet away, but it feels like they are sitting on my shoulder. Although the fences are almost three hundred feet behind me, I struggle with the tight squeeze of claustrophobia. Flashing phone cameras leave me light-headed. My dry and red eyes can't focus. I rub them with the balls of my hands. Kyle pounds his catcher's mitt and repeats, only louder this time, "Bring the heat."

I want this first warm-up pitch to be a strike. I want to get off to a fast start. My feet are parallel with my shoulders. My fingers grip the glossy baseball tight.

From behind me, I hear a loud belly laugh, the kind that sends milk down a little boy's nose.

Kyle stands up, "Biggie, pitch from the stretch. Do you know how to do that?"

I turn my shoulders and place the inside of my left foot on the mound. Behind me I see the runner at first base is the one laughing. Watching him chuckle at my simple rookie mistake only makes me want to beat them more.

All throughout my idiotic quest, Laser forced me to pitch from the stretch at least half the time. "Just in case a batter gets on base," he would say. I felt foolish doing it then and I still do now.

Calmly, I snap off seven more warm-up pitches, each one requiring little effort or mobility from Kyle.

During the past year, Laser told me a lot of things: keep your head up, legs straight, arm warm, and so on. He also said baseball has no clock. Oftentimes during hundred-pitch practices, my patience would wane. Throws would come faster and faster as I yearned for blue Gatorade or cold water. Laser would tell me to slow down. He would repeat over and over that I could take all the time I needed. *There is no clock in baseball.*

Remembering that, I stand tall with my feet on either side of the rubber and close my eyes. When I dreamed about this day, I felt myself surrounded by a perfect early-summer breeze, a Finch breeze. If some guy from Canada felt the gust on his face, he would feel heat. If some guy from Florida, Southern California, or a desert stood here, he would be freezing, but to us in Finch, the wind is perfectly uneventful. Now as I stand here, the wind barely exists. Instead, a faint mist hovers over the grass—the quiet before the storm. The chemical smell of the treated grass hides the musk smell so evident in my nose, just as when I put back the mower in our garage.

While baseball has no clock, I do have to open my eyes, squeeze the baseball, lift my elbow, arc my back, lift my leg, and get this guy out.

"Here we go," I whisper.

My first-ever high school pitch is bunted out in front of the plate. I stumble off the mound, but keep my balance and reach the rolling ball first.

"Throw to first!" Kyle screams.

I pick it up and cock my arm, but it fails to move. I just grip the ball and watch the kid race up the first-base line, chin up and knees chugging. Our first baseman stretches out his gloved hand and waits.

"FIRE IT!" Killer yells.

I grit my teeth and throw. The ball arrives a split second before the runner.

"Nice throw," Kyle says. "Let's not make it so dramatic next time."

The base runners move up to second and third. If I allow a hit, both could score, and St. John's would take the lead.

The out calms me and lifts a lot of stressful weight off my shoulders. The next batter, a small kid with baggy pants, steps in the box.

I fire a pitch: strike one. Then another pitch, even faster: strike two. And then I grit my teeth and let the next pitch fly. The umpire, as if someone lit a firecracker below his ass, explodes out of his crouch, swings his arm like he's speed-painting a wall, and yells, "Strike three!"

Kyle pumps his fist, and Killer belts, "Two down!"

As my head spins toward Killer's excitable roar, I see our senior third baseman hunched over not in pain, but in laughter. When he sees my eyes, he bites his lip to stop his laughing. My guess is he's laughing at the perceived absurdity of my unhittable fastballs. As I scan the rest of my teammates, I see others smiling like the Joker from *Batman*, cheeks high and mouths partially open and curled.

They might be surprised, but I'm not. One more out and I've cleaned up Jet's mess. Five minutes after Kyle seemed a hundred feet away, he now sits right in front of me. I feel like if I stretch my arm a little bit more than possible, I could pull and snap back his catcher's mask.

Then I hear it. Only a couple people shout it, but I hear it.

"Biggie! Biggie! Biggie!"

Once again, deep breaths calm my demeanor as I regenerate my self-confidence. Now poised on the mound, I feel like I'm immortal. Okay, maybe not eternal, but at the very least, I feel like a good baseball player. No! A *great* baseball player. I feel like I belong on this mound. It feels more like home than the synthetic mound under the dome, thirty feet from my bedroom.

I rock and fire, and the batter swings and fouls the ball straight back. The ding of the aluminum bat startles me.

"That's the only time you're going to touch the ball," I whisper to myself.

The cheer has gotten louder as more and more fans join in. "Biggie! Biggie! Biggie!"

I find myself listening more than concentrating. I've heard

experienced athletes say they can't hear the cheers when they're on the field and in the zone. Since this is my first real athletic experience, I hear the fans loud and clear. I try hard to block it out and concentrate, but it sounds so amazing.

The ball feels smaller as if I could wrap my fingers around it, bury it, hide it. With the tips of my fingers, I spin the ball in my palm and dig my cleats into the dirt. Again I grunt as the ball races to the plate.

The batter swings and the ding returns, only louder. The base hit screams to right field, easily over the outstretched arm of our second baseman. The runner who was on third base scores, while the runner who was on second is rounding third. Jet scoops up the ball and in one motion fires the ball to the plate.

"Get down, Biggie!" Kyle yells over the deafening St. John's fans' cheers.

Like a second-grade tornado drill, I drop to my knees and cover my ears. The ball skips off the grass and lands in Kyle's glove. The runner tries to slide around the tag, but Kyle slams his mitt on the runner's knee inside a cloud of swirling dust.

Before my eyes focus on the scoreboard, which now says the game is tied at 7–7, Killer places his face in my line of sight and claims, "We're going to score a lot more runs, Biggie. It's all good."

As I sit in the dugout, Maddux hands me a blue Gatorade. "You've got to go tell Jet thanks for picking you up," he claims.

"What?" I ask between gulps of Gatorade.

"It's baseball stuff," he continues. "You have to tell a player thanks for picking you up when they save your ass."

"Really?"

He just nods like a bobblehead.

I get up and tap Jet on the shoulder, "Hey, man, thanks for picking me up."

"Keep firing, Biggie, you big old son of a bitch. We're winning this title," Jet says with an unnecessary punch to my chest.

My ass plants back down on the dugout bench next to Maddux.

"It's insane out there," I mutter. "There's lights and noise everywhere. It's hard to breathe."

"You got to throw the pitch, the Wiffle ball," Maddux says.

Elusive Gatorade soaks my chin as I try to get the last ounce out of the plastic bottle. I belch and wipe my chin clean with the back of my hand.

"Coach said only fastballs," I inform him.

"He doesn't know about the Wiffle ball. Trust me, the pitch is unhittable. I mean jeez, Biggie, that's why we are here—to throw the Wiffle ball. Remember?"

I do.

✻ ✻ ✻

After Finch fails to score in the bottom of the sixth, I'm back on the mound. I feel a lot more comfortable pitching from the windup and more relaxed knowing there aren't any base runners behind me.

Maddux told me that the heart of the St. John's lineup is coming up and if I want to avoid a big inning, I'm going to have to throw the Wiffle ball. I'm hesitant to defy Coach Phillips, but Maddux is right. We just spent nine months perfecting the magic pitch.

As the first batter steps to the plate, Kyle puts down the sign for a fastball and, just like I had seen in the movies, I shake it off. I'm throwing my Wiffle ball. As if I'm going back in time to the first-day-of-school Wiffle ball game, I place my fingertips in the proper positions. With my left hand in my glove and the baseball hidden inside it, I bring my glove to my mouth and calmly blow on it. I step back and I begin my windup. I snap my wrist and release the ball. It starts outside. Kyle slides to his right just before the baseball spins back to him. He catches it right in front of the outside corner of the plate.

"Strike one!" the umpire yells.

The batter shuffles forward in the box. Kyle sees it and quickly and emphatically drops one finger between his folded legs. I throw my fastest one yet and it catches the outside corner.

"Strike two!" the umpire yells.

Again, the batter dances in the box.

Kyle again asks for a fastball, but I shake him off. He looks into the dugout for a split second, but comes back quickly and makes an upside-down peace sign in front of his crotch.

Nine months after my parking-lot perfect game, I still remember where the holes were on that Wiffle ball and the right amount of pressure to make even this sturdy baseball dance.

Once again, the ball starts outside and hooks over the plate. Just like last time, it's going to catch the corner and the umpire will jump up and send this batter to the bench. Kyle reaches forward to catch the ball and my mouth starts to tingle.

But right before Kyle can snag it, the batter leans over and swings. The ball connects with the barrel of his bat and soars high into the air. There is no ding this time. The bat releases a dull thump. I watch it fly to left field, and it looks like it's going to go foul. I attempt to lift my hand and pray it into the stands, but before I can do anything, even breathe, the ball bounces off the foul pole. Home run.

My shoulders drop. The St. John's crowd screams so loud that my brain can't create simple thoughts. The clapping rattles between my ears. I have to bend over and press hard on my ears to clear my head. While the St. John's fans' cheers and clapping are ear-popping, I still hear Coach Phillips yell from the top step of the dugout, "Biggie, what did I say? What did I say? Throw heat and get us in the dugout!"

CHAPTER 36
THE VILLAIN

After a running catch by Jet ends the inning, I walk off the mound, eyeing only dirt and grass. As the players surround Coach Phillips, I walk through the dugout and into the hallway. I rip off my glove and let it fall to the ground. I place my forehead and elbows against the concrete wall and they slide, along with the rest of me, to the ground.

I blew it. I knew it was a bad idea. That's why I quit the team. I'm not ready to be a pitcher. Killer talked me into coming down here, but maybe he did it on purpose to teach me a lesson. Worst of all, I didn't listen to my coach, who told me not to get fancy. Instead I listened to an eleven-year-old.

"Biggie, you've got to come and cheer for your teammates." Maddux appears in the hallway.

I get up. Shoulder hung, eyes glazed.

"No," I say.

"Biggie. I'm not kidding. You have to go out there. It's the bottom of the seventh. You need to be with your team."

"No, I don't."

"Listen to me," he says.

I walk toward him.

"What? You said I need to listen to you. Who are you? C'mon, tell me who you are."

"Biggie," he says, backpedaling.

"You said you were going to teach me an unhittable pitch," I mumble, closing in on him. "You said I could throw a perfect game. You said I could do something no one has done, not even Aaron Abbott. This is all your fault. You convinced me. You told me to throw the pitch, even though Coach said not to. You told me you could teach me a pitch that was unhittable. This is all your fault."

"The pitch worked on the first guy," he says.

My volume increases, "It's all your fault, but here's the thing: no one knows that. Everyone out there thinks it's my fault. Hell, maybe it is my fault. After all, I listened to you."

Despite the fact that I weigh 150 pounds more than him, Maddux, all of five feet, stands tall and steps toward me. "You need to be with your team," he says. "You need to be a good teammate."

In one quick motion, I pick him up by his armpits and toss him up against the tunnel wall. His torso convulses in my hands. With his legs swinging in the air, we are at eye level.

"Listen to me!" I yell. "You're a kid. You're not a ballplayer. You're not on this team. You're a glorified batboy. No! You are just a batboy, a kid who picks up bats. You're not a coach. Do you hear me? You don't know anything! Do you hear me? You don't know anything!"

Tears glaze his eyes and start to flow. His cheeks glow red and his lips shake.

"Why are you so mad?" he asks.

I feel like a monster, huffing and puffing with a small boy in the palms of my hands. I set Maddux down.

"I'm a laughingstock. I cost us this game," I say with my back to my little brother.

"The game's not over," Maddux says.

I head down the tunnel to the locker room. I feel lucky that I have my truck. It's just a few steps away. I can easily grab my stuff, race back out the door, and be gone before anyone notices. The nightmare will be over. As I enter the locker room, I immediately turn on the sink and splash water on my face.

All I can think about is that note my mom found nine months ago in my backpack. Why did I put that note in my backpack? If I'd folded it in my pocket, none of this would have happened. I wouldn't have thrown up on YouTube, almost strangled a redneck, gotten beat up by a girl, or blown a title chance for my classmates at Principal Park.

I pound the sink with the side of my fist.

"Fuck, fuck, fuck!" I rotate obscenities with sink punches until the side of my hand aches too much to continue.

On the floor I see my Yellow Jackets cap lying there upside down. A banner stain of sweat covers the brim and inside. My hand reaches for it, worried that it's ruined. I'm mad that the cap may be soiled so I rub the blotch in faint hopes that it would disappear. Sweat transfers to my fingertips. And then I catch a glimpse of myself in the mirror.

I stand up straight and place the hat back on the top of my head.

It's weird how reality can just slap you in the face. In the past nine months, I played catch almost daily with Maddux and Laser, tried out for the Yellow Jackets, got cut, made the team, received a uniform with Laser's retired number, sat in the Iowa Cubs bullpen, struck out two batters, and gave up a home run, but only now, rubbing the sweat off the inside of my black and gold Yellow Jackets cap, do I suddenly feel like a baseball player.

As I look at my reflection, the first thing I see is the cap. Then I see my face, worn by running sweat and flying dirt. Then, the uniform top, "Yellow Jackets" spelled out over my chest. To see it more clearly, I take a step back and then another and then another.

For years, I have hated mirrors. The reflecting glass is nothing more than a bully, and the worst kind. In the schoolyard, kids call you names—"fat ass," "dumb ass"—mostly they pick a word and throw "ass" on the end, but what do they know? They're just mean, dumb kids. A mirror, however, knows all. When it calls you fat, guess what? You're fat. When it calls you ugly, guess what? You're ugly. A mirror never lies. And as I keep stepping backward, I can see more of my uniform—my black belt, my long baseball pants, and finally as I bump my back into the locker-room wall, my black, dirtied cleats.

A small smile appears as I think about Coach Phillips cutting me. "How do you like me now?" I think, happy that I proved everyone wrong. But the smile fades as I try to think of others who doubted me, who said this day would never come. I try to remember other moments when people laughed at the idea of Biggie playing baseball, but I can't think of any.

Suddenly, my chin drops and my lips dry out. It's a cold, lonely feeling when you realize that the person in the mirror is the villain in the story. This is the guy. This guy, now five feet from me, stalked a girl online, ignored and shut out classmates, lied to his mother on a daily basis, looked down on his stepfather, and threw his little brother up against the wall, just for telling me to support my teammates.

When I said I wanted to be a ballplayer, Maddux jumped on board. Although I embarrassed him at the first tryout, Laser trained me anyway. Even Kyle told me to try again after I lost some weight. Shit! Even Killer drove three hours to tell me I could be just what Finch needed to win this tournament. No one doubted me. No matter how much I want to believe that this world is full of cold, selfish bullies, the simple fact is that I'm the one who treats others with disrespect. I'm the selfish one.

For the second time in nine months, I look straight into a mirror and make promises.

"I'm going to be better person," I say. "I have to say I'm sorry to Maddux."

I run out of the locker room.

As I head out the tunnel, the ceiling rumbles under pounding feet. I feel like a four-year-old experiencing his first thunderstorm. As I reenter the dugout, everyone is standing, leaning against the dugout rail or pacing back and forth. At first glance, I don't see Maddux. My teammates are congratulating Christensen, who stands on first. The sophomore hears shouts of, "Way to get us started," "Now we go," and "Get him home, guys."

As Jet walks up to the plate, I see Maddux sandwiched between two players twice his size. He's not screaming or pacing. He just stands there and watches Jet take a few practice swings. As I walk toward him, Maddux finally yells, "Speed kills, Jet. Put it in play and keep it going."

As I reach Maddux, he uses the protective dugout bar to pull himself up and yells, "C'mon, Jet."

"Maddux," I say.

He doesn't look back. "C'mon, Jet!" he repeats, either ignoring me or blocking out everything other than the game.

"Maddux!"

He looks up and over his shoulder, his hands still pushing and pulling the fence as if the motion is creating the electricity to energize Jet.

"I'm sorry," I say. "I didn't mean any of it. You do know a lot about baseball."

"I know I do," he says.

"So what do I do now?" I ask.

"You just cheer," he says. "You need to fire up Jet. It's the bottom of the seventh. You have to cheer as loud as you can."

Maddux follows his own advice. Like a raging madman, he opens his mouth and lets out the loudest animal-like scream I've ever heard. If his fingers weren't curled around the fat, red bar, his fists would be pounding on his chest.

I look out and see Jet circle the sky with his bat. He's batting left-handed now, not right-handed like he did in gym class. He's ahead in the count, two balls and no strikes, and there is one out. The pitcher throws the ball, and Jet reaches out and slaps at it. The ball skips up the third-base line. The St. John's fielder snags the ball and pumps his arm, but doesn't even try to throw out the two-time small-school state champion in the 100-meter dash.

As Jet crosses first base, he flexes his chest, tilts his neck, and just screams to the sky.

"We need one hit, Killer," Kyle yells out as Killer steps into the on-deck circle.

"C'mon, Killer!" Maddux cheers.

I want so bad to cheer for him, but I just can't. Instead, I clap my hands tentatively and place my cleats on the top step and look into the crowd. Practically everyone who lives in Finch is in the stands, clapping their hands and chanting, "Yel-low jack-ets, yellow jack-ets."

As I look for Annabelle, Mom, or, yes, I know it's crazy, Courtney, I hear, *PING!*

I twist my head and see the baseball fly high over left field. The cheers are deafening, and every member of the Yellow Jackets jumps out of the dugout.

Killer jogs slowly to first. With a tight grip, he still holds the bat. Christensen and Jet stand still a few feet from their respective bases, and the St. John's left fielder stands up against left-field wall.

Then, the world stops. As if God hit the mute button, we all stand in silence.

CHAPTER 37
PLENTY OF GAS

From three hundred fifty feet, it looks like the left fielder is leaning against the wall when he reaches up and catches the ball. As he throws the ball back in, the crowd behind me and the players beside me go quiet.

Tagging up, Christensen races to third and Jet to second as Killer fires his bat to the ground, leaving it there for Maddux to pick up. Killer pulls open the Velcro of his batting glove like a nurse rips off a Band-Aid.

"In the dugout." The umpire orders that I take a couple small steps back to the top step.

"Now or never, Kyle," Maddux says.

Kyle steps into the box. Resting the bat on his shoulders, he stands upright and blows a pink bubble.

"Kyle," I yell.

He looks at me, and I freeze. Not a word appears from my mouth. He grins and looks at the pitcher. Under my breath, I say, "C'mon, one hit."

The St. John's crowd chants its pitcher's name. Morgan, I think. Our crowd claps calmly and says next to nothing. Most just have their eyes open and hands clasped. As I look down the dugout, everyone leans against the fence and breathes slowly. Three games, all close, have worn the team out. Finch has played twenty-seven innings in three nights. Over the past two days, there have been too many rallies, big hits, highlight catches, costly errors, and brain farts to count. After letting out every last bit of energy in a feeble attempt to scream Killer's fly ball over the left-field fence, no one, not Maddux, the players, or the fans have any cheering fuel left in the tank.

Well, not everyone is gassed. Someone was resting on his bed during the first two games and sitting on his ass in the bullpen for much of this one.

I raise my fists and yell, "Kyle, we just need one hit! C'mon, No. 10, one hit!"

The first pitch is high, and Kyle bends his back and drops his shoulders to get out of the way.

"Kyle, he's scared," I continue. "He is just like the rest of us. He knows you're going to win this game. C'mon."

Although, the umpire banished me to the dugout, I step back onto the dirt, look up at the crowd, and start clapping my hands above my head. "C'mon, let's go," I yell to my neighbors.

Slowly, everyone starts to clap with me.

"C'mon, Kyle," I yell again.

The next pitch is right down the middle, but Kyle doesn't swing.

"Kyle, Kyle, Kyle!" I try to start a chant…and it works.

The cheer gets so loud that we can no longer hear the clapping hands or pounding feet.

"Nine, get back into the dugout," the home-plate umpire orders.

I start to jump, pumping my fists, chanting, "Kyle, Kyle, Kyle!"

Laser grabs my shirt and pulls me into the dugout.

"Don't get kicked out," he says.

After regaining my balance, I look at Kyle, and he's laughing. Although he's twenty feet away, it's like we're back at our locker telling jokes.

Kyle swings at the next pitch and lines the ball to center field. The outfielder races in and my heart stops beating, my lungs forget to pump air, my lips lock, and my clinched fists rise slowly into the air.

The outfielder dives face-first at the dropping baseball. The ball hits the grass and bounces over his glove.

Elbows, shoulders, and knees thump my back and legs as Yellow Jackets race toward Kyle at first base. As Jet, who easily scored the winning run, picks up Kyle, I look at the scoreboard and smile when the seven changes to nine. Above the box score, it says, "Congrats, Finch!"

A long row of Finch fans, who are clapping and cheering "Best Team Ever," wait for us in front of the locker room. Girls from my school are high-fiving and hugging the players. Nothing too passionate, mostly a quick two-arm wrap around the neck. By the time the player can place his arm on her back, she has let go and moved on to the next guy.

I give high five after high five, receiving a few hugs and a bunch of "Way to go, Biggie" compliments.

I have dreamed about having one girl after another press her boobs up against me, even if it's just for a split second. But the two hours of stress weigh on me, and I'm barely awake going through the line.

At the end of the line is Annabelle, who is talking with Jet. From two feet away, I can see him blatantly stare at her breasts, which are hidden by only a thin piece of gold fabric with the words "Finch Softball," stretched out over the front. Annabelle has no problem wearing shirts way too tight for her gifts from God.

As I walk up to her, I don't wait for her to decide between hug or high five. I place my hand right in the middle of her back and pull her tight up against me.

"You know you were the one that told me I should play baseball," I whisper into her ear.

She pulls back. "I don't remember that."

"I do," I say. "It was the first day of school."

"Oh yeah! Wiffle ball."

"Yep," I say.

"Well, I'm glad I did."

She's so beautiful. I know I have to let go. I can't hold on to her forever, but I just want to rub her back a few more seconds before I have to say good-bye. As I pull my hand away, she gets on her tippy-toes and kisses me on the cheek.

"I'll always be sorry about…you know," I say. "I want you to know that."

She smirks and says, "You should be."

And with that, she's gone.

"Biggie," Coach Phillips squeezes the top of my shoulder.

"Go into the office; I'll be right in," he orders.

I turn around and hope that he will give me more time on the field. For someone who has yearned to be alone most of his life, I am so happy to be on the diamond with the celebrating players and family members. The air buzzes with delight and elation. It's intoxicating.

"I will, sir, but can I just stand out here a little longer?" I ask.

"Sure, Biggie," Phillips says. "Oh, and you might want to look at the scoreboard. Every day, I planned on erasing you from the roster, but Laser kept sharing this tall tale that you would come back some day. He just wouldn't let me take you off."

I look up at the massive outfield scoreboard and there it is.

WP—Henry Abbott (1–0).

"Let's keep that loss number at zero for awhile," Coach says as he walks away.

"Perfect," I whisper.

CHAPTER 38
EIGHT TEXTS

I sit down in the blue leather chair in front of the cluttered Iowa Cubs manager's desk. My back curls and my eyes look down at my knees. Why does Coach Phillips want to talk to me in private? Am I getting cut? Was this a one-time thing? I should have listened to him. He said fastballs. What was I doing?

"Biggie, how's the arm?" Coach walks in.

"Okay," I say.

"Your fastball looked good."

He settles on the edge of the desk. His chin, filled with black and gray stubble, hovers right over my head.

"Coach, I'm so sorry about the hit. I should've listened to you. I just thought the pitch was unhittable. I was wrong."

"Shut up." He takes off his hat and rubs the bald spot on the top of his head. "How can the smartest kid in this school be so mentally weak? How can the strongest kid in school have no backbone?"

My body tingles as I wonder if I should answer either of the questions or follow his order to shut up.

"Is it a girl?"

"What?"

"Why are you doing this? All of this?" he asks. "Why are you here, playing baseball after all of these years?"

He was right. It was a girl. Strap me up to a lie-detector test and the only passable answer was Annabelle. But I couldn't say that. Reason No. 2 may be to get the attention of my step-dad or my real dad, but I can't bring myself to admit that either. I exhale a long breath, look up, swallow some rancid cigar breath and say, "Because I want to be a champion. You aren't anybody in this town if you're not a champion, and I want to be someone."

That was the coolest thing I've ever said, I think, feeling really proud of myself. I'm almost more proud of those words than my game-winning pitching performance. Before Coach Phillips can respond to my awesome response, two men walk in the office. Leading the way is Finch mayor Marty Blaine, and right behind him is him. Aaron Abbott.

"Marty, Aaron, I'm just talking to my pitcher right now," Coach says.

"Aah, don't mind us, Coach," Mayor Blaine says. "We're just looking for that trophy."

Aaron limps. It's not pronounced, but I notice that he pulls his right leg with every step. He's tall, really tall actually. I feel a slight urge to stand to see if I tower over him, but I remain planted in the chair. I always imagined that when I saw him, he would look rough.

His face would be covered in a five-o'clock shadow and his clothes would be dirty, like he just got out of a fight. I supposed I always imagined him as a loser, a bum whose time had passed.

In reality, he looks wealthy and clean-cut, with a black Polo shirt and olive green shorts. He walks, limp and all, in flip-flops. He doesn't look big, more lean, in shape. Part of me always hoped he would carry around a big gut, and my obesity was hereditary. Nope, he looks great. I am fat, and became fat due to shoving my face with junk food and spent free time reading and playing video games.

"Sorry, guys, the trophy's gone. It's getting engraved," Coach says.

"Yeah, they probably already had St. John's engraved on it. Oops!" Mayor Blaine says before releasing an over-the-top belly laugh.

"Thanks for making the trip, Aaron," Coach Phillips says.

"I saw the sweep yesterday and got on a plane this morning. This is a big win, Coach," Aaron says.

"Thanks," Coach responds.

"And this is the winning pitcher." Aaron looked down on me. His eyes look just like mine.

My mind is blank. I can think of nothing to say. I guess I said it all last night.

"He kept us in the game. That's for sure," Coach says.

"Well done, No. 9." Aaron places his hand in front of mine, and I shake it. As he grips my hand, I wish I hadn't, but I did.

"You need to put some ice on that shoulder," Aaron says.

I nod my head and remain silent.

"Well, we'll let you get back to it," Mayor Blaine says. "You bring that trophy by when it's engraved."

As Aaron walks out, he places his hand on the top of my shoulder. He pats it twice and then squeezes it, almost as if there's a meaning behind the squeeze.

"See you guys at State," he says as he lets go.

I watch him walk out and close the door. Two fingers from Coach Phillip's hand pull my chin back around.

"You're only going to worry about me right now." Coach Phillips's eyes are inches from mine.

"Well, you missed two weeks of practice, most of which was training to get everyone in shape. Looking at you, I can tell you did what you had to do to get in shape, but as a gesture to the guys who busted their asses for two weeks, you'll carry everyone's bags to the bus on road trips. I told the guys to leave their stuff by their lockers and you would take care of it."

"Yes, Coach," I say. "Of course. It's the least I can do."

"Now hit the showers," he orders.

I get up, but before I reach the door, I look back and blurt out, "I'm going to throw a perfect game."

He nods a couple of times and exhales. "Don't forget the bags."

Before getting dressed, I reach for my phone. It's been a personal record four hours since I fiddled with it. I sit down and start looking through the text messages I missed. They're all from Courtney.

First one says, This might sound stupid, but it looks like you're pitching in the bullpen.

Second, They just called your name.

The third message is a picture of me on the mound.

Then, there's a picture of the crowd cheering for me.

And another picture of me. Below it says, After the strikeout.

The sixth message says, Wow, you throw hard.

Another picture. This time, I'm leading cheers.

The eighth message says, You were amazing.

My eyes water and my hands shake so much that I fumble the phone. As it lands on the concrete floor, it slides under the bench.

Every hair on my body tingles as I reach down to pick up the phone. I pray that she's still at the stadium.

With the phone lodged between my hands, I take a deep breath before slowly typing. Whether it's nervous energy or water on my fingers, I keep hitting the wrong key. After several stop-and-starts, I finally ask, Where are you?

As I wait for a response, I slide on my underwear, shorts, and my lucky blue shirt. Before I bend over to pick up my towel, my phone vibrates.

With my eyes closed, I whisper, "Please still be here."

Sliding my thumb to see the response, I see, I'm outside Gate B.

I hurdle the bench and push open the door. With wet hair, no shoes and no idea where Gate B is, I race past Coach Phillips.

"Biggie, the bags!"

"I won't forget."

Leaving wet footprints, I maneuver around fans young and old until I'm outside. Before I see the sign for Gate B, I see her.

She's alone. Her eyes scan the crowd. Her half-zipped blue sweatshirt covers her chest. Even on a humid night, her dark hair lies straight.

Her eyes see me. She adds a small smile to her half-wave.

Eight months of daily running doesn't keep me from losing my breath as I get within the vanilla scent of her perfume.

"I looked for you," I say.

"Jenna and I were hiding from what's-her-face," she says. "We were sitting with the enemy."

"How did it go?" I ask.

"You were awesome. When you—"

"No. How did last night go?" I interrupt her.

She leans in a little and says, "You were right about him. All hands."

It happens fast. In less than a blink, my lips touch hers. As she rubs my neck, I place my hands on her cheeks.

I've never kissed a girl before, so I have no idea what I'm doing. Her lips are soft but flavorless. For years, I dreamed of kissing Annabelle, a Chapstick addict. So I expected to taste cherry, but Courtney's lips are flavorless. Flavorless and really soft.

She steps back. How long did it last? Who knows? Maybe two seconds, maybe ten, but it didn't last long enough.

"So you like the PDA, I see," she jokes.

"Sorry," I whisper.

"Don't apologize. It was nice," she says.

"You saw the home run?"

She steps back, looks stunned, and says, "Oh, my God. One more inch and it would have gone foul."

CHAPTER 39
MADDUX AND MATH

I love summer. I don't have to worry about schoolwork. I can read comic books and contemporary fiction. Deep into *Fight Club* by Chuck Palahniuk, I stare at Maddux, who sits next to me in the backseat of Laser's SUV. The family, me included, are headed south to Springfield, Missouri, to watch Laser throw out the first pitch for the Springfield Cardinals, a minor league team he played for a couple of seasons. I have never seen a minor league baseball game, so I'm excited to see how much harder pro pitchers throw than me.

After making some friends playing Little League, Maddux told Mom that he wanted to go to school. He actually said he wanted to get straight *A*s like his older brother. I was there in the kitchen when he said it. It was really cool. To help him with his goal, I've been tutoring the little guy since summer vacation started four weeks ago. I'm giving him a crash course in subjects like math, science, history, and language. I enjoy tutoring him and think that being a teacher might be a good profession for me, maybe even a coach. I want to work with the sorry players, not cut them. Have those players, not just the talented ones, lead us to state titles.

"Is this right?" Maddux asks.

Through the eraser crumbles is a fraction problem. "Is this supposed to be four?" I ask.

"Yeah, why wouldn't it be?" he says. "You just add two plus two— the easiest math problem in the world."

"It's not four," I inform him and return to *Fight Club*.

He takes back his work. "I thought it was too easy." He blushes a little.

"What is the only rule when it comes to math problems?" I ask.

"Do the steps," he says with little pep. He's tired of me reminding him not to take shortcuts. "I keep getting four."

I drop the book, keeping my thumb planted on page 187. "Look at this. What do you subtract here?"

"Um," he ponders and guesses. "Thirty-five minus seven?"

"No, you skipped a step. Look back."

"Oh, I didn't multiply the two. So it's thirty-five minus fourteen, and then it's twenty-one divided by seven equals three."

"Don't skip steps," I tell him.

"Wow, that's was easy," he says, although it took him ten minutes and four wrong answers.

"Oh, trust me, it gets harder," I honestly say.

"I like math," he says. "I think it's my favorite subject."

I stretch back on the comfortable leather seat and spread out my legs. It's a lot easier to get comfortable in a car now that I don't weight three hundred pounds. I reopen *Fight Club* and find my spot.

"Hey, Biggie." Maddux interrupts my reading. "You should learn how to hit. I could teach you."

"There are DHs." I keep my eyes in the book.

"Yeah, but you're a big guy," he says. "You could hit the ball five hundred feet."

"This is coming from the same kid who told me I could throw a perfect game. In case you haven't noticed, I'm still looking for a perfect inning."

"I looked at the record books," he continues the sales pitch. "No one has ever hit three home runs in a game. With my help, you could be the first, and then I would hit four and break your record."

"You think?" I ask with a strong dose of sarcasm.

"Yeah! I admit a perfect game in pitching was a pipe dream. Too many outside factors: the umpire, your teammates, the weather, lots of stuff. Dad, what do you always tell me about hitting?"

"It's just you and the ball," Laser says from the driver's seat.

"It's just you and the ball," Maddux repeats. "Look, I've hit a lot of home runs. Home-run hitting is different. You can make mistakes. It's okay. Hell, you could hit home runs in three at-bats and strike out in the other three. Home-run hitters strike out all the time. I'm telling you. Mom, what do you think would happen if Biggie connected with a baseball?"

"It may never land," she jokes from the passenger seat.

"Never land. Did you hear that?" Maddux asks, knowing very well I did. "What do you say? Want to hit some home runs?"

I peek over the top of the paperback and ponder his suggestion.

"Biggie, you don't have to be perfect," he says.

"All right," I agree. "Let's buy a bat."

And Maddux smiles.

ACKNOWLEDGMENTS

Biggie is my debut novel. But it wasn't supposed to be. While in graduate school at Hamline University, I spent three years working on another book. For whatever reason, I couldn't get any of my instructors to tell me the book was finished. After a rough critique, I asked Mary Logue, one of my instructors, what I needed to do next. She told me to give that manuscript a break, put it away and write something else, anything else. I took her advice and wrote a short story about an overweight teen who somehow throws a perfect game of gym-class Wiffle ball. I originally intended to just write that short story, but Mary told me to keep going. Mary, without your wonderful pep talks, Biggie would not exist.

I have to thank my Owatonna family. It was at the *People's Press* newspaper that I fell in love with writing. I especially want to thank Jeffrey Jackson for giving me my first writing job. I also want to thank all of my instructors and classmates at Hamline. I have been so lucky to be surrounded by so many talented writers.

To Sara Megibow and everyone at Nelson Literary Agency, thank you for all of your hard work. Sara, I'm so grateful that you found my story in a stack of queries. I would not want anyone else championing my novels. To Kelly Barrales-Saylor, my editor at Albert Whitman, thank you for believing in a book about a shy, overweight teen from a small town in Iowa. Working with you and your teammates has been amazing. And to Pamela Carter Joern, thank you for your insight when I was first starting my novel.

Thank you to my family for all your encouragement and support through the years. And to Beth, my motivator. You have always believed in me and pushed me to be my best, with the perfect mix of compassionate support and brutal honesty.